PURCHASED FOR SEDUCTION

DARK BWWM GREEK MAFIA ROMANCE

THE GREEK MAFIA ROMANCE BROTHERHOOD

JAMILA JASPER

ISBN: 979-8-3302-8375-0

Copyright © 2024 by Jamila Jasper

All rights reserved.

No part of this book may be reproduced in any form or by any electronic or mechanical means, including information storage and retrieval systems, without written permission from the author, except for the use of brief quotations in a book review.

Thank you to my Patreon subscribers for your support with this book. I could not have done it without you. www.patreon.com/jamilajasper

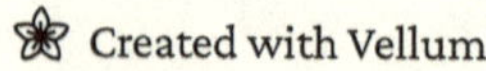 Created with Vellum

GREEK MAFIA ROMANCE BROTHERHOOD

Purchased For Submission

Purchased For Pregnancy

Purchased For Seduction

DESCRIPTION

The hot guy Latrice met in the world of social media "influencing" is a narcissistic mafia killer...

Galanos is blond, vain, and only interested in collecting followers, panties, and bodies.

Latrice wants nothing to do with a cruel, unhinged mobster once he exposes his true colors.

Trapped on a Greek island thousands of miles away from everyone she knows, leaving isn't easy without Galanos' help.

But when facing rejection for the first time, and from a plus-sized black woman no less, Galanos refuses to let Latrice leave his multi-million dollar Greek mansion...

Mob life is not as glamorous as it looks online, and Latrice's love/hate relationship with a mobster drags her on a non-stop roller coaster of adventure.

Book #3 in the completed mafia romance trilogy. Check your undies at the door for this sizzling black woman/white man mafia romance with a plus-sized female lead and open-door spicy scenes.

This unhinged, dark, and full-length multicultural romance novel is a NO cliffhanger, NO cheating romance with an African American plus-sized lead character and guaranteed HEA.

Thank you to my patrons for your ongoing support. This new edition is only made possible because of your support.

*Here's to manifesting your **happily ever after...***

Click here to subscribe:
www.patreon.com/jamilajasper

CONTENT AWARENESS

BWWM Dark Mafia Romance

This is an adults only read for fans of diverse romance, dark romance and high-heat relationships between black women and white men.

<u>When I say dark, I mean DARK</u> so expect mention of the following topics: sexual assault, abuse, rape, BDSM specifically the D/s relationship dynamic, unprotected relations, some bondage but no torture, piercing or other gore. Mention of spanking/domestic discipline, dirty talk, kink, murder, violence and more.
There is one scene that toys with white male submission but mostly the book is a hardcore alpha male who does whatever it takes to conquer his chosen queen.

As this is a fictional story, Jamila Jasper does not condone any of these actions. **<u>Don't try any of this at home.</u>**
<u>Please always use protection and do what you can to care for your sexual health.</u>
<u>Remember this is a work of fiction.</u>

CONTENT AWARENESS

There is copious amounts of oral, PIV as well as eating the B-U-T-T in this book so if this isn't your cup of tea, **gift it to your homegirl who likes getting her booty ate with no crumbs left and move on to another work**. Thank you for your time.

YIAYIA

14 YEARS AGO

My grandmother issued a straight command as I stumbled through the gates, an excited smile plastered on my perpetually freckled face, "Come, Galanos."

"Yiayia! The puppy followed me home!"

She smiled. Yiayia was always beautiful. Even in her old age. I spent all my days with her. I went to school *sometimes*, but whenever I wanted to skip, she would scream at Papa and keep me home on her lap. I would brush her hair. I would zip her dresses. I would sit at her feet in the grass.

As I walked into her garden she smiled at me and then the dog.

"If you want him, he's yours."

I stooped down to touch the puppy. A surge of warmth flooded me. I would protect him and make him mean. And that way whenever Loukas and Stavros decided to push me down a hill or hit me, my little pup could fight back.

"I want to name him Harry Potter."

"Sure. You will need to take good care of him."

"Okay."

I touched the dog. I still remember how the puppy smelled and how excited he was. *I'm sorry.*

For six weeks, I spent every minute of my time with that dog. I loved him. I loved that dog more than I loved anyone. When Yiayia was busy with her friends, I played with the dog. My siblings were too old. Cassia still lived with her mother.

I was alone — except for Harry Potter, who eventually became *Harry*. The last time I saw the dog was a bright, sunny day. I should have been in school, but I demanded the neighbor's son skip school as well to play with me.

I had a brilliant idea of turning Harry into a bloodhound who could help me hunt down my "prey" — the friend I'd invited — and then we would play fight with sticks once I found him. Usually, these games ended better for me than my friends.

We got to stick fighting after Harry got distracted by a butterfly and we brought the stick fighting inside. Yiayia and her friend from church were drinking tea. She grabbed us by the collars and thrust us along the route we'd entered, grumbling at the tracks at first and then outright yelling.

I thought she'd hit me, she was so angry. But then her anger subsided and I thought I was safe. Relief flooded through me. I could always offer to clean it up, even if Yiayia never let me clean up.

Once her friend and mine left, she sat in the kitchen quietly sipping tea while I played with Harry on the porch.

"Galanos. Go inside," she said, coming out of the kitchen with a calm expression on her face and a wicked look she cast at Harry. I knew she wanted to hurt him from the look on her face, although someone less practiced might not have recognized her rage for what it was.

I remembered not wanting to leave Harry. I begged and cried. She never raised her voice, but she kept insisting. Eventually I left. Once I was inside, I knew what was coming.

I tried to cover my ears. Two gunshots later and I knew what she'd done. A sick feeling overwhelmed me, but I couldn't allow myself to vomit. She'd make me clean *that* up. But back then, I couldn't bring myself to push hard against her. I was a child... *impotent* to the commands of my grandmother.

When she came inside I was pacing and telling myself that I'd punish her. That I'd *shoot her.* But I was only a boy. So I did what boys do.

"You're a BITCH!" I yelled — a word I'd picked up from Lou fighting with his girlfriend at the time.

Yiayia said nothing.

"You're an old bitch! I fucking hate you! I fucking hate you, cunt."

Once I'd finished that sentence, I'd run out of swear words. I was six. I thought cunt, fuck and bitch were plenty.

"Are you done?" Yiayia asked calmly, as if she hadn't just executed my beloved pet. *My only friend.*

"BITCH!" I yelled emphatically.

"Do not overreact. I killed the puppy to help you understand something, Galanos. You respect your elders, first. And second, you never become attached to living things. They will always die or disappoint you."

"I hate you," I seethed, meaning every word of it. I imagined squeezing her neck and watching her eyes bulge out. The thought made me smile. *That's my diagnosis, isn't it?*

"I know. You hate me now. Come, I will get you ice-cream and teach you how to hurt that little friend of yours properly. I don't want a display."

I didn't want to put Harry out of my mind. I wanted to be angry with her. But I was six. And Yiayia was the only parent I knew. Whatever she did must have been right, so killing Harry must have been right.

I still miss that dog. I got his name tattooed somewhere most people don't see. Yiayia wanted me to become cold. I think it worked.

The only person who casts doubt on that is *Latrice Boyd.*

ONE
SUNKISSED MELANIN

atrice's skin melts like butter in the sun. She's lathered every inch of her body in jojoba oil as she lays on the pool deck, going through her phone. She's curvy... and dark. Darker than both Tisha and Fallon.

"Dating anyone new this week?" Latrice snipes at me as she scrolls through my social media account on her phone. I posted last night's party — the one she didn't attend. An after party for a job well done.

Stavros and Fallon went away with Adrian for a month after my first job. No more Adamos brothers, no more innocence. I'm not their shit head little brother anymore. But there *was* more killing involved in ridding ourselves of the problem. More than any of us wanted. Yiayia would have loved the blood and glory of it.

I miss her. It's been ages since I've seen her. She doesn't know about Latrice. *She can't ever find out.* But I like having Latrice around. I don't know why.

And it's *my house.* Latrice is my *friend,* so I can keep her wherever I want, anyway. I don't need my grandmother's opinions on my friends.

Stavros doesn't have regrets about what happened, but my brother still has the voices.

He has returned with Fallon in time for the baby shower and they're in a better mood than I expected. Better than Tisha and Lou.

Loukas and Tisha constantly fight over food and whether Tisha can name the twins after her favorite basketball players: Steph and Klay. During a heated moment, she calls Michael Jordan "wack" to Loukas' face. They have a screaming match that ends with Carlotta telling them off for the entire night with Helen at her side shouting drunken insults at Loukas about his "deformed head".

She had the right idea but the wrong message.

"I don't date," I tell Latrice.

If Latrice knew what my relationships with women were like, she wouldn't be my friend at all. All my relationships are dark. Kinky. Filled with nasty sex. Latrice probably likes men who buy her flowers and beg for her attention, not men like me: utterly psychologically broken.

Unlike my brothers, I embrace the darkness. I prefer it. I like women who call me *master*. I like women who dance with the devil and then come home with me to make hard, passionate love until morning.

Latrice wouldn't understand. Or she'd probably throw something at my head.

"Right," she says, "You're too much of a *freak* for dating."

Her loathing stings. *Why do I care what Latrice thinks?* She's a friend and not a particularly high-status one. Sure, she does the social media thing — and she's successful at it — but otherwise Latrice is *normal*. Possibly even boring. Not boring to me. I can bring the wild side out of her with a bit of cajoling.

I'm only saying...

I don't have to worry about what scumbag guys she brings around because frankly: there are none.

We can just hang out together. No competition. No desperation. I don't have to play games with her. I wouldn't say I *feel* anything around her. But I don't have to *be* the shit head little brother for a change.

And she loves lying by the pool. So she's automatically well suited to spending the summer in my villa. I wish I could be more like her. *Normal.*

But I'm not normal. Yiayia had me tested when I was a child.

"What's wrong with not dating?" I say to her, "There's no *point* in it."

"Falling in love," Latrice says, shrugging, "There's that."

"Why would I date? Why would *you* date? We're young. We just need fucking, cocaine and… sunshine."

Greece has an abundance of all three. I love my fucking country. Maybe I should get the flag tattooed on my ass. I'll ask Cass what she thinks. I'd ask Latrice but… then I'd have to talk to her about my ass and she normally hates when I bring up my ass. I don't know why. It's perfect…

I close my eyes and stretch, flexing every muscle in my chest and abdomen. I love a good stretch. Latrice pretends not to look at me. She *likes* my body — it's the rest of me she has a problem with. Tisha forced us together and now Tisha grumbles around, pissed we became best friends.

She hisses to Latrice about how she can be friends with a "stupid misogynist like Gal" and she warns me that if I put a hand on Latrice, she'll "castrate me like a market goat".

Tisha fancies herself a countryside Greek woman already and she hasn't even birthed a Pagonis brat yet. She'll be insufferable once the twins are here.

Loukas will be worse: fussing over them and expecting me to babysit.

"You are so shallow," Latrice complains, "I don't know why I hang out with you."

The pool begs me to jump in. I lie on the deck, working on my tan, letting my blond hair turn white from the sun. I love the high-lights. They make my face look even better.

"You *love* me," I whisper.

I want it to be true. I don't have an explanation.

"I do *not*. We're friends. And I don't even want people knowing about that."

"You have to admit that I at least have the best pool," I say lazily, yawning and stretching again, this time twisting my hips and groaning before flopping onto my stomach lazily. I wonder if Latrice could get me a drink.

I'd prefer a blowjob. But she definitely won't agree to that.

Latrice nods and flips over. Some of that oil drips down her curvy thigh and I think my cock will burst out of my shorts.

"True. If Tisha didn't introduce us, I would have run out of body positive content in London," she says, "Now I can post pics in my bikini, tan by the pool, eat the best food in the world and spend all day getting verbally harassed by a blond *sociopath*."

"Whatever. You love me."

She starts saying something else but I hear something more interesting.

"Shut up, Latrice," I growl, "I can't hear Fallon's argument with Stavros."

"What possessed you to buy the villa next door to theirs? I visited you when you shared a wall with them... I remember how they were."

I nodded, thinking about the constant loud sex. After Adrian, they have only amped up their nightly lovemaking routine.

Since the Adamos incident, it's like they're trying to break their bed. Again.

This argument seems to be about Fallon's new sex swing. I turn to Latrice and figure I had better put her to use before this gets too disturbing to listen to.

"Can you cut another line for me, babe?"

"I hate when you call me that," Latrice complains, "Anyone could hear and think we're dating or something. And I'm not helping you snort cocaine."

"Don't sound so offended. You would be lucky to have a taste of Pagonis cock."

Latrice sits up, her breasts spilling out of her pink swimsuit. I didn't know they made bikini tops for breasts this large. I can't help but stare.

It's Latrice, so she'll slap me if she catches me, but she's too busy telling me off to notice my eyes lewdly attached to her enormous breasts. Damn. They must be what... S-cups? I wonder if I could fit the entire nipple into my mouth...

Latrice snaps me back to reality. *Fuck.* Why can't I stop having sexual fantasies about her?

Latrice says, "I would rather die than date you."

As she huffs, the breasts swing past each other. I'm not thinking about a single word out of her mouth. Words are useless. Tits are better. But it's Latrice, so I have to play it cool.

"Right, because you're so much better than me," I grumble, standing up. She gazes up at me, her expression quickly changing to a scowl.

"Try eating a sandwich, Gal. I can see your hip bones poking out of your trunks."

"Can you see anything else from down there?"

I grab my crotch and Latrice shrieks, jumping back.

"Gal!" She yells, "That's not funny!"

"My hip bones are fine. I don't need to eat a sandwich. I need a swim. Will you jump in with me?"

"No."

"Too bad."

I run over and scoop Latrice up, which shocks her.

"Gal, put me down!" She yells as I carry her to the edge of the pool at a full sprint.

"Gal, you're crazy!"

"Grab on!" I yell one last time as I leap into the air and leap into the pool holding Latrice.

We sink into the water. I'm holding her. I have to. I grab her hips and her thighs wriggle against my body as we both find our way to the surface. I rise from the water, a natural swimmer while Latrice anxiously paddles and then floats on her back, gasping for breath.

TWO
0% CHANCE

'm going to kill you," she gasps as she grabs for the edge of the pool. I hop up and lean over, staring down Latrice's bikini top and pretending that I'm not. If Yiayia knew I was like my brothers... spending all my free time with a *black* girl... she'd go ballistic.

But Yiayia also taught me the most important lesson in life: *I can do whatever the fuck I want.*

"You aren't," I tell Latrice, shaking water out of my hair, "Without me, you'd never have any fun."

"I still never want you posting about me," Latrice warns, "My audience is *body positive*. They'll think I'm a total sell out if they know I spend all my time with Galanos Pagonis the fat shamer."

"You say my name like it's dirty, babe. And I didn't shame anyone. I simply said that it isn't healthy for cats to be obese and it makes them ugly."

"You also got cancelled for being racist," she says.

I roll my eyes.

"That was exaggerated. I was singing along."

"You get how that's still wrong?" Latrice huffs.

"Okay," I shrug, "I was wrong. But what else is so bad about me?"

"You posted a dick pic to your social media and nearly got the entire account deleted."

"That was an accident," I grumble, "Plus, if it didn't look good, you wouldn't still remember it."

Tiger and I did so much coke I barely remember posting the picture. I didn't even remember taking my dick out. But there were girls. Lots of girls. Fuck. Latrice is giving me that angry little beaver look.

"Stop it," Latrice protests, her American accent flattening the "O" sound to a crisp. I like her voice, all deep and gravely, with a bit of a twang to it.

"Fine. I don't know why you care what those people think. They don't understand how hard it is to be an influencer."

"You realize we spent three hours by the pool," Latrice says.

She's always trying to teach me about 'privilege'. I don't get why she wants me to feel so sorry about it. Why would I feel sorry about being better than everyone? Whenever I ask this, she slaps me. I will continue investigating…

First, I need to remind her that tanning by the pool is *excruciating* labor.

"Yes," I explain, "We spend hours by the pool. That's because I have to look perfect. That's the hard work. Looking perfect 100% of the time."

Latrice rolls her eyes.

"Perfect. Just because you fit the beauty standards doesn't make you *perfect.*"

"So you don't like the looks of this?"

I flex every muscle I can at once, showing off to her. Latrice, for all her ministrations, is a heterosexual woman. She can't help admiring my perfectly chiseled physique, nearly forgetting for a moment that she truly believes she's a better person than me. Our friendship has to be a secret because to her fans, she's an angel and I'm the devil incarnate.

"You are such a show off."

"I'm not a show off," I say, kneeling on the edge of the pool and offering my hand to Latrice. "I'm *perfect*. Blond. Tanned. Hot. Any woman I approach would be crazy to say no to me. I can fuck any girl I want."

"This is exactly why I don't want people knowing we're friends."

"Yes," I say, "And the mafia thing."

"That too. But your family is less... *murderous* than I expected. I think Tisha influenced y'all. That girl has a heart of gold. Did I tell you about the summer she fell in love with a chicken?"

I scoff. Latrice doesn't know my family the way I do if she thinks they're all cotton candy and sea breeze. She doesn't know what I've done either. But that's how I want it.

Latrice is wrong about us. Even Tisha has a dark side.

Latrice doesn't know I've killed. She can't ever find out. I had to do it. Family is everything. Carlotta always got me great deals on coke and I enjoyed beating the shit out of a few of her boyfriends. Even the people I hate and torment are precious to me. Now that I'm older, I *understand*.

Yiayia needs me like this so I can do the dirty work required of Pagonis men. Liquor plagues Loukas and voices plague Stavros. Helen and Cass are both Pagonis women — sharp, commanding, but insistent on keeping their brothers at arms length. They are not suited to this work anyway.

Our family needs a man who can kill and plot and keep his cool. Yiayia wanted that person to be me. She finally has her wish. It's nice to forget what I do for a while. And focus on a beautiful woman... who I can never touch.

Latrice sits on the edge of the pool next to me. I'm eager to sneak off to the bathroom to do a bump of coke. Latrice doesn't *do drugs*. She prefers getting high on life.

I prefer stimulants and alcohol. I quit smoking when Carlotta lost her eyesight because she quit and needed support. I miss cigarettes. I have a secret stash for emergencies, naturally. But I mostly quit for my niece.

I'm not the devil incarnate, even if Latrice and her legions of fans think so. I may not be an angel, but I put my family first.

"Listen," I ask her tentatively, knowing that Latrice will probably say 'no' to my request, "I need you to come to the nightclub tonight. I *need* you."

"What? Why?"

"Because...I need assistance with a very important task. Plus, I need a date. Carlotta's dating some creepy Vogue Italia model, Cassia's bringing Sandros, and Antonio's boyfriend is in town. I can't be the only one not to have a date. I'm a Pagonis."

Latrice rolls her eyes.

"You're so narcissistic."

"Women like it."

She glances at the water bashfully, the long hair from her wig dusting the surface of the water. Her round face scrunches up as she considers my request regarding the baby shower.

"You have to tell your family we're just friends," she says, "I don't want people to think we're dating... like *ever*. It's already weird enough that I'm staying at your place."

"We sleep in separate bedrooms."

"Probably because I lock my door," Latrice mutters.

"What are you implying, Latrice?" I lean forward and smirk, biting down on my lower lip and causing her to glance away nervously.

"I'm not implying anything. And I don't want *you* implying anything either. But I guess I'll come with you. I don't have anything better to do."

"Perfect," I tell her, "Thank you, babe. Come inside with me."

"I'll stay out here," Latrice calls, "it's nice out."

"Cassia's bringing some friends tonight. It should be wild."

"Too wild. Y'all need to learn how to chill. I don't want to wear an Adidas tracksuit and party until 10 a.m. every damn weekend. I'd better catch up on my beauty sleep. "

"That's Thessaloniki, babe. You need to find a nice man to go home with."

Latrice wrinkles her nose and mutters, "Ew."

I grin and tease her more.

"Latrice," I ask, "are you gay? I am okay with all homosexuality."

"Shut up. Just because I don't want to screw some gross guy at a club doesn't mean I'm a lesbian."

"I've never met any of your boyfriends," I tell her. Which is true. It's why I like her. No idiot guys around to get in the way of hanging out. Latrice is *always* there when I want to chill with her.

"I've only ever hooked up," she says, "it's not a big deal. Shut up, Gal."

We're getting into uncomfortable territory. Latrice hates talking about this stuff with me. She'd hate it more if she knew how sexually depraved I was.

Not wanting her to find out is the main reason I haven't forced the issue of screwing her, even if I think about it constantly.

"Sex?" I ask, "How many guys?"

"Gal, stop."

"What?"

"I hate how you get like this," she snaps, standing up, "You do this all the time. Sex. We're not talking about sex. You and I... we're never going to go there. So drop it."

"We're friends," I snap back, "Friends talk about sex."

"Not us. Because you're a shallow prick who sleeps with anything who walks and I have feelings. The last thing I want to do is make this shit confusing. I know people don't tell you 'no' but let me be the first."

"I'm not fucking attracted to you, Latrice," I tell her, "Now. Can we chill for a bit and head out tonight? I'm starving."

"So am I," Latrice mutters, "But I'll stay out here a while longer. You go change."

I walk away from her red-faced. My Pagonis temper embarrasses me. I shouldn't snap at her. She's Latrice. The best friend I've had in ages. Yiayia didn't like me having friends but she wouldn't like me having friends like Latrice.

Tisha's cousin happens to be a plus-sized body positive influencer with a follow count in the millions, near mine.

Her manager agreed to let her move to Greece and document her "expat life" and we've spent every day together ever since. Best friends? Maybe. As close a friend as Galanos Pagonis could have.

I shouldn't push Latrice. She barely wants to be friends with me and she'd never entertain the idea of anything more. We keep our friendship secret and I don't mind.

I'm lying to her, anyway. I mean, I'm usually lying to someone, but this time it's my best friend. I'm not fucking attracted to her? Lie. I think about her all the time. I have screwed all the models I could get my hands on for the past two years and I've chased a high that I could never achieve.

I know what I want but... I bite down on my lower lip and think about Latrice's comments. Maybe what I think is admiration is only disgust. I don't understand people. Or feelings. I only understand desire — that heat beneath the skin, the racing of my heart. The wanting.

From the moment I saw Latrice, I wanted her. I knew she would be perfect for what I wanted. I sensed it on her, like a shark smells blood miles away in the water.

Tonight, I'll have her. I have it all worked out — the way I'll tell her how I feel. She'll move my coke, she'll spread her legs and she'll beg me to fuck her. I have every detail planned. How I'll kiss her. How I'll spread her thighs and allow her flesh to spill into my hands as I bury my tongue in the deepest cunt imaginable.

Ah, Perfection.

Nothing could ruin tonight. And then I'll take her to Tisha's baby shower and she'll agree to be my girlfriend. Maybe even my wife. It'll be easy once she realizes that she's addicted to my cock. **There is a 0% chance this plan will fail.**

I'm a Pagonis after all and I always get what I want.

THREE
GOLDEN

get ready for the night out. Black trousers, a green silk shirt halfway undone. Gold rings. Gold chains. A gold earring. A necklace with a spoon in it, packed with as much coke as I can fit.

Gel in the blond hair. I look like a young, blond Stavros. He hates that he can't party as much as I do anymore. I mean, I'm sure he loves his kid but he must miss women.

Cassia bursts through my side door with Sandros, who has grown into a hulking giant since Loukas took over his workout routine. I don't like that I can't push him around anymore. I prefer lean muscle to Loukas' bulky gains.

"Gal. Nice outfit," Sandros grunts.

"My jewelry costs more than your parents house," I tell him, because I'm an asshole and that's what they expect from Yiayia's favorite, "Look at the rings, Sandros. This one I took from Giorgio Adamos' finger. Solid fucking gold."

Sandros can't help but admire the rings because he grew up worshipping my family. He stares at Cassia like a little pup. Sandros doesn't mean to be a beta male, but he can't help it. He didn't have my upbringing. He didn't have Yiayia.

"Shut up, Gal," Cassia mutters, yanking the baggie of drugs from my hand, "Carlotta's coming with her new boy toy, so I need to be super high. He's a creeper. The way he talks about her…"

"I thought he was a Vogue model?" I say, thinking about drugs and cigarettes.

Remember that you quit. Remember for Carlotta.

Carlotta has horrible taste in men, probably because her father is a psychotic drunk who fucked her best friend, but who am I to judge? If Loukas is a monster, I'm satan's right hand.

"What does he say about her?" Latrice asks, scampering out into the living room. Cassia's face brightens once she sees Latrice, now wearing a pink wig and a black wrap dress that leaves *nothing* to the imagination. She fills it out so perfectly with ample curves spilling over. I adjust my crotch and move behind the couch so none of them can see how hard I get when she walks into the room.

"You look *so* good. And he's got a blind fetish," Cassia reports in a hushed voice, "I'm serious. He's creepy."

"Tisha and Loukas will sort him," I reassure her, "They're equally murderous."

Cassia groans, "Are you still hung up on Tisha?"

I shrug and move one of my gold rings up and down my index finger as I say, "I fingered her and she didn't even fall in love with me."

"Isn't he entitled, Latrice?" Cassia scoffs, "And don't talk about fingering her. If Lou heard you, he'd castrate you."

"He *tried once*. That stupid incident in the kitchen where the girl screamed rape."

Latrice gets visibly uncomfortable and buries her face in a glass of wine. Cass never knows when to shut her mouth. Yiayia was right to sell her to Ofek. We're close half the time, but the rest of the time I want to slaughter my annoying younger sister. We're roughly the same age. Different mothers. But Cass's didn't abandon her.

"You tried to rape her," Cassia accuses, "You were *laughing*."

"She told me she had a fetish, I was obeying orders!"

Cassia snaps, "If someone ordered you to jump off a bridge, would you do it, *idiota*?"

Cassia's been sprinkling more Italian into her dialect because she spent one week vacationing there at Van Doukas' invitation. He creeps everyone out except Cass. Stavros suspects she's working for him now, but Cass would never tell if she had another source of income. After her failed marriage to Ofek, she never trusted any of us properly.

"Listen," I explain, "I didn't rape her. I've *never* raped anyone. I get laid plenty on my own. I'm *literally* the most attractive person in a ten mile radius."

"Yet Tisha rejected you..." Cass mutters.

"I'll fucking kill you, Cass."

Sandros perks up like a pit bull and steps up to me.

"Careful what you say to her. She's my woman. I'll protect her."

See what I mean? Puppy. I don't warn a man when he touches my woman. I start by punching him in the face and then I work from there.

"Back off, you stupid moose," I tell him, "we're siblings. This is how we express love."

Cass skips the drugs and passes the baggie to Sandros who follows. I take two bumps and Latrice declines one.

Carlotta arrives with her walking stick and her boyfriend, Evan. He's seven-feet-tall and built like an Olympic swimmer with black hair, a large Persian nose and shoulder length hair. He says "namaste" a lot and dresses like a cult leader.

"I'm here with my beautiful *sightless* love," He says, walking up to me and hugging me before kissing me on the lips. I push him off.

"Watch it," I snarl, wiping the wetness from his lips off mine aggressively.

Where does she find these simians?

"*Namaste,* family of Carlotta. My beautiful prophetess ensures that there are plenty of psychedelics and other experience enhancing drugs for our night's festivities. Pray tell, where may I find a bump."

His American-Italian hybrid accent makes me shudder. I give him drugs to shut him up for a few seconds. He takes a tab of LSD and smokes an entire spliff before doing three bumps of my coke stash.

This rich asshole is yet another dick in a long line of Carlotta's boyfriends. We all miss that attendant of hers.

Poor Carlotta couldn't handle him and abandoned him on the Ethiopian coast after the hospital transferred Yiayia back to Greece.

If Lou finds out how much of a cunt Evan is, he *will* kill this man. Even with the distraction of Tisha and the twin fetuses. I can't believe that tiny little thing can fit twins inside her.

Tisha. I hate that everyone knows how wrong that went for me. I had a crush on her, while my creep older brother was sliding into her bed at night. Embarrassing. But I've moved on. I don't stay stuck on women for long. Except Latrice. Months of waiting. Months of planning. Months of finding the right moment.

My new obsession is the only thing I can think about. She's not like my normal obsessions. It's not only lust. There's something else that I've never experienced before. Similar to what I feel for my family but... different.

It's something unique to her. Latrice. Black. Curvy. Gorgeous. I'm high enough to stare at her without caring if she notices me. I'm high enough to imagine her riding me. Kissing me. Fellating me.

She flips hair from the pink wig over her shoulder. I have plans for her tonight... sexual plans. I could never marry her, obviously. Yiayia would never approve. But I can fuck her. I can *take* her. I look forward to it.

Carlotta hangs on Evan's arm, skipping both drugs and cigarettes and taking a shot of tequila instead.

"Let's party! I'm losing my best friend to motherhood in a few months and I need to let loose. Gal, caffeine pills for later?"

"Ready and waiting. Latrice? Ready to rave?"

"You people are crazy. I might come home early."

"Nonsense. We'll keep you dancing all night until you find a guy to go home with."

And I need her to move a shit ton of cocaine. I can't have Latrice out of it.

Latrice laughs and lightens up a little, "Are you going to be my wingman, Gal Pagonis?"

"Yes. And you'll be mine. Find me a girl to go home with."

"What happens if neither of us find someone?" Latrice says.

I scoff, "Babe, I'll go home with a girl tonight. The night's not over until I've fucked someone hard."

Latrice pushes me off her. She hates when I talk like this and she usually yells. Tonight, she's quieter than normal. And has more of an attitude. When I tell her she has an attitude she calls it a *micro-aggression* but I don't know what that is.

"Everything okay?"

"My latest post. Someone posted about it on a gossip blog and theorized we knew each other."

I put my arm around her and pull her against me. She leans into me but pretends to be disgusted by the sensation of my firm, perfect body resting against hers.

"Well, we know each other, so they aren't wrong."

"I'd ruin your brand too," she says as we walk along the cobble-stone streets toward the club. A stray dog barks at Cass, who insults the dog's mother and grandmother in one broad curse.

"You wouldn't ruin my brand," I say, "You are... unique."

"Everyone who follows you and who you interact with is stick thin, blond and covered in muscle. Let's be real, Gal. We should keep our friendship secret. Be on the lookout for any phones."

"I don't care, Latrice," I groan, "I just want to dance... do drugs and find a girl to fuck. If we fuck other people tonight, we don't have to worry about gossip. So can you relax?"

"Fine. But don't say I didn't warn you."

"If I fuck up my social media money, I'll just do what my brothers do... kill people."

"What would I do?" Latrice snaps, "Work as you're damned maid?"

"I would keep you busy, babe."

Latrice scoffs and folds her arms before chastising me again, "You'd never. You're too soft-hearted."

"Literally no one thinks that about me."

She's the type of girl who sees a lion chew on a living gazelle and calls it 'cute'. She'd have to be to find me soft-hearted.

"They don't know you like I do," Latrice says. Hm. Maybe all the sun has damaged her. I put my hand to her forehead to check for a fever and she swats my hand away. No fever, I guess. It's a good moment. Latrice, beautiful, standing so close to me, and nothing horrible happening for once in my life.

I want to tell her. Now. But I don't. I have a plan, and I can't screw it up.

FOUR
BETTER THAN SEX

Antonio shows up at the villa with two bottles of wine.

"I'm eighteen bitches!!!" He yells at the gate, "I can finally get into the club with my *real* ID!"

Latrice buzzes him in. Antonio's wearing a mesh tank top and jeans. He has both his nipples pierced like we're in London and not Greece. He's looking to get his ass kicked. Luckily, despite my concerns, Antonio appears capable of handling himself.

I hope he did his damned research about the night club. If we sell in the wrong clubs to the wrong people, we could create serious problems that fuck up our cocaine empire. Selling party drugs cut with Johnson & Johnson baby powder to British tourists has supplied both of us with plenty of *pura vida* South American cocaine to last the summer.

I don't want to say goodbye to easy money. I don't want Latrice to ever worry about it. I want her in my villa forever, really. She will be my best friend, lover, then wife and basically... I can have all the fun I want. Loukas would tell me it isn't much of a life plan but what does he know?

"Woo!" Latrice screams excitedly at the sight of Antonio, "Party time!"

"Yes, queen! I love your hair…"

Antonio kisses her on the cheek and lifts his boot.

"Look at the platform on these, sis. They are fierce as fuck…"

"Where'd you get them?"

Antonio shrugs, "Doesn't matter. Let me make you a cocktail in your mouth."

Antonio shakes up the Peppermint Schnapps he carries in one hand and tells Latrice, "Open up!"

She only listens because it's Antonio. My nephew doesn't have his father's eyes but he's like Loukas in nearly every other way. Except sexual preferences.

Antonio came out to me when he was fourteen and I was sixteen. Some Thermopolis asshole pushed him into a wall and called him a horrible name. I saw the bruises and helped him get revenge.

I've looked after my nephew ever since, still giving him shit once in a while for liking cock. But he's my blood and my best friend. He's busy with boyfriends now, but his newest will meet us at the club later.

Antonio cheers as he squirts a mouthful of chocolate sauce into Latrice's mouth and pours a shot of Schnapps. Latrice closes her mouth, cheeks bulging like a puffer fish and then she swallows.

"Holy shit. That was good."

I roll my eyes and snap, "I don't want you pouring your cum drink into my mouth. Coke? MDMA? What are we selling the scumbags tonight?"

Latrice unlocks her phone and starts tapping around like she usually does when we start talking drugs. Or *the family business* as I call it. Antonio sets down his bottles and drags me out. I brush his hand away once we're in the foyer.

"You talk about this shit in front of Latrice?" Antonio scolds.

He's Loukas' son alright. My *nephew* forgets his place often. I know how Yiayia would handle this. I opt for a more *Loukas Pagonis* option.

"I can do whatever I want," I snap, "Drugs? What do you have?"

"I need to move this."

He reaches into the pockets of his pants. Three ounces of weed in ten Euro bags. Then fifteen bags of coke.

"I'm taking one for myself," I say, "charge me later."

"Fine. But we need to move the rest."

"No way we're getting this shit in the club after the Adamos incident."

Antonio rolls his eyes and insists, "We're fine."

"Are you sure we can sell here?"

"Who cares? Who the fuck will get in the way of Pagonis business."

"Antonio. Promise me you looked into it."

Antonio folds his arms and starts sounding like his sister when he insists, "If we don't sell drugs how are we supposed to get spending money?"

"You could always fuck an old guy," I tell him.

Antonio pushes me.

"Fuck off, Gal."

"Latrice," I tell him, "We can use Latrice to get it in the club. She's not Greek. She has huge tits, she can fit this between them."

Antonio shakes his head and disapproves sharply, "No. She's not Greek. Which is exactly why we can't get her involved in mafia business."

He's just like Loukas. Too cautious, too caught up in his own self-loathing to be useful.

"She's my friend," I snarl, "If she won't fuck me, she has to be useful to me somehow."

Antonio snickers.

"That bothers you, doesn't it? The one girl on earth who won't sleep with you?"

"Shut up."

"We can't use her," Antonio whispers.

"Give me the drugs, pussy."

He hands the drugs over with a glare and I put a hand on his shoulder before I warn him, "Tell Loukas and I'll tell him what I saw you doing last week."

"Papa knows," Antonio says, but he's not sure. I don't know how Loukas could miss it. Antonio's never been subtle. I still like keeping my nephew on his toes.

"I'm bringing a 9 mm tonight. Stay armed. You never know when an Adamos cousin might return to Thess for revenge. We can't all stay home screwing our wives like Lou and Stavros."

"You are the most bitter uncle in existence."

I reach my finger into the bag and do a bump. It's good shit. Clean shit.

"Fuck," I gasp, "It's perfect. Better than sex."

"No, Uncle Galanos," Antonio says, "nothing's better than sex when it's with the right person."

Latrice walks into the room with her arms folded.

"What are you two still whispering about?"

"Drugs," I tell her, "I need your help."

"*My help?!*"

"You sleep in my villa, you use my pool, nothing in life comes free. Hide this in your bra."

I withdraw everything from my pockets and Latrice has a nearly cartoonish reaction.

"You are fucking kidding me."

"What?"

"I thought you were a crack head lying about all that mafia shit."

"Do I look like a fucking crack head? Put the shit in your bra. Now."

Latrice rolls her eyes.

"I'm not doing what you command like one of your little girl-friends."

"I don't have girlfriends," I snap, "I have sex slaves."

Latrice flashes me a look of utter disgust. Her loathing shouldn't have the effect on me that it does.

"I'm not one of your *slaves*."

She sounds so disgusted with me. I hate how that makes me feel. Like I want her more. I yearn for her.

"I can tell," I snap, "You're not nearly obedient enough."

"Are you listening to yourself? You have *slaves*? Earth to Galanos. I'm black."

"What does that have to do with me? I'm Greek. Will you help me with the drugs or not?"

"Will you stop being an asshole if I help you?"

"Yes."

But I'm lying. I'll never stop being an asshole, especially not to Latrice. I can't ever confess my true feelings to her because then she'd find out the truth about me. I'm exactly as sick as she suspects. And worse. My reputation in Thess amongst women has landed me in a few scrapes. I only have Yiayia to thank for weaseling out of them.

"I'll help," she agrees, "But if anything happens to me, I will *kill* you."

"We own this town, babe."

"I am *not* your babe."

But you could be.

"Whatever. Take the fucking drugs. Hurry."

Latrice is uncomfortable all the way there. I go in through the backdoor after showing the bouncer my Pagonis ring and flashing my 9mm. Latrice follows behind me, apologizing.

"Did you just *threaten to kill that guy*?" She squeals.

"Come," I tell her, grabbing her wrist and dragging her down the back hallways to the VIP rooms. I have a room reserved five days a week. Once we're in the room, I lock the door behind us and she takes the drugs out of her bra. I still have mine in my pocket.

"Great," I tell her, "Think you can move half of this?"

"I'm not selling drugs, Gal," she protests, "I brought them into the club but you have gone *way* too far. I only came here tonight so we could hang out and have a good time."

I roll my eyes and take another bump. I need to be a lot higher to handle Latrice's protests. And to have the social skills to move this much fucking coke.

"You brought them into the club. Why not sell them?"

"It's illegal."

"It's only illegal if you get in trouble."

"That's not how the law works," Latrice says, getting more frustrated, "I'll leave you here with your family business. I'm going to hang out with the others."

She lunges for the door.

"Latrice, wait."

"What?"

She turns around, pressing her back to the door. I am *so close* to telling her.

"Stay here," I say, "They won't expect us downstairs."

I take my shirt off. Latrice stares.

I make my bold proposal. The one that will be impossible for her to refuse.

"I'll fuck you, I'll eat you out. Then we can have a good night."

Latrice's voice changes and she gets serious, "Galanos, put your shirt back on. Seriously."

"Why? I've got a perfect body. I have a perfect cock. So sleep with me, Latrice."

FIVE
A BLIND GIRL & A PREGNANT WOMAN

Latrice gazes at me in horror. I've revealed a part of myself to her. The repulsive, nearly sociopathic Galanos Pagonis that I normally try to hide.

My mother had me tested before she ran out on us. I was two points away from the diagnosis.

Oppositional defiant disorder. It's likely Galanos could become a sociopath. He's still young. With a proper environment, he could still become a normal boy.

That was all my mother needed to hear before she left. Papa was already smacking her around. She just needed a little push.

Mama tried to get in touch with me since then. I sent her dog shit in the mail. Mama was one of Papa's sluts. A desperate Greek skank like all the girls I know here. Loukas and Stavros might have liked me better if I had their mother. Not some slutty teen girl who played stepmom when they were already adults.

I hate my mother. I hate that my brothers and sisters know how she didn't want me. I hate how they treat me like the extra child. They like Cass better because she's more like them. I'm blond. Gangly. Different.

It's what makes Latrice so... refreshing. She doesn't know me as little shitty Galanos. She likes me. Except she has that angry beaver face again and I'm doing something wrong... I don't know what.

"Get your clothes off," I demand, "Now."

"I'm leaving, Gal," Latrice snaps.

I cut back at her, "Why won't you do it? I see how you stare at me."

"Why won't I sleep with you?" Latrice says, shutting the door again, "Let me count the reasons. Number one, you're a sociopath."

"I'm *almost* a sociopath."

"It doesn't matter," Latrice huffs, "Number two, you're completely shallow and only go for skinny blond Greek girls."

I interrupt her again. Why is she being so annoying? Why isn't she doing what I want...

"That's not true," I snap, "I only introduce white girls to my grandmother because she's racist. Why would I put someone I cared about through that?"

Latrice snorts and then twists the knife, "Number *three,* you don't *care* about anyone but yourself."

"I care about my family," I snap, "I killed for my niece. And I'd do it again."

Latrice pauses. Fuck. She's caught me in a lie. I told her I'd never killed before and "forgot" to mention the incident with the Adamos brothers.

Fallon took Adrian to America to meet her family while Stavros worked the job.

He had to risk the voices to save Carlotta. Tisha refused to leave Greece while we hunted. She gained five pounds from binge-eating chicken fingers nightly while we worked.

By the time we got back to the city, Tisha was nearly about to pop and Fallon was desperate to get pregnant again.

We have so many men on payroll now to make up for the gap left by the Adamos family that my brilliant accountant of a brother — Lou — cut our salaries.

Everyone under twenty-two had their salaries cut. Antonio sells drugs and I split the money with him and sell too when I need spare change. I've been eyeing a new part for my AR-15 and Tiger wants to take me to Russia to hunt foxes.

I have my contracts from the social media followers, but really, that's how I meet girls. *Depraved* girls who won't whisper about me around Thessaloniki. Unlike Stavros and Loukas, I don't make my sex life a family problem.

Carlotta gets money by stealing from Tisha. For a blind girl, she's a remarkable thief, but not remarkable enough. Carlotta thinks Tisha doesn't know. Tisha allows her to steal a monthly stipend of exactly €17,400. You would think Carlotta might figure it out eventually.

The weight of the silence pains me as Latrice realizes how many times I lied to her. I might have 'forgotten' several more times than I let on.

"You lied to me," Latrice says, her voice dripping with rage. But she isn't surprised.

The angry beaver face changes. She's *sad?* Or horny? Probably sad. I'm horny. It's impossible not to be horny around her.

"Not exactly," I tell her, "I didn't *like* killing him. That part was true."

"Number four," Latrice hisses, "You're a monster."

Okay, she's definitely not horny. Latrice flings the door open again.

"Latrice, wait..."

She glances back at me, hopeful that I'll apologize. *Never show contrition or any signs of weakness.* I straighten my back and point at the drugs on the table.

"Get the fuck over here and take these downstairs. If I don't have €3,000 by the end of the night, you'll have to sleep over at Tisha's."

"You don't have to act this way, Gal," Latrice grumbles, grabbing up the bags and stuffing them into her purse, "You don't have to act so cold just because you're afraid of rejection. If you want people to like you, try being a better person."

I grab her forearm before she can duck out of reach and I squeeze.

"I didn't need you to like me," I snarl, "I need you to do what women are good for. Get me my *fucking* money. Now get out."

Latrice storms off with the drugs. I think she'll have my money. I don't scare her even when I try. She gets angry and then she comes back to me. I can't figure out why she keeps coming back. I guess at the end of the day, I must be an amazing friend.

But I can't get her to love me. Even when I try. What is she talking about a better person? What's better than Pagonis man? I'm as tall as Loukas now (but not as tall as Stavros).

My hair's perfect. I have an incredible body and I eat exactly 1,550 calories every day — including alcohol — and work out three hours daily. *Better?* I don't know what Latrice could mean by that...

A better house maybe? The villa was €10 million. It's nice enough I think... I follow her and consider ways to improve myself. If that's what Latrice wants, I can do it. Become *better*. Once she has my money, I'll tell her about my new commitment.

She's downstairs whispering to Antonio, probably getting his advice on how to drown me in my own pool. Tiger's spinning at the club tonight — Eurotrash techno that only sounds good when you're high out of your mind. I'm in luck. Three bumps in and I'm starting to feel it. The sheer bliss of cocaine. I hurry downstairs and scream.

"WOO! Galanos Pagonis in the house!"

The crowd erupts in cheers. I buy a round of drinks for the entire club. Party. Man I fucking love to party. I see Latrice in the corner of the club talking to a group of girls. Money changes hands. Shit is going well for me. Antonio stumbles out of the bathroom with a few drag queens who all look *very* happy.

Drugs keep this nightclub alive. Drugs keep Greece alive. I didn't bother asking Antonio where he got the drugs from. Loukas' son is a Pagonis too. He has a right to acquire drugs from wherever he wants. I hope he was right about the club being safe. We're making money fast with worse coke because this isn't a typical Pagonis stomping ground.

Thank you, Tiger...

I watch Latrice moving around the club again. Tisha shows up at the entrance of the club with a bottle of water. Carlotta and Evan run over to her and Carlotta hugs her tightly. Tisha probably snuck out for one last night of partying with the twins.

I'll shit myself if she brought my idiot brother. If Lou finds out what we're doing, he'll kick my ass.

Downstairs, everyone makes way for the pregnant woman and a few people cheer when Carlotta and Evan help her up onto a table. Tisha yells, "I'm nine months mother-fucking pregnant y'all! Take a shot for me!"

I guess this is one of her old party palaces with Carlotta. Their partying days will be over soon once Tisha finally doubles over and pops out some babies. Maybe I can pay her to name one Galanos. I grin as I imagine Loukas losing his mind or perhaps even wondering if the child is mine.

The crowd cheers as they keep dancing. A blind girl and a pregnant woman dancing on the bar. If Loukas could see this, he'd have ah heart attack.

Ah well, I'll bring it up at the baby shower if it gets boring. That should spark things. A cute girl comes up to me. She smells like coconut and the ocean. Fuck. She's sexy and her nipples poke out of her dress.

"Hey," I say, ready to ask her to come upstairs to the VIP room with me. She looks tight.

"Hey," she says, "Are you Galanos?"

"Yes."

She giggles and wraps her arms around me. I put my hands on her hips and she giggles as she comes close to me.

"That easy, babe?" I murmur, "What's your name?"

I love this part. Her body is small though. Smaller than I'd prefer. And she smells like liquor. But she's sexy. I bet she'd scream.

But as the woman presses her lips to my ear, she doesn't kiss me or answer my question.

She whispers, "We have your African prostitute behind the club with a gun to her head. If you aren't out there in 2 minutes, my brothers will put two bullets in her skull. How dare you sell coke in our territory, Pagonis scum. We had a deal."

She punches me in the stomach as hard as she can, taking me by surprise. I double over and struggle for breath. Fuck. Fuck, they have Latrice. And since when did we make a deal about this club? Fuck. I don't have time to think about that. *They have Latrice.*

My heart leaps into my throat as adrenaline courses through me.

I run. I don't think my legs have the capacity to go as fast as they do. I run behind the nightclub and whip out of my gun, skidding to a stop as I hook my finger around the trigger.

It's too late. *Fuck.* Three guys. AR-15s. They have Latrice and worse, they have four guns pointed at my head. I drop my 9mm into a puddle. Rain pours over us in a sudden cloud.

SIX

OUR DARKEST CHAPTER

The men put a gun to Latrice's head. I can't play games anymore. They have Latrice which means nothing is going according to plan. I've played with fire and now the flames are licking at my heels, pushing me into peril.

I recognize them. The Stathakis brothers. *Fuck*. And then I remember. I'd been in a drug-induced haze when Loukas warned us about this. But he'd warned us. Antonio should have reminded me who we were fucking with. I wouldn't have brought only a 9mm and my *best friend in a pink wig*. I would have brought men. Reinforcements. Greek bastards who wait in the VIP room to blow a hole in Stathakis skulls.

These are the assholes Lou cut a deal with to keep Yiayia safe in the Thessaloniki private hospital facility. They are unstable. Powerful. Growing in strength. But like our family, the Stathakis brothers are not unwilling to negotiate in either diplomacy or violence.

The ugly one appears to have lost taste for diplomacy. And he looks like a horse.

Horse snaps, "Step onto the boat."

"No," I say, "We won't. Kill us here if you're going to and have my family descend on you like wolves."

Latrice lets out an anguished sob, "Gal, no!"

I'm trying to call their bluff but Latrice isn't helping. Rain. So much rain. It sticks my shirt to me and I can smell the liquor on all of us. My head hurts. I need more cocaine so I can think straight. Or more liquor.

"Get onto the fucking boat, Pagonis or I'll blow the bitch's brains out," Horse threatens again.

Fuck. My grandmother has a way of getting into trouble with people but that trouble rarely ends up on my doorstep. This was my doing. Antonio had a job to do but I am the older male.

You are the boss, Galanos. You can shoot your way out of anything.

"We're listening," I say calmly, "Don't hurt her. You don't have to. We can talk this through. It's a misunderstanding."

That's my biggest priority. I don't want these bastards to do anything to Latrice.

"Misunderstanding, Galanos? I fucking know you. I fucking watched you grow up. You're an entitled little shit. I told Loukas to make sure you stayed away and here you are... so *get on the fucking boat with the bitch.*"

I step onto the boat with my hands up. We need another way out. Latrice follows and cries as she gets on the boat. I'm silent. Thinking. And realizing there's no way out, a new gnawing sensation works in my lower abdomen. I'm painfully aware of how vulnerable we are and worse, how vulnerable I've made her.

I won't be able to tell Latrice sorry before we die. Before they shoot us and toss our bodies in the ocean.

They're quiet as they pull away from shore, leaving us on the deck. We're a few hours away from sunrise, so it's still dark, which is bad. I don't know if I can swim to shore in the dark. If I could get away.

But even if I could get away, I would have to leave Latrice behind. I'd take a bullet before doing that.

We can hear the nightclub from the boat and then there's silence as we're far enough away from shore. They kill the motor. Latrice whimpers. I want to comfort her but I still need to think. I can't afford to have her sobbing and crying.

I have not lived a good life, have I? It's been all drugs. All partying. No falling in love. No children. And now I'm going to die and leave behind no *heir*.

Poor Yiayia tried to trick me into getting many village girls pregnant. They were all too thin and pale to work for me. Too *vanilla*. Maybe I should have had a child. The chance will be gone after tonight.

I'll be a body. An *ugly* distended corpse.

The men shine their lights around the deck. There's a large fishing chest in the center but no weapons. And no way out. I have to pray that Antonio is sober enough to figure out I've disappeared too long.

He's Loukas' son, hopefully he inherited his father's competence and not just his ability to get on my nerves.

"Bend over the chest," Horse says.

I'm not thinking. I'm enraged. Or maybe a part of me sees what's coming. There are many types of punishments in the mafia. Some are less discussed than others. I have a feeling Horse wants to subject me to a *lesser discussed* punishment. I'm sorry for what I say next, but the heat gets to me.

"Fuck you," I snarl.

The man slams the gun into the side of my face before I can say anything. I yelp as blood gushes from my cheek, filling my mouth with the metal taste. I spit and yell a curse at them in Greek. The gun hits me again. I throw a punch and the man grabs my necklace, yanking it off. The stupid thing bursts open and a sprinkling of cocaine dusts my face like fresh snowfall.

Stick and Stone push Latrice face down over the chest next to me. They hit her with their gun and I panic. Hurting me is one thing but

Latrice has nothing to do with this. She wouldn't be here if it weren't for me.

"NO! Don't hit her!" I lose my mind as I watch what they're about to do to her. Horror hits when I know they mean it. There's nothing arousing about the situation. They're going to violate us before killing us. It hits me what the gnawing sensation in my stomach is. *Fear.* I must have felt it before. Long ago. When mama kissed me goodbye. When I moved in with Yiayia.

They're going to rape her and I can't stop them.

For all my depravity, I never lied about that to my family. Rape is abhorrent. Dreadful. Blood rushes past my ears and my tongue turns into a cotton ball.

I struggle and they slam a gun into my face again. I fight and they snarl, "One more move and the bitch is dead!"

There's only dread. Nausea. I can't stop fighting for her, even if I can't move. I thrash and scream and use every muscle in my body to try to break away and stop them.

I'm yelling at them and begging them, but it's like another person is yelling. I'm outside of myself. Lost.

"LATRICE. LATRICE I'M SORRY."

She's whimpering and crying still. The sound claws at me and I can feel my own blood pouring out of my wounds. I'm not in enough pain. I'm not in the pain I deserve for hurting her like this.

Loukas always says I'm too fucking young and dumb for his own good. Today, I glimpse how true it is.

"Let her go. Let her go," I plead, "She's American! You want the fucking CIA down here busting up all our operations?"

They lift her black dress. I keep arguing. Yelling. Not that black dress. I liked that dress. The one that left little to the imagination. And then they rape her. Stone doesn't care that his cock is out in front of a bunch of men he works with. There's just this: hurting a woman, overpowering her. Humiliating her.

Not Latrice. She's *an angel.* She doesn't deserve this. I throw myself at them and earn another punch in the face and then one in the ribs. I hear my ribs crack.

Latrice screams. I yell at them to stop. I go crazy trying to fight. *No. They can't do this.* But the men push me down and they stick a wad of cloth into my mouth.

There's nothing I can do now because it's my turn. With Latrice subdued, I'm next. I may be twenty and large, but I can't fight off multiple men. With guns. I yelp as I feel the first one. I cry louder than Latrice. Pain. Red hot pain. Her screaming. And then mine. I sound like a little girl. And I cry worse than one.

I don't think it will ever end. I think they'll kill us both, unloading the guns into our heads after the rape. But then its over and the sea is eerily quiet again, as if the torment never happened. They sail as the attack on us continues and by the time the last one beats the center of my back with a wooden pole after ramming into me, we're several miles from Thessaloniki.

I feel warmth trickling down my leg. Blood, I tell myself. It's blood. Latrice whimpers but she can't move. The men take her and throw her overboard. *She'll drown.* And then they take me and throw me overboard too. I'm nearly too weak to swim. My ass hurts. My legs hurt. But Latrice isn't a good swimmer — not as good as Pagonis.

If I don't pull myself together, I'm not the only one who will die out here. She'll die out here too. I've done enough to Latrice. I can't allow her to die. *I have to save her.*

My mouth fills with water. I sink beneath the surface and hear the boat's motor chugging beneath the water. I kick and grab hair. Her wig. *I'm close.* I reach further and grab her arm. I pull Latrice up over my shoulder. I don't care how heavy she is, I *will* bring her to shore. I will keep her alive. Adrenaline surges through me and I find my strength through the pain.

I'll stay alive for her. I'll *protect her.*

I'm a Pagonis and I will survive this. I will kill the men who hurt us. And then... I don't know what I'll do. I will either have Latrice or I will have nothing. My only purpose right now is saving her. Keeping her alive. *Healing her.*

Because my selfishness caused this to happen to my best friend. I swim for forty minutes against heavy currents to shore and when I spread Latrice's body on the beach, her dark lips are blue.

I touch her and feel a pulse. She's breathing. Her heart's slow but she's alive. I push down on her chest and by some miracle there's no water in her lungs. She's just unconscious. I wish I was unconscious. I'm naked and *cold* and I still have to get us out of here, wherever the fuck we are.

Her wig hangs off her head and I remove it. I push on her arm, desperately trying to wake her as salt stings my wounds and my soaked hair sticks to my neck. *I need her alive.*

"Latrice," I murmur, "wake up."

My voice catches in my throat. She looks dead and I'm the one who did this to her. She stirs a little. But not enough. We can't stay out here for long. It's nearly morning. I drag her to a little house on the beach front.

There's an old woman staring at us from the window. I'm naked and dragging an unconscious woman down the beach. It's bound to draw a few stares. She shuts the blinds and I can't even mouth the words, "Help."

But then the door opens and the woman runs out with two blankets. She touches my chin and then she lifts my gaze to hers.

"You look just like her," She whispers and then she kisses the beads around her neck.

"Help us," I say, "Please..."

The woman recognizes my family. We're recognizable. Beautiful. And I heard that Stavros ran around one of these coastal towns with his cock exposed, adding to our legend. I didn't fact check this one, but my brother is insane and well-endowed enough to have done it.

The woman asks, "Pagonis?"

I nod.

"Come," she says, "Bring the girl inside. You'll catch a cold out here. I'm Mrs. Andino."

"Galanos…"

Inside, Mrs. Andino sets Latrice to warm up on the couch, stripping her naked and wrapped her in blankets. I pull my blanket tight around my shoulders as she pours me spirits. Brown liquor hits me in the right spot as I lean back in the chair, painfully exposed. This old woman looks like she's birthed several children who are now older than me. She smiles warmly.

"I knew your grandmother. She was a good friend of mine. What have you gotten into… Come on. Come on."

I nod and find my teeth chattering. I glance over at Latrice, whose chest heaves and then falls. I can't sit for long. It hurts. Fuck, it hurts. I stand up and wrap the blankets around me.

"I should not impose," I ask the woman, pleading on behalf of my family name, "If you could lend me a small sum, €2,000 I could repay you."

I learn that €2,000 is not a small sum of money. And the woman refuses to let me leave. She feeds me fried fish, grape leaves, espresso, tea, bread, olive oil and cheese before giving me a hoodie and sweatpants that belonged to her eldest son. She hands me another larger hoodie for Latrice, who sits in silence, her eyes vacant and distant.

I've never felt this way before and it takes me nearly an hour to realize what I'm experiencing is *guilt.*

She puts Latrice and I in her guest room. She lets Latrice lie there first and then leaves me to sleep next to her. There's only one bed and my best friend glances at me nervously.

Terror catches in my throat. The woman doesn't ask what happened to us but she can tell its bad. I can't get into bed right away. I climb into her shower and I scrub. I scrub my skin until I'm pink and then I throw up in the shower drain twice. Latrice sits on the bed and she's still staring off into nothing when I leave her for the shower.

They raped Latrice too.

I can barely breathe when I return to the bedroom, but she's awake, sitting up in bed with her round face gazing at me. Her eyes are covered by the shadows but I know she's crying because I am too.

"It was a dream," she whispers, "Please, Galanos, tell me this is a dream."

I say two words I rarely ever mean. This time, I mean them, "I'm sorry. Latrice. This is my fault."

"They... they raped you too," she stammers.

"Mrs. Andino has offered us rest here. Let us sleep tonight and think about this tomorrow. We're alive. What matters is that we're alive."

"There's only one bed."

"You don't have to—

"No," Latrice says quickly, "I want you next to me. I wouldn't have made it out of there alive if it weren't for you."

I nod and she moves over. The guilt strengthens. I lie next to her, careful not to touch Latrice's body. But my friend wraps her arms around me. Her thick thighs spread apart as she wraps one leg around me. I relax into her. She holds onto me tightly and sobs softly. I don't want her to let go.

I've saved her from death but there's more I'll need to save her from. The *aftermath*.

I turn around and face her, hugging her as our foreheads press together. I don't want to kiss her and ruin the moment but my pain surges in my chest and I want to *do* something. I want to release something.

"Don't," she whispers, "Not now. It's too soon after."

"It's my fault," I murmur, "It's my fucking fault. I'm so sorry. I promise you, Latrice. I will find the men who did this. I will kill every fucking Stathakis."

I use my thumb to wipe the tear away from her cheek, "I promise Latrice. I'll kill them."

She clings to me and I don't want to let her go. I *can't*. I've never had her this close to me before. As it turns out, nothing went according to plan.

But I have Latrice with me. And she's alive. We're in pain, but we're alive. Shock gives way to sleep.

In the morning we hold each other and we don't move for hours. We're both awake, making small adjustments to our bodies, but saying nothing. *Trauma.*

I thought I was immune to trauma.

Latrice finally says, "that little old lady must be wondering what happened to us."

What happened to us? A drug deal gone bad. Both raped and left for dead. I pulled Latrice out of the ocean and we're stuck here, relying on kindness from a stranger.

I sit up and Latrice moves away from me.

"Your chest has bruises on it."

"They probably broke my ribs. I just need to walk it off."

"I think you need to go to a hospital."

"Leave it, Latrice. I'm fine."

She gets quiet, which makes me regret snapping at her. She slips into some clothes and paces toward the door.

SEVEN

TWENTY-TWO

Latrice lingers at the door. I don't know if she means to shatter my heart or if that's an unintended consequence.

"I was a virgin," she whispers, "I lied to you. No guy I liked ever liked me back."

My stomach flips again. I want to hold her. I want to take away all the pain I caused.

"You're twenty-two how could you be a virgin?" I whisper.

I can't imagine it. I can't imagine that was her first time. My cheeks flush with shame. I have to find a way to fix this.

"Please," she sobs, "Don't make this worse. I wanted my first time to mean something. I wanted it to be with someone like..."

I cross the room and I want to hold her. But she's made it clear how she feels about me. I'm shallow. Repugnant. Monstrous.

Unlike my brothers, I embrace villainy. It's easier to be the villain. But it's hard when I'm looking at her. Latrice. Broken.

"Someone like who?"

"You'll laugh," she says, sobbing more, "That's what makes it so horrible."

"Don't cry," I say, praying I sound comforting, "Come sit. Don't run off."

"I'm starving," she sniffs, "I have to get something."

"Come. Now."

She obeys me. I enjoy inspiring her obedience, even if now all I want to do is protect her. Latrice sits close to me and shakes her head.

"Explain," I command.

"I can only talk to you about this because you're a friend, Gal. I've never been this close to a guy. Ever."

I shrug and say, "I've been close to plenty of women. I can handle it. I've got sisters."

"I know," she says, "But I still—

"You're full of half-sentences," I murmur when she trails off.

"We should be responsible, shouldn't we? About what happened?" She says, her voice catching in her throat, "We need to see doctors. They could have..."

I take her hand in mine. As a friend. And to stop mine from shaking.

"I don't want you to worry," I whisper, "Don't. What happened to us was horrible, but I will make sure we survive. Do you understand?"

She sniffles and nods.

We work up the courage to leave the room and Mrs. Andino prepares coffee and breakfast. She is a resourceful Greek woman and once we're done, Loukas and Stavros show up together in a Jeep. I don't know how she found a way to contact them.

But my brothers show up alone, without their wives, which means I'm in trouble. Shit. I put my arm around Latrice and lead her out of the house. Stavros and Loukas stride toward me.

Stavros is red. Loukas is calm, which is more dangerous. Stavros takes his hand and slaps me across the face. Hard.

"Fucking idiot," Stavros snarls, "Are you a fucking idiot?!"

"Latrice, get in the car," Loukas says, "I don't think you should see this."

"I want Gal to get in the car too," she protests. She's smart enough to see the ill intent written all over my brothers' faces. They want to punish me.

"Get in the car," Loukas says, "Because we won't stop ourselves."

"You don't understand what happened," Latrice says, but it's too late. I don't fight back as Loukas slaps me too.

The men took the fight out of me. I know what Yiayia would recommend. The whip, Galanos.

"Get off him!"

Latrice lunges. Loukas carries her into the car and locks her in. Stavros pushes me.

"What the fuck is your problem? Antonio is your fucking nephew. Tisha's fucking pregnant! She was nearly killed!"

"I don't know what happened," I say. I sound slow and sloppy. My head hurts. I need more coke. Or something better.

"That's the best excuse you have?" Loukas snarls, "We should kill him, Stavros."

"No," Stavros says, "No. We won't. You don't know what happened at the club? What do you know then? Where the fuck were you?!"

My throat tightens.

"Stathakis men raped Latrice," I murmur.

My heart races. I don't bother mentioning what they did to me. I'm a man. My brothers would laugh. They would make fun of me for how I cried. They might make fun of me for how my ass hurts.

They might say I was less of a man. I'm already less of a man to my brothers. I don't have their respect. And now I have shame. Deep shame.

Loukas' face falls. Stavros mutters a half-curse, half-prayer and kisses the talisman on his neck. Neither of them glance back at her.

"Raped? She needs a doctor."

"Yes. She does," I whisper.

"And you're not the rapist?" Loukas mutters.

I wince and want to slap my brother in the face as shame courses through me. Those men used me. They hurt me. Maybe I deserve it. But I don't deserve my brothers staring at me like I'm a maggot.

"No! I'm not! So can we get the fuck out of here?! I fucked up. I get it. Fuck. It's not like either of you were any fucking better at my age."

I storm off into the back seat and sit next to Latrice. My face hurts but they didn't break my nose which my brothers easily could have. They've done it before.

Stavros has done it at least twice. Thankfully, I got a nose job after he made a mess of my face. I slump back in the seat ignoring the searing pain in my ass. My chest tightens as I remember the violation. The screaming. I can't breathe.

"Latrice," I gasp, "I'm sorry."

I feel like if I don't say it, I'll die. I deserve to die anyway. I pressured her to sell the coke. She probably wanted to stay home eating barbecue and watching reality TV. I could have done that. I don't always have to be full on Galanos Pagonis.

Her fingers interlace with mine. It doesn't feel friendly.

She answers, "Breathe, Gal. Breathe."

"I can't," I whisper, "I've fucking hurt you. How the fuck could I do that?"

"You didn't do this," Latrice whispers, "Just breathe…"

Stavros and Loukas get in the car and drive us to the villa. They take Latrice aside and talk to her discreetly about the doctor's arrival.

My brothers are both fathers now and they act like it. Latrice storms over to me once they've finished.

"You didn't tell them?" She snaps.

I have half a bottle of whiskey in me at this point.

"Tell them what?"

"I'm not the only one who needs a doctor. Gal. Seriously. They could have given you something."

"I don't want my brothers knowing," I snarl, "And if you tell them, I will slit your throat."

She takes my whiskey and pours it on my face.

"I'm not scared of you, Galanos. If you want to die of a preventable illness because of your pride, that's your choice."

Before she can slither away, I grab her and pull her close. I'm drunk and I want to hurt her. Or kiss her. I can't tell which.

"I'm ashamed," I admit, my heart pounding, "Is that what you want me to say? Yes. I'm ashamed. I screamed like a bitch while men raped me and I did it in front of a woman who—

I let go of her and opt for not finishing my sentence.

"Get out, Latrice. And don't tell them. I can handle myself."

For all my snarling and carrying on, I am attentive to her when the doctor arrives and I think Latrice forgives me — or she's lying in wait to punch me in the face or push me again. The doctors draw her blood and examine her. I can't sit down throughout the entire appointment. Pain. Searing pain. But liquor helps.

I don't remember much of what happens after the appointment. But then it's morning and Latrice walks into my bedroom with a smile on her face. I don't feel like smiling.

"What's wrong with you?" I groan.

"It's the baby shower in an hour. You've been in here since yesterday."

"I don't remember."

"Gal, get up!"

"Ugh..."

I sit up and Latrice tosses me a shirt.

"This is hideous," I mutter.

"You are such a diva."

"Are you wearing pink."

"It's a baby shower, not a funeral."

"Fine. Get me something pink."

"We don't have to match. I still don't want people thinking there's something going on with us," she says.

She's still worried about that? I haven't looked at my phone since that night. I keep a spare but I don't want to see what the world has to say to me or about me for a change.

My sex slaves may be awaiting my commands but they'll have to keep waiting.

I get out of bed and shut the door behind Latrice.

"Trust me, there's nothing going on between me and any woman until my asshole stops throbbing."

"Why won't you see a doctor?" She begs.

"Damn it, Latrice. I can walk it off," I say, "I don't need a doctor."

"I'm not walking it off. I'm talking to Fallon. She's been trained to deal with this sort of stuff, and she's helping a lot. She's texting me."

"Right. You want me to talk to my sister in law about getting raped? I am a Pagonis. I'm a fucking man."

"I don't care who you are. We went through trauma."

I hate that word. And I hate that Latrice has seen me like this.

I get into the pink clothing.

"Listen," I groan, "Get me whiskey and three pills from my drawer. If I'm going to make it through this party, I need a lot more help."

EIGHT
#PLUSSIZE

Latrice gets the pills for me. I can finally move around properly once I've swallowed them. Latrice folds her arms and waits for me in the doorway.

"You aren't the only one having a hard time," she says, pain in her voice.

"How many times do you want me to apologize?"

"That's not what I meant. I meant... we should be there for each other."

"Like friends?"

"Yes, Galanos. Like friends."

"I don't have many friends Latrice, and the ones I have I treat like shit."

"You don't treat me like shit," she whispers, "you saved my life."

"I got you into trouble in the first place."

Latrice shakes her head and whispers, "Stop it, Galanos. Let's just... help each other. Okay?"

"Whatever, babe."

I don't mean to sound so cruel. Even if it's what she expects from me. Latrice rolls her eyes.

"Come on. You don't want your family to worry."

She gets me out of bed and links arms with me. She's close. The last time I had her this close was right after it happened. She smelled incredible and she smells better now. She acts... fine. Like she's ready to brush this off. Maybe Fallon really is helpful.

"Why are you still here, Latrice?" I grunt as a strange movement causes pain to sear through my ribs. They're probably still broken. Fuck. Aren't these painkillers supposed to make this bullshit stop?

Latrice appears to have given me normal medicine instead of "the good stuff".

She pulls away from me and scowls. I want to pull her close and ravish her. But that angry beaver face gets in the way of everything.

Or maybe it's my selfishness? If I was that selfish, my ribs wouldn't hurt like hell.

"I'm here because we're friends. That's it," she says smoothly.

"Friends? I'm the worst kind of friend. I got you raped."

She pushes me and I yowl. Fuck! Did this little wench have to slam her palms into my ribs.

"OW!"

"You deserve that!" she yells, "Not everything is about you. You didn't cause this! These men caused this. They chose to do this. And they want us to be afraid and ashamed. I won't be."

She's so frustrating. How can she brush this off? These bastards didn't only rape her... they took her. They took Latrice from me. Not everything is about me. Sure. But if it's not about me, then it's about her. I hurt her. I caused this.

But Latrice still has this love-hate thing going on. The pain in my side causes me to think she's leaning more toward 'hate'.

I sneer at her, "Is this part of your 'body positivity'?"

"As a matter of fact," she says, "it helps."

I grunt.

"Get my gun, babe. You're right. We'd better go."

"You're bringing a gun to a baby shower?!"

"In case Loukas doesn't like the gift."

"You're going to kill him?!"

"No, babe," I lean over and kiss the top of her head, "I'm going to give the baby the gun."

"Galanos, a gun isn't a gift for a baby."

"Why not? They're boys."

Oh great. I've mentioned gender, so I can tell Latrice will give me another lecture. She spent a week haranguing me about calling women 'toys' when she first arrived in Greece.

"So boys get guns and what do girls get?"

"Chastity belts."

She lunges for my ribs and I pull away, wincing anyway.

"Ouch. Monster," I mutter.

"You deserve it."

"Gun, babe."

She retrieves the gun and I stick it in my holster. Latrice won't let me drive because I'm 'too drunk'. Whatever. I lean back and take a selfie in the passenger seat while she drives to Loukas' villa. We probably could have walked but I always bring a car to a Pagonis get together in case I need to make a hasty getaway. It's more common than you might expect.

Papa sits on the porch of Loukas' villa, eyes red from crying as he smokes. With his mother in the hospital he spends all day making awkward social media posts about trips they took together. They have a strange relationship.

When I approach with Latrice, I keep a safe distance from her. Papa stands up and puts his hand on my shoulder.

"Galanos. It's been a while."

Papa wipes his nose on his handkerchief.

"How is she?"

"The doctors think they're ready to bring her out of the coma soon. Tomorrow."

"Tomorrow?"

My heart quickens. That's soon. I never planned on seeing Yiayia.

"We don't know if she'll survive."

Latrice slinks past our father-son conversation into the house. Tisha squeals when she sees her and I hear Loukas chastising his young wife about prematurely peeking beneath the gift wrap. Papa puffs his cigar and then fingers the gold chain around his neck.

"Be careful, Gal. When my mother wakes up, she will be in a sensitive state. Understand?"

"Yes."

"I heard about the incident with the Stathakis men."

His hand tightens on my shoulder. I'm not scared of my father, but I'm wary of him. My siblings think he's soft, but I know the back of his hand well enough to know he is thoroughly Yiayia's son.

"What did you hear?"

"Don't be smart," he mutters gruffly, "you took a risk and it didn't pay off. Don't let your brothers intimidate you. Handle your business. Here."

He sticks a piece of paper in my hand.

"That's where you can find them."

"Papa..."

"Get your revenge. Be a man."

I walk inside and I hear Antonio and Carlotta coming in through the front gate behind me. Antonio screams, "YASSS, Work it Carlotta!"

Papa laughs and takes his granddaughter in his arms. Apparently they've worked out their differences.

Carlotta has enough Cartier bracelets to sink a U.S. Naval Ship to show for it. Papa has always liked women who could spend his money and doting on Carlotta makes him happy now that he doesn't have Yiayia to obsessively trail.

Once I'm in the villa, I can't contemplate the address in my pocket. My siblings are here and I have to be the man they expect to see. I'm no longer in pain. But I'm thirsty. Vodka thirsty.

"Tisha! You look like a turkey on Thanksgiving," I greet her, "I am glad you made it out alive."

"Shut up, Gal," she says, giggling and munching on some spicy looking chicken wing, "You look great. I love the matching outfits."

"We're not matching," Latrice and I say together.

"It's like you two are dating," Fallon agrees, "In that lovey-dovey phase."

Fallon and Tisha exchange glances. At least I think they do.

"We're friends!" Latrice protests, "Gal happens to own a lot of pink for a guy. I don't like what y'all are getting at."

Tisha hugs Latrice who gives her a big hug back. Latrice hands me her phone and asks, "Gal, can you take a picture of us?"

I take the picture and Latrice uploads it with the caption.

Baby shower with my girl. 9 months preggo and her body is perfection! #plussize

I have to do everything in my power not to press the little heart button next to the photo. She looks fucking amazing. With Tisha's bulging stomach right next to her, I can't stop fantasizing about Latrice like that.

Her breasts would become... *enormous.* I catch my hardness growing as I lose myself in the fantasy.

But I can't do anything so I try to think of something unsexy. *Raw eggs sliding down an old man's hairy chest at the beach.*

Latrice is obsessed with keeping our friendship a secret to a disturbing degree. It's confusing why she wouldn't want to brag about hanging out with me. But I suppose it's relieving.

She's not a gold digger. It's why we're friends — that and the fact that she puts up with me at all. Most people can't, unless they're monsters like I am.

But the social media stuff...it's one line I won't cross with her. She loves this stuff. The pictures. The fans. The love letters from girls who hate themselves.

I suppose I have those too. Love letters from girls who hate themselves.

I walk outside to Loukas' pool deck and take a selfie holding my gun.

9mm poolside. Rating tits in my inbox. #hotchicksonly

My sex slaves are very responsive. My cyber submissives...

NINE
.JPG

Katie: IMG_456.jpg
Katie: I would die for you.
Katie: Master, what do you want from me.
Galanos: This is boring.
[This user has been blocked.]

Cyber slaves don't work anymore. I stare at pictures of tits and none of them stir me. My stomach hurts. Too much alcohol.

I can't want these women. For years, I've satisfied my needs in the digital world with women willing to subject themselves to my depraved desires. Fame helps. They beg for me. They plead for a chance. I feed on their desperation and obsession.

The thought of them makes me numb now. After what happened, I feel different.

I don't want to feel any different, but I can't help it. I need to get rid of all these women. I dump all of them. Each of my cyber submissives disappears from my life in an instant. The beauty of the internet. I'm not a little kid anymore. I've done real shit and I've seen real shit and now I need the real thing. A proper woman to love and possess. I want her. I've wanted her for so long. I've denied myself because... I know how my family will react. Especially my grandmother.

I still want her. I'd still do anything for Latrice.

But not yet...

I spend most of the baby shower passed out on pain pills by the pool. I get up to sing Happy Birthday, which is not a baby shower tradition. I make Tisha cry by telling her the babies might not like basketball and then beg her forgiveness when Loukas nearly punches me again.

Stavros and Fallon take me aside and ask if there's something wrong with me. Fallon uses her counselor language, which makes it hard to fantasize about sucking on her lower lip. I tell her that and Stavros nearly breaks my nose. Latrice begs him not to, and he tells her, "I don't know why you're so in love with my idiot brother."

In love? I assume I imagined that part in a drug-induced haze. Latrice hauls my ass back to the car around midnight. The address Papa gave me burns a hole in my pocket.

There's another reason I want to drink myself into oblivion. I need to kill again. I need to take revenge. It should be easier for me. I'm almost a sociopath, right? I have killed before.

I need to do it for her. To keep her. I haven't admitted to Latrice that I can't bear to let her go. The idea of letting her go terrifies me. If Latrice stays in Thessaloniki, even if we're only friends, she will walk down the street and know that she is safe and I've paid my debt to her.

Yiayia never wanted me squeamish around a trigger. She knew what my life would demand from me. A drug deal gone bad only ends in rape if teaching the Pagonis family a lesson means something.

When I wake up, I am dreaming about a woman's mouth around my cock. It's what I want more than anything right now. Sex. A picture to jack off to? My head fucking hurts. And then there's the fact that I dumped all my girls. All of them? Fuck. How many pain pills did I take?

I groan and throw my door open.

"Finally," Latrice mutters.

"How the fuck did we get home?"

Latrice sits at the kitchen counter eating toast and peanut butter.

"It's 4 p.m."

"Fuck."

"I drove you here."

"Latrice, get me pills."

Latrice makes one of those judgmental and sassy little snorts.

"Latrice, I asked for my fucking pills."

"I threw them out. No more pills. No more alcohol. No more cocaine."

"YOU FOUND MY COKE?!"

"Calm down. I made coffee."

"Coffee?!" I can hear my voice getting shrill, "Only a damned American could think cocaine is equivalent to coffee!"

"Calm the fuck down, Gal. Sit."

I sit and take the coffee.

"Sorry. I'm... in a weird mood."

"You're withdrawing," Latrice says, "Fallon said you might act like this. It might also have something to do with the fact that you broke up with all your sex slaves."

"What? What are you talking about?"

"Don't bother lying," Latrice says, like she's at least smart enough to expect me to lie 50% or more of the time.

"I'm not lying."

Yet. I'm not lying yet.

"Right," Latrice says scornfully, "Well, you announced it to the entire house several times and talked about it on the ride home, detailing all your sexual fantasies and proclivities and then you showed me every single one of the girls you talk to and made me have a hoe funeral for them."

"I'm quitting drugs," I mutter.

"Yes," Latrice says, "You are. You're quitting drugs and you are getting your act together. I mean, why the fuck am I here? That's a good question. And yesterday, I finally figured it out."

"A hoe funeral?"

"Focus," Latrice snaps, "I am here, still here with the world's biggest dick head, Galanos Pagonis, because... you need me. And all I need is for you to admit it."

"Latrice, I tell you I need you all the time. Why do you think I ask you for pills, alcohol, food, and sexual favors?"

"Number one, you never say that. You are literally never nice to me."

"Yes, I am!"

"No, you're not."

"You want me to be nice?"

"Yes."

"What do I get in exchange?"

"God, you are so stupid," she snaps.

"Right," I mutter, "This is who I'm taking kindness lessons from."

"I tried to tell you the other day but... it felt like a bad time."

"Hurry," I grumble, "This caffeine is nothing like cocaine. So either sprinkle some powder in it or put me out of my misery another way."

"I wanted to lose my virginity to you. Platonically."

"What!?"

"It was a dumb idea I had, but I thought... I... The reason I took the stupid drugs was because I thought if I sold them, it would make things easier later..."

"You turned me down."

"Because you were an asshole who offered to eat my pussy before we ever kissed. That's weird, Galanos."

I'm speechless. Latrice shrugs and shakes her head as she continues, "It doesn't matter, anyway. It was just a stupid fantasy. See? Now we both know embarrassing shit about each other."

"Right."

"It's cool," Latrice says, "You don't have to worry about me having feelings for you."

"That's not what I'm worried about," I say, "I'm worried about... I haven't cum since before... what happened."

"Gal!" Latrice shrieks.

"What? I thought we were talking about sex."

"Yes, but I don't need to know when and where you're cumming."

"That's the point. I'm not cumming in or on anything. And now, I can't even masturbate because I dumped all my sex slaves."

"Can't you watch porn like a normal person?"

"No. Porn is boring. I like..."

My cheeks darken. This is embarrassing, and I shouldn't talk to Latrice about this. I have better things to talk to her about, anyway. Like Yiayia. She doesn't know much about Yiayia, and I hope that she never finds out.

Latrice isn't finished with me, and she presses on, saying, "What?"

"You don't get it, Latrice. I need control."

"Why? No offense, Galanos, but you have money out the ass. You're crazy rich, blond-haired and blue-eyed. What do you not have control of?"

"You don't know how I grew up. Why I'm like this."

TEN
KITTEN

"Let me get this straight," Latrice repeats slowly, "You're traumatized your grandmother killed your dog and now you can't attach to anything... or anyone."

"It wasn't only the dog. I had four cats. Three other dogs. A squirrel, once. A toad. Several lizards. A ball python. Monty Python did not deserve that."

"She sounds like a monster," Latrice says. I scowl. A monster? Latrice doesn't understand. My grandmother was preparing me for the world. She was always preparing me. She just didn't want me to be weak. Any grandmother who cared about her grandson would have done the same. I'm a Pagonis, we can't afford to be weak.

I especially can't afford it now. With the information from Papa, I have business to handle. But the appeal of Latrice is nearly impossible for me to resist. I'm curious... She might think she wants a night with me, but... Latrice is too good. She's nothing like my slaves. If I could remember their names, I might miss them. One was a redhead. I might miss that...

But how could I, with Latrice standing here? Moving me to care about someone other than myself for once. But speaking ill of Yiayia crosses the line.

"You sound like my brothers," I snap, "She isn't a monster."

"Gal," Latrice whispers, "Maybe I could help you. Platonically. And you could help me... *redo* what happened on the boat."

"With what? Don't get all Fallon on me."

"Not therapeutically. Sexually."

"Shut up, Latrice. I'm not falling for this feminist consent trap."

Latrice folds her arms, jarred out of the moment by my political correctness.

"What the hell is a feminist consent trap?"

"One of your little schemes," I snap, "Where the feminists trick you into rape. I've heard all about it."

She pushes me a bit too roughly. I raise a single suspicious eyebrow. Is she serious? Could it really have been that easy? I didn't have to force her or coerce her — or worse, beg. She would just offer herself to me.

"You are delusional, Galanos," she says, but I know that when women chide and needle you, it's their way of showing how much they care. I enjoy being the scoundrel they think I am. I enjoy them pretending that they don't like it.

"Or am I too smart to fall for your games?" I tease.

"Sex. You wanted to have sex with me. I wanted to have sex with you... eventually. Maybe not in a gross club VIP room."

"I've had some of the best threesomes in VIP rooms."

"Okay! Enough about your threesomes," Latrice says, "This was a bad idea. You're Gal... you're... off-limits for a reason."

"Am I?"

I move in close to her, and lean in, raising her chin so her gaze meets mine. Her worried look brings a smile to my face.

"Listen, Latrice. I'd love to fuck you. Seriously. But... a night with me won't be like a night with any other guy."

"You are such a dick," she hisses.

I keep holding her cheeks.

"I'm serious, babe. I do shit that's probably illegal."

"Like what?"

My heart pounds. She's curious. Not scared. Fuck. I was right about her. Why is it always the chicks with the loudest mouths who melt like butter in your hands?

"I have a dungeon, first," I say, "I rarely get to use it but... it's ready. Not for your first time."

"A sex dungeon. That's very 50 shades. I think we're past that."

"I play rough, babe. Really rough. Pain. Everything."

I don't know how I can talk about sex right now. I'm still in pain. And not the good kind.

"What type of pain?" Latrice whispers. Her voice trembles, but her thighs clench together. I imagine her juices coating her inner thighs and leaking out of her as I describe all the filthy things I want to do to her. If I do this too long, I'll lose control.

"Well," I whisper back, "It depends on if you've been a good girl or a bad girl. Good girls get to cum. Bad girls get to scream... then cum."

"You can't control when a woman cums," Latrice hisses. But fuck, why does it sound like a challenge?

"A good dominant controls everything about his sub. Her clothes. Her hair. Her body. Her cunt. That's what I meant when I said I don't have girlfriends. I can't handle it. A woman who gives herself in submission to me gets more than my cock. She gets my protection. My heart."

"You weren't in love with all your cyber sex slaves," Latrice hisses.

"You're right," I tell her, "Because the woman I love will wear a collar. At all times. She will have earned the right to stand by my side and I will have earned the right to claim her publicly."

"It sounds very... fucked up."

"Right," I whisper, "It does, doesn't it? But does it make you wet?"

"Gal…" she whispers, "Maybe we shouldn't talk about this before we both do something we regret. This was a bad idea."

"Come on, Latrice," I murmur, "friends? Us? Seriously. You're a body-positive feminist and I'm a narcissistic murderer. There's only one reason we're here."

"Your pool?" She whispers.

"Babe, you know that's not the right answer. We're animals. Fucking. Lust. It's the only thing that matters to us."

I lean forward and take her lower lips between my teeth to prove I can. She kisses me back, lunging forward and giving way to the desires she doesn't want me to know she has. Fuck. She's a good kisser. She has the fullest lips I've ever touched. The thickest thighs.

I pull away from her suddenly, nearly losing control of the dominant Galanos who never yields.

"Latrice," I murmur, "I've never been with a black girl. Not sex. Not BDSM."

"Okay," she whispers, "I'm just a normal girl."

"Right," I murmur, "Right…"

I remember that's why I like her. She's normal. Gorgeous. Everything I want and everything I'm too afraid to touch.

I pull her toward me again and kiss her. I don't know why it scares me. Touching her. My brothers both have black wives. Papa doesn't care. I caught him trying to pinch Tisha's bum once, but she ran away and Loukas nearly gave him a black eye.

I touch her thighs and find my hands burying between the folds. Fuck. There's so much of her and it feels perfect. Soft. Arousing. Feminine. Yiayia would kill me if she knew. She made me promise to be the good one.

"Marry a Greek girl. That's all I want from you. Don't *disgrace* me."

I pull away from Latrice for a moment and press my forehead to hers, catching my breath. My heart pounds so fast I'm nearly in my throat. Sex has never felt so wrong. So urgent. I need her. Who the fuck cares what my grandmother thinks? I'm 20. I'm *hard*.

"Gal," Latrice whispers, raking her fingers through my hair, "I want to know what it would have felt like. If it had been you..."

I kiss her neck and murmur into her ear, "This is a horrible idea."

"Why?"

"I told you, Latrice. Sex slaves. I need that from any woman. I would turn you into that."

"You ain't calling me no damned slave," Latrice mutters, slipping into her more American accent, which she sometimes does when I annoy her.

"It doesn't matter what I call you. I can call you something else. It's not real slavery, so you don't need to get all social justice."

"Shut up, Gal..."

"Okay. Fine. I could call you my kitten. My pet. My toy..."

"Your toy..."

Her voice drips with skepticism and my heart races with fear of rejection. I've never *feared* rejection the way I do with her.

"Do you like that one? I prefer kitten. You're all soft like a kitten."

And I could protect her like a kitten too. I kiss her forehead and Latrice pushes me off.

"Gal... If I do this... will that screw up the platonic part of things. I feel like... this is a bad idea."

"Not for me. I can fuck and cum in whatever I want and maintain whatever platonic feelings you want."

I am such a liar. I already love her. Sex will only turn that into an obsession.

"Right," she mutters.

"If you were my kitten, I would tell you to stop overthinking things and give me your cunt. I've waited long enough. Your sir needs cunt."

"Sir?"

"All my women call me sir, kitten."

ELEVEN

ALL THE MONSTERS

"Don't we need a safe word?"

Five little words, one step closer to gaining what I need. Her consent. Her agreement. I have never gone into this without a contract. I have never broken a rule. And when I cross a line, my slaves will pull me back to where I ought to remain. My heart pulses at the idea of making Latrice sign a contract. Official documentation that she belongs to me will make owning her sex so much better.

"We need many things. But it will make sex better. Can you wait for me, kitten?"

She nods. I lean forward and kiss her.

"I will think about your cunt when I'm gone tonight."

"Where the hell are you going?"

"I'm going to take care of family business. When I get back, I want you to wear that black dress with the cleavage. Pantyhose. I enjoy ripping it off. I want you to get a silk tie from my closet. Pick your favorite. I'll use it to tie you up. Natural hair. No makeup. Cum once before I get home."

"We haven't even had sex and you're making demands," she complains.

"Don't be a brat, Latrice," I murmur, "I wouldn't want to punish you. Consider it a test. To see if we're a suitable match."

"I get to make demands too," she whispers.

"Like what?"

"Get a damn STD test."

"Okay, kitten. I will do what you ask."

I lean forward and kiss her. Latrice gapes at me.

"What the hell was that?" She whispers.

"What?"

"You never agree with me like that. I've never seen you act like that."

"It's balance, Latrice," I tell her, "I always take care of my women. You... and your pussy... you're mine."

I touch the side of my head and Latrice dry swallows.

"But natural hair?" She says, "Since when?"

"Since I realized that there's probably nothing hotter than fucking you in your natural state. I've never experienced it and I want to."

"Fine," Latrice says, "Whatever, weirdo."

"Don't forget the pantyhose."

I kiss her cheek and then force myself away from her. An STD test. Right. I call the doctor and go into his office. I explain what happened, and he responds neutrally. I'm not the first in my family to sit here. The examination is thoroughly humiliating and by the end, I'm ready to blow a hole in every fucking Stathakis I can get my hands on. There's no more hesitation about exam results. The humiliation from the doctor provides a reminder that I need to finish things.

Yiayia might be dying. I have to do this in her honor, if for nothing else. She believes in revenge. My nephew is ready to help for a tidy sum. The little shit is a bigger hustler than Carlotta or Tisha. But he bats his dark lashes and gets what he wants.

I pick up Antonio outside the bar. He guides me to an alley where he knows a guy and opens the trunk of a beat up old Volvo. He has two AR-15s for me and enough ammo to blow the estate the fuck up. I have no problem with the weapons, and an enormous problem with Antonio's sartorial choices for our evening plans.

"Are you seriously wearing heels to go murder people?" I snap at my nephew.

He shrugs, "Don't hate on my fabulous life, Uncle. It's not my fault you're old-fashioned."

"We're like a year apart, Antonio. And what the hell would Loukas say if he knew I took you to kill people in a mesh tank top and 6-inch stilettos."

"Whatever. Tisha's an expensive stepmother and papa spends all his money on her. I need an income and you pay well."

"You know what. I am a dangerous influence."

"Do you see my fucking shoes, Galanos? €4,000. It's fucking Prada, baby. I need money and papa only cares about Carlotta's education. What about my education? I'm an artist. I need to live the life of the streets. That's the education I need. And it's expensive."

"You live the life of a back alley hooker," I mutter.

Antonio shoves his elbow into me. Hard. I forget that he's strong.

"Watch your mouth, uncle."

We drive to the Stathakis estate and park a couple miles out, making Antonio's heels more ridiculous.

"Are you going to click all the way up there like it's the fucking Yellow Brick Road?"

Antonio sticks a cigarette in his mouth and slings the gun over his shoulder. He's remarkably silent in the shoes. We get close to the compound. There's loud music blasting and then the men...

"All of them?" Antonio whispers. I nod and we solve our problems. I'll spare you the gory details out of respect. Despite Antonio's heels, we have the element of surprise. The men are overconfident that the bitch they raped won't come back. Guess again, the bitch is back. I kill the ones I remember first. The others I kill because I can, not because I need to. The gun's hard work to hold up by the time we're finished.

We fire our guns for fifteen minutes and then we check the house. Antonio fires the last shot at a Stathakis brother passed out in the bedroom upstairs. Antonio is not happy about having to kill a man in an already weakened state.

I check the upstairs bedrooms and don't find anyone else. I send Antonio to sweep the house. I hear him calling to me from downstairs.

"Uncle Gal! Uncle Gal! Come see this."

I hurry downstairs, expecting to see Antonio at the other end of a gun. But he has... a puppy.

"What the hell is that?"

"He was in a crate in the pantry. He looks new."

The puppy squirms and tried to escape from Antonio. He looks like a typical mutt. A fluffy tail. Brown fur. Floppy ears. My chest tightens nervously as the dog yaps.

"We should shoot it," I mutter.

"What the fuck is wrong with you?" Antonio yells, "You can't shoot it. But he looks hungry."

I crouch down and the dog approaches me, whining and pressing its nose to my fingertips. My heart catches in my throat. I hate that I'm sweaty and smell like blood, but I forget all of that when the pup's tongue lavishes my finger in kisses.

Antonio laughs and then stiffens his back, towering over me with his high-heels, "Shit, we'd better get out of here. And I don't want to be here when you kill the fucking dog."

"I'm not killing the dog," I snarl, "I'm bringing him with me."

I lift the dog, who presses against my chest. I hold him there and make the promise I made to all my other pets. I won't let you go. I won't let anyone hurt you. I don't want to lose anyone else. If I do, things will get so dark that I'll never return.

In the car, the puppy runs around the backseat, probably ready to piss itself. I haven't had cocaine in a long time and fuck, I could use some.

"You good, Gal?" Antonio asks.

"Yeah. Get the guys to clean this shit up."

Antonio clears his throat and then asks, "My money?"

"Check your account."

Antonio checks his account and nods.

"Great. How's Latrice?"

"She's fine."

"I don't know what she sees in you. Seriously. Like, I'm gay. I should get it."

"You *should* get the fuck out of my car."

"Don't leave me this far from town," he complains, "What kind of cheap date are you?"

Fine. I drive my annoying nephew back to his place and take the guns and the new puppy home. The puppy runs through the door and I flick the lights on. Latrice sits on the living room couch. She's asleep, poor girl. But she's done what I asked.

Pantyhose. Black dress with the cleavage. Her hair. I crouch next to her, smelling of death. She'd hate that. Fuck, she's beautiful. Something strange happens internally whenever I get close to her. I crouch down next to her. She's beautiful. Too beautiful.

"Latrice," I whisper, half-hoping I can wake her up. Half-hoping I don't. If I wake her up, I'll do what I promised. I'll make love to her. I'll break her. I know what I told her, but now that I look at her sleep, there's a tug at the better part of me. The part I normally ignore.

She doesn't wake up and I take it as a sign. Tonight, I'm not meant to have her.

"Sleep well, my love," I whisper, "I've taken care of all the monsters."

I take my sweaty and bloody shirt off and hang it over a stool in the kitchen. 200 pushups. 100 pull ups. 300 crunches. Shower. Then

I feed the new puppy. He nips at my heels and acts quite the little cunt already.

Once he's fed, he climbs up next to Latrice and falls asleep on the couch. I hope she likes dogs. I've never asked. Tomorrow, I'll handle her, the dog and a far worse beast than both — my grandmother, freshly awake from a coma.

TWELVE

DON'T FEED THE TROLLS

wake up to the dog yapping at me. I've fed him before and the pup has already adapted to his new circumstances. I'm food-guy. I groan and he yaps even louder.

He looks like my first dog. He's a cute one. A fluffy tail. Floppy ears. I love dogs with floppy ears. He's only a pup, so he might grow out of both. I like his brown fur. I groan and roll out of bed.

I hurry out of my bedroom and search my kitchen for some proper food for the creature. What on earth did I feed him last night? I was too busy thinking about the Stathakis job and avoiding the woman on my couch.

I crouch down with some leftover chicken Tisha deposited in my refrigerator. The pup runs his tongue over the chicken.

"You need a name," I mutter, "What should I call you? Claws? Thunder? Odin?"

I hear a little half-snore, half-sigh from the couch and my chest tightens. She doesn't know about the dog. She doesn't know that she fell asleep last night and missed her chance with me. Rather, I spared her. A moment of weakness on my part doesn't mean I need to damage the best friend I've had. Especially when I need a friend.

I peer out into the living room. I put a blanket over her this morning and she's snuggled nicely beneath it. I wish I could be that blanket. She must be so warm...

Latrice. What am I doing with her? And why is there always this strange... thing in my stomach when I'm near her? It's not lust. It's like another part of me is permanently horny.

I hop over to the couch across from hers, and I only mean to close my eyes for a moment. I must have been sleeping for much longer.

I hear Latrice shrieking, "Galanos! Why is there a puppy in here?!"

"Quiet, Latrice," I groan, "I'm exhausted."

"It's two in the afternoon, lazy ass."

I try not to point out that she just woke up too. She flings a pillow at me when I don't explain. The puppy whines.

"Hey little guy?" Latrice says to him in a cute little voice, "Did Gal forget to feed you because he's a little sociopath? Good boy..."

She scratches his ears, and I roll my eyes at her. I guess she likes dogs. I act like that doesn't make me happy when I reply.

"He'll be a brutal killer one day. I know it."

"Gal. He's a puppy. He's going to be a sweet doggie. Aren't you boy? Where the hell did you get this dog?"

"Taking care of our problem last night."

"Our problem?" Latrice sounds skeptical.

"Our attackers. You don't have to worry about them anymore. Antonio and I handled it."

"Handled it?"

"I promised I'd look after you."

I glance at my phone. Nice. A text from the doctor. No STDs. But he wants me to do a follow up HIV test in six months. Latrice must have the same thing. Then I look at social media for the first time in ages. After last night's workout, I'm sure I look great.

800K notifications. 453.4k comments. Fuck. What the hell did I do last night? That's a lot. Even for me.

"Hey have you been online?" I mutter to Latrice. Maybe she

knows. Her community of 'love and light' hippies might be up to canceling me again.

"No. I'm officially detoxing with my social media tribe," Latrice says proudly, sounding suspiciously like Fallon's been sending her these self-help memes.

"Please don't call those millions of desperate women your tribe before I've had a shot of espresso," I mutter bitterly, earning an irate expression from Latrice.

"You'd better get up and get your own damn espresso," Latrice says.

"If you were properly mine, you'd watch your tongue before speaking to me like that," I mutter without thinking.

"Or what?"

"I'd punish you, obviously."

Latrice isn't sure if I'm joking or not.

"You'd better watch your mouth, white boy."

"Coffee. Please... I'm desperate."

She grins when she hears that I'm desperate. I watch her move toward the kitchen in that dress. I was right about that dress. She looks fucking fantastic. I imagine going over to the kitchen and bending her over in front of the Nespresso machine. Having my way with her and dripping lukewarm espresso over her nipples before sucking it off.

Thank fuck she doesn't know how much a pervert I am.

I slide my phone open to check my notifications and post a "good morning" selfie. There's nothing women love more than blue eyes in the morning. But the first thing on my feed is something Latrice will definitely want to see...

Celebz Expozed Blog

Hey gossipers,

HOT new pics emerge of Gal Pagonis @RealGaPa and body posi influencer Latrice @plussizedlatrice in Greece.

EXPOZED... their SECRET relationship. RACEPLAY

INVOLVED!? Several of Galanos' ex-girlfriends speak out
about racist allegations, fraud, domestic terrorism and more.
"His six-pack isn't real," — @Katiekinz24_2233
Love you guyzzzz — C

Unbelievable. My six-pack is 100% real. Fucking Katie. I should have let her down more gently. Latrice sits next to me with an espresso for me and I turn my phone over so she can't see it and snatch the coffee from her, pouring it down my throat before the temptation to act out my nipple fantasy takes control of me.

"Most people say thank you," she snaps.

I'm tempted to pin her down and thank her with my tongue between her legs. I stare at her like I'm considering it but whisper, "Thanks, babe."

"Galanos..."

"Listen. I have some news... and I don't want you to freak out."

"Spit it out, white boy."

"There may be a social media problem."

"What?"

"Someone has accused me of faking my six-pack."

"That hardly seems distressing enough to warrant your concern. You have five million followers."

Shit. My follower count.

I continue, "Listen. Why don't you see for yourself how bad it is?"

I hand my phone to Latrice, who glances over at me suspiciously.

"What the hell did you do? You would never give anyone your phone."

"I trust you, babe."

"Stop it, Galanos."

"Whatever. Open it..."

She reads the website and my phone falls to her lap.

"This is bad."

"It's fucked up."

"I haven't turned my phone on in a week. Gal! You've gained 2 million followers."

"I have?!"

Unable to look away from the train wreck, she scrolls over to her page and shrieks.

"What?!"

"I'm down to 800K followers?!?"

"Are you serious? That's not possible."

I grab my phone back from her (rudely). Latrice punches my shoulder as I hold it out of view to read the comments on her latest upload.

_@kemeticmenswisdom: I knew she was a bed wench. This fat hoe will do anything for white dick.

"Let me see!" Latrice shrieks.

"NO!" I say, "This is horrible. They're celebrating me for being a hero, and they hate you for associating with me. It doesn't make sense."

"It's my right to see it."

I get up and open the sliding door and hurl my phone into the pool.

"It's gone now."

"I still have my phone," she protests.

"Not for long you don't..."

Latrice screams at me as I race into her room and destroy her cellphone. I might be going a little too far...

THIRTEEN
MY LOVE BUNNY

"YOU SHOT MY CELLPHONE?!"

The puppy barks and yaps at us. I set the gun on her dresser after firing three bullets into Latrice's phone on the bed..

"We need a maid in here," I mutter, "And we need a name for the dog. Stop worrying about the fucking phone."

"Gal, I don't think you get it. I need this money. I need my cellphone. And now, I need to move to your other guest room."

"Why?"

"You don't need social media. You're rich. This is my *job*."

"Work for me."

"What?"

"I'm hiring."

"What would you be hiring aside from a sex slave?"

I smirk. Latrice clasps her hands over her mouth. But I don't stop smiling.

"You're joking, right?"

"Fuck what they have to say about you. I can take over the

Stathakis business lines with Antonio and you can take care of my needs for one night. I'll pay handsomely. Let me look after you, babe."

"Gal... we're friends. If I 'work' as your *sex slave*, that will be impossible. I would never do something like that. I'm not one of your stupid hookers."

"Are we fucked up enough to do the impossible?"

Latrice gets close to me and stares into my eyes.

"I don't know," she says, "I'm normal. Except for the part of me that thought sleeping with you was a good idea."

"I'll give you some time to think, kitten."

Her face gets all funny when I call her kitten. Latrice likes it, I can tell. It gets her wet when I treat her small and feminine, when she's clearly wrought like iron, the way I am. I run my fingers over her lips, careful to keep her involved in the game.

"This time, you won't be asleep when I get home," I say firmly, testing her obedience. Latrice is the type that fights back. Always. I like that about her.

"Please tell me you're not killing people again tonight."

"No. My grandmother's awake. I need to go see her."

"Yiayia? Do you want me to come?"

"No!" I say, perhaps a bit too sharply, "You'll be better off here. Trust me."

The puppy runs over to Latrice and starts whining at her feet. We have more important to things to worry about before I leave. The pup needs a name, and he probably needs a walk. I scoop the pup up and kiss the top of his head as he nestles into my arms.

"He needs a name."

"He's yours," Latrice says, "you name him."

"Will you take him for a walk?"

"Sure."

"He looks like an Odin," I say, "Let's call him Odin."

Odin runs straight to Latrice, who squats to scratch him between the ears. I lean on the counter and look down at her playing with him. I want her to agree to my sexual proposition so badly, I'll pay her anything. It's not only because I need orgasms. Every part of me wants Latrice to stay with me. Here.

In my fucked up brain, a contract is my one chance to convince her that even if I'm a little more evil than she'd like... I can make her happy.

Latrice snaps me out of my reverie with an unpleasant question I have no interest in considering.

"Galanos. Did you hear from the doctor?"

I nod and keep my voice steady as I answer, "Six months we'll know if we have HIV or not."

"We don't," I whisper, taking her hand and pressing it to my lips, "We can't."

She rises to her feet as I take her hand, and then she sighs and says, "Wishing isn't great protection. Do you ever freak out about what happened to us?"

I shake my head and kiss her hand again.

"No. I killed the men who laid their hands on you and if any other feels the temptation to do the same, I'll kill them too."

"Right. Gal. This is crazy. I can't do anything like this. I can't... listen to you talk about killing people. Or think about it."

"Do you want me to stop killing people?"

"I don't have a right to demand that," she says, "We're only friends."

I let go of her hands. I hate the reminder. There's so much more I want from Latrice than friendship. The horrible things that happened to us only make me want her more. She seems okay, but I know she's hurting. She can't help hurting. She's innocent. Normal.

My chest catches with guilt for what I've done to her. Not anymore. No one will hurt Latrice anymore.

Odin barks at Latrice and wags his tail, demanding more petting.

"He's like you," she teases, "A demanding little alpha male."

"Alpha male?"

"Don't let it go to your head," Latrice mutters, "It's not a compliment."

It's definitely a compliment.

"Whatever," I say to her, "You spend the day with Odin and consider my offer. For the privilege of being my cum receptacle, I pay well."

Latrice wrinkles her nose and says disdainfully, "Cum receptacle?"

"Is that too degrading?"

"Yes," she mutters, "Asshole."

"Fine. My love bunny. My sex kitten. Whatever you prefer."

I grin and hope that I can convince her. I have to convince her. This is perfect. She needs money and I need my plan to pay off.

If I get nothing else out of the horrible incident, at least I want Latrice. She rolls her eyes.

"I hate that you're making me consider this."

"Trust me, babe. I pay well."

"My career's down the toilet. Wouldn't the smarter thing be fixing it?"

I grin and shake my head, fluffing out my perfect blond hair before telling her, "Something tells me, you'd rather have a night with Gal Pagonis."

"You are annoyingly cocky."

Cocky? Maybe. Correct? Definitely. I can tell Latrice wants me.

"I'll see you later."

I bring a gun, because it's Yiayia, and I tell Latrice to prepare herself to read my standard one-night BDSM contract, which I'll supply her with later. It's crazy how my brothers think all I do is sit around the pool all day. Sometimes, I hatch plans. Brilliant plans.

I can turn a press leak into getting exactly what I want. Latrice served up to me.

Soon, Latrice will be in love with me. I'll worry about falling in love with her later. What does love feel like, I wonder? I'll ask Stavros and Loukas after the hospital today. They're always giving me annoying brotherly advice. They can make themselves useful for once.

I drive over to the family villa. Papa and Helen are arguing over politics, but then Papa tells Helen that he wished she had a child and they're now arguing over Helen's fecundity. I'm surprised anything that enters my caustic older sister doesn't shrivel up and die.

"Hello, shit," she greets me, immediately demanding a cigarette.

"Helen. You look like an ugly skeleton today. Is your crack dealer out of town?"

"Shut up. We're going to see Yiayia. She's been asking for you and refuses to see any of us until she's seen you first."

"How long has she been up?"

"Several hours. Lou and Stavros are at the hospital. Fallon's home with Adrian and Tisha's probably at the hospital, but Lou told her not to come."

"Cass?"

"She left with Sandros this morning. She's still angry with yiayia and wants nothing to do with her. They're both stubborn."

Helen shrugs like she's given up on being angry with Yiayia, which she probably is. Our grandmother can be difficult for my siblings. I get to the hospital where Lou and Tisha are pressed up against his car in the parking lot.

She has him pushed against the car and she's kissing his neck while he fondles her ass. Stavros is asleep on the hood of his car.

"I smell Galanos," he mutters.

Tisha jumps off Lou, who gives her butt another pinch like the dirty old man he is. I'll give him a pass. Tisha is fucking sexy while pregnant. I bet Latrice would look great pregnant. Maybe I can work that into our contract, even if it's only for one night.

My heart races thinking of the contract. I expected her to reject submitting to me, but because of her mild disapproval; I wonder if a part of her craves it.

Not every woman craves submission. Some want to press stilettos into your testicles or drag their nails down your back. Not my circus. Like every Pagonis, I yearn for control and the one place I take complete control is in the bedroom.

My older brother's annoying voice snaps me out of my fantasy. I wonder if Loukas knows how much I want to punch his smug face...

"The golden boy is here," Loukas says, "Go on and see her so we can get this nightmare over with."

FOURTEEN
THE COOKIE JAR

Tisha grabs my hand and hisses, "Don't tell her about Latrice."

I give Tisha a dark look. I don't have to listen to her. Since her pregnancy all she cares about is Loukas and her babies. She doesn't have a clue what's going on with me or Latrice.

"I don't talk to Yiayia about my personal affairs, and I can tell when you all have been talking about me amongst yourselves."

"Hurry," Loukas snarls, "We've been out here for hours and I need to get home so I can fuck my wife."

"LOU!" Tisha snaps.

Loukas grumbles, "I can't take watching you prance around in those tight clothes any longer. Hurry."

"I get it. You have sex, Loukas. I'm proud," I mutter sarcastically.

I walk into the hospital. The nurses and doctors either stare or get out of my way. I don't mind either. I haven't visited my grandmother enough.

I figured she was in a coma. How would she know? And there was Latrice. I had Latrice as a great distraction.

I didn't want to see my grandmother lying there, all old and half-dead.

Yiayia sits up when I enter the room. Her hair looks great, but she looks older. My grandmother's frown is deeper than usual, but once she recognizes me, the frown falls away.

Maybe I am the favorite. But I've suffered every minute.

Yiayia folds her hands in her lap and calmly greets me, "Hello, handsome."

Yiayia might have been my first introduction to dominance and discipline. She expects the same of me whenever I enter a room. Yiayia understood the value of both dominance and submission, although I doubt she ever submitted to anyone in her life.

I kiss her twice on each cheek and then kiss her ring. I pull a chair up next to her and sigh.

"You pulled through," I say.

She'd hate any emotional sentiment from me, even if I want to hug her, smell her hair and tell myself that she's not going anywhere. I know how my brothers feel about me, but she was the only mother I had.

Helen was always off getting her heart broken, and my mother didn't want me. Yiayia gets straight down to business — plotting against Tisha West Pagonis.

Loukas hasn't told her yet, so Yiayia doesn't know how I acted against her. At least if she knows, she's behaving strangely calm about the fact that I disobeyed her direct orders and allied with my brothers.

I hate that my grandmother makes me nervous. Even if I'm her favorite, I understand her better than my siblings. I know that she's unstable and more dangerous than they realize. They didn't grow up under her thumb. I did. My back has the scars to prove it. My head swims as I search her eyes for recognition or loathing. I've become an expert at identifying all of those in her.

Yiayia sneers, "That little negro girl will have to work harder to kill me. I trust I don't have to worry about her anymore?"

How much does she remember? I remember to always show a tough face around her. There's nothing my grandmother despises more than weakness. Well. She hates Tisha and others of her color nearly as much.

I don't know why YiaYia is so racist. I think she's wrong about the race stuff. I may be an idiot, but we are all people.

"You have nothing to worry about," I say to her.

"Good. How are you?"

"I'm here to find out how you're doing, Yiayia. I spent every day praying for you."

"Unlikely, my child."

She touches my cheek and smiles, warmly. Her smile could make you so desperate. Her smiles were so rare.

"I am glad you're here," I whisper.

"I am glad that you are stronger than your brothers," she says, "How do I look? Did they have someone brushing my hair properly?"

"You look great."

"Galanos... Something has happened to you. I'm sure of it."

"I'm fine."

"You need to eat more."

"I can handle myself."

Her smile is suspiciously warm as she responds, "Yes. You can. Girlfriend?"

"Yiayia, we don't need to talk about my love life. My brothers are here. They want to see you. They want..."

"Forgiveness?" Yiayia suggests.

I try not to smirk. Forgiveness? Yiayia is the one who wronged them. She's wronged all of us, really. I just handle her better because I'm not as stupid as my brothers. And I'm almost a sociopath, so I suppose I relate to her. I don't need a test to know what Yiayia is.

"They want to talk. They want our family to stop killing each other."

"Family?" Yiayia reaches out and grabs my forearm, digging her nails into me. I don't react. If I react, she'll dig deeper. My eyes meet hers, unafraid. I know I can reach for my gun. But I also know I can't shoot her.

I don't hate Yiayia the way my brothers do. I love my grandmother.

She hisses, "No one who brings a black-skinned slut into our bloodline is family."

"Yes, Yiayia. I understand."

"Your mouth always twitches when you're angry," she says, "What have I said to deserve your outrage, eh?"

"Nothing, Yiayia."

My phone buzzes and I know it's Latrice probably accusing me of playing mind games with her over the sex slave thing. I have to ignore the buzzing while yiayia's staring at me.

"Are you becoming sensitive to these so-called people and their plight? They bring it on themselves."

My jaw clenches and if I'm not careful, she'll notice that her usual banter is getting under my skin.

"Yiayia... I understand your feelings, yes? But I need to go home. I only came to see you because... I wanted to make sure you were okay."

"I knew it," she says, "There's a woman."

"I'm going home and it's none of your business."

"Are you finally tired of your cyber sluts?"

I think Yiayia knows too much about me. I scowl, which she enjoys almost as much as she enjoys pushing me to the brink of genuine anger.

"I'm rid of them. I'm ready to settle down."

"You're much too young for that. Whoever this girl is, I'd like to meet her."

No. She really wouldn't.

"I'll send in Loukas and Stavros," I mutter as Latrice calls me when I don't answer her. Maybe discipline would be good for her...

I kiss Yiayia's cheek and answer the phone with a snarl as I leave the hospital.

"What?"

"Gal…" she whispers, her voice coming across soft and vulnerable.

I melt. Shit. I sounded too harsh and tempestuous. As usual.

"What's wrong?" I ask her.

She's in danger. My heart lurches when I hear Yiayia shriek, but there's a more important woman I have to care for. Latrice. Loukas and Tisha enter the hospital. I wonder if Loukas wants her to have a heart attack. Knowing my brother, he probably does. I'm still on the phone with Latrice.

"Stay on the line and tell me exactly what's happening," I snarl, going into full protective mode over her.

Did Tisha know her gorgeous, curvy cousin would have that effect on me when she introduced us?

"I need you back here."

"Get the gun I have in the cookie jar."

FIFTEEN
A CONTRACT WITH THE DEVIL

"What?" Latrice snaps, her weak voice giving way to that angry voice she always uses to talk to me. I like the damsel in distress — the secret behind every powerful woman — especially her.

I dream of the hidden side of her I can own. I dream of Latrice belonging to me.

"Get my gun if you're in danger."

"I'm not in danger. I'm just... this is embarrassing..."

"Tell me," I command, wanting to protect her — and wanting her to give me a good reason to get out of this damned hospital and avoid my grandmother's probing.

"I'm having a panic attack. I was. I just... I feel out of control. You're the only one who... you went through what I went through."

"I'll be home in ten."

"You're at least twenty minutes away."

"I said I'll be home in ten," I snap.

I break several laws on the drive back to the villa and nearly run over some kids who really ought to be in school. I probably taught them a valuable lesson. I hurry into the house to find Latrice slumped over the counter, a spoon buried deep in some ice-cream.

How the hell did she sneak ice-cream into this house?

I grab the ice-cream and throw it into the trash.

"Galanos! What the hell is wrong with you. I'm having a panic attack. Well, I was. Then I had ice-cream. How was your grandmother?"

"Who gives a shit?" I snap, "Panic attack? What happened? Are you okay?"

Latrice glares at me and I'm confused again. Why am I always getting people all wrong?

"Why are you acting like that?" She snaps instead of answering my question with any sense about her.

"Acting like what."

"All gross and protective."

My cheeks darken.

"I'm not gross. Ice-cream is gross."

"False," Latrice teases, "Ice-cream is delicious. And you are probably going to prison for running every red light on the way here."

Hm. Latrice knows me too well, I think.

"Remind me why I let you stay here and sass me," I mutter bitterly.

"Because. We're friends. That's what friends do. They help each other."

"Friends..." I mutter, "Friends about to make an arrangement, perhaps?"

Latrice sighs.

"This is a horrible idea and we both know it, don't we?" I say, praying that she'll disagree.

We exchange glances and now I can see that Latrice wants me. She wants me as much as I want her, and it makes my cock ache to go slowly with her. I don't even get why she likes me. I'm... horrible.

But now that I've seen Yiayia, I'm ready to succumb to any horrible idea Latrice and I come up with. She's the one person who makes me feel utterly out of control, and sex is the one place where I control everything. Where I have to.

My wires got crossed. A few screws fell loose. And Galanos Pagonis grew up to need high-adrenaline super-dominant sex. The type of sex that would scare off a good girl like Latrice.

"It wasn't a horrible idea," she says, "Maybe if I had something to think about other than all the horrible shit we've been through... it would help."

"Okay," I mutter, "This one is *definitely* the feminist trap, right?"

"No, stupid," Latrice snaps, "I'm serious. Listen, it's unconventional but..."

Her round face contorts into a scowl and then relaxes into a smile. A pretty smile. Latrice is beautiful. You don't see girls like her in Greece. Not with her cheeks, her nose or her smile. And especially not her curves. Those are insane. I love touching her. Feeling her. Squeezing her. It's incredibly hard to focus on anything when she's near me.

"Tell me," I command again.

Her back straightens as she obeys. Maybe not such a bad idea. She's mostly obedient. But that's the fun, isn't it? Getting a girl that's mostly obedient and turning her... docile. I bite down on my lower lip, willing my heart to calm down so I can think straight enough to get exactly what I want from my best friend.

"I want to feel out of control... I want to let go. But I'm too uptight to let myself drink my pain away like you. I want to let loose. I want to experience a rush..."

"And you trust *me* of all people?"

Perhaps Latrice suffered a severe head injury. I scan her head for signs of it, and she only shows me that angry beaver face again.

"Yes, you idiot," Latrice snaps.

"If you were mine, you wouldn't call me an idiot. I'd train you better than that."

"Train me?"

I pat her head, which annoys her because she finds it condescending.

"I don't play without a contract, babe. Even if it's only for one night."

Latrice grins and shakes her head.

"I didn't know you could read," she teases.

"Laugh all you want," I tell her.

"You aren't joking."

"Not even a little."

"Fine," Latrice says, challenging me, "Let's see your contract."

"Think you can handle it?"

Latrice rolls her eyes, and I hug her before grabbing a sheet of paper and a pen.

"You're writing it down on a piece of paper?"

"It's not legally binding," I tell her, "If I fuck up... well, you could show the cops the bruises and start a mafia turf war that would turn Greece into a tinderbox."

"Bruises?"

Rather than cowering in fear, Latrice peers over my shoulder as I write. I scowl and push her off.

"Stay over there. And have something healthy to eat, like a banana. I'll tell you when I'm ready."

"Yes, daddy."

I scowl at her.

"What? Isn't that what you need me to say."

I've got to get her more obedient than this... and Daddy? That's not my thing.

Dominant & Submissive Contract Between Galanos & Latrice

1. The submissive will refer to Galanos only as Master.

2. The submissive will await Galanos in bed for a night of kinky, raunchy sick fun at Galanos' discretion

3. The submissive will wear dresses and nylon tights in Galanos' company

5. The submissive will obey all Galanos' directives without question or subject herself to punishment at Galanos' discretion

6. Galanos will not abuse or harm the submissive beyond reason

7. Galanos will pay the submissive €50,000 for one night of play

8. The submissive may terminate the contract at her discretion, but she will forfeit all income and benefits of Galanos' protection

9. The dominant may terminate the contract at any time if the submissive fails to comply with his orders.

10. The submissive may terminate the contract if the dominant fails to live up to his end of the contract

11. The dominant and submissive agree to the safe word *Euthanasia.* At any point when they hear this safe word, either party will immediately stop the interaction.

12. The dominant will provide adequate housing for the submissive according to his tastes and expectations of his submissive for their night of play and the aftermath

14. The dominant expects the submissive to dedicate herself fully to studying his pleasure and her own during the duration of their contract

15. This contract will hold both the dominant and the submissive to the aforementioned standards for a 24 hour duration.

I slide the contract over to Latrice, who tentatively glances down. She's right to worry about what sort of terms I could write into a contract. The good thing is, there's nothing legally binding on a contract like this.

We need to trust each other. The contract is just the physical manifestation of our commitment. This may push Latrice to her limits. Hanging around a bad boy all the time may have tempted her to take a walk on the wild side, but Latrice might look at my hastily drafted contract and balk.

Her finger pressed to the page, traveling beneath each line.

"You aren't serious," She says, without a hint of reaction to her voice. I wet my lower lip, my heart pounding with uncertainty that I didn't normally experience when it came to sex slaves. Most women beg me for a chance to submit.

Latrice's healthy skepticism arouses me.

"I'm serious."

"Euthanasia?"

"You'd never say that during sex," I point out, "perfect safe word."

"It's sick."

"The contract or the euthanasia bit?"

"All of it."

"Fine. I'll rip it up."

My cheeks darken with embarrassment. See? This is why vulnerability is stupid.

She drags the contract away from me before I can get my hands on it and rip it to shreds — along with my dreams of conquering the one woman I never thought I could.

"Not yet," Latrice says, "It's a contract, right? That means I get to make *amendments*."

SIXTEEN
LATRICE'S AMENDMENTS

DOMINANT & SUBMISSIVE CONTRACT BETWEEN GALANOS & LATRICE

Dominant & Submissive Contract Between Galanos & Latrice

1. The submissive will refer to Galanos only as Master.
2. The submissive will await Galanos in bed for a night of kinky, raunchy sick fun at Galanos' discretion
3. The submissive will wear dresses and nylon tights in Galanos' company
5. The submissive will obey all Galanos' directives without question or subject herself to punishment at Galanos' discretion
6. Galanos will not abuse or harm the submissive beyond reason
7. Galanos will pay the submissive €50,000 for one night of play
8. The submissive may terminate the contract at her discre-

tion, but she will forfeit all income and benefits of Galanos'
protection

9. The dominant may terminate the contract at any time if
the submissive fails to comply with his orders.

10. The submissive may terminate the contract if the dominant fails to live up to his end of the contract

11. The dominant and submissive agree to the safe word
Euthanasia. At any point when they hear this safe word,
either party will immediately stop the interaction.

12. The dominant will provide adequate housing for the
submissive according to his tastes and expectations of his
submissive for their night of play and the aftermath

13. The dominant expects the submissive to dedicate herself
fully to studying his pleasure and her own during the duration of their contract

14. This contract will hold both the dominant and the
submissive to the aforementioned standards for a 24 hour
duration.

15. *The dominant will remain humane for the duration of the
contract and will look after his health once the contract is terminated*

16. *The dominant and the submissive will abandon their social
media accounts for the next 24 hours and the ensuing weeks.*

With a few extra agreements in place, we agree on something.
Finally.

Latrice is especially stern about the last part of the contract. No
social media. She has a point there. I can't post a picture of my big
toe without legions of super-fans begging to suck it for me.

Neither of us needs that.

"Ready to sign it?"

"Signing my soul over to the devil? Sure."

"Scared?"

I put my fingers on her shoulder. Latrice nods. I don't mean to scare her so much. My brothers always tell me I look and act like a serial killer.

"Is it because I'm cold?" I whisper.

Latrice glares at me before rolling her eyes and saying, "Yes. You're cold. But it's more than that. We're... friends. It feels... I dunno... Incestuous."

"It's sex, Latrice. Don't overthink it."

"Maybe sex means nothing to *you*."

I flinch at the accusation and she notices despite herself that her words genuinely prickle me.

"Sex doesn't mean nothing to me. And if you're going to be like this, don't bother. Submitting to me is an honor. I can't force it on you."

Latrice scoffs, "Do you ever listen to yourself?"

Our eyes meet and I can *see her* for probably the first time. I sense her fears. I sense her attraction. I sense that she wants this but I'm the problem. Galanos Pagonis. She looks at me the way people in Thessaloniki look at me. I'm like a monster to her — a Rottweiler that she expects to turn on her at any moment.

I want to tell her not to fear me, but I know she should.

"I want you, Latrice."

Her thighs clench together and her eyes flutter shut.

"You don't know how insane it drives me to hear you say that."

"Is it wrong?"

"Months, Gal. I spent months in your house watching you parade bimbos out of here, hearing your stories about all the girls you've *used* for nude photos or exhibitionism. I find it hard to believe that you want... me."

I kiss her shoulder and Latrice's throat tightens. Gorgeous, Latrice. She doesn't understand how I love. Why it's so dangerous for me to love. My encounter with Yiayia today reminded me that even touching Latrice puts both our lives at risk. My. Grandmother isn't a rational woman.

"I can prove it to you," I murmur hoarsely, "Sign the contract."

Now I sound like the devil. I hand Latrice a pen and her hand hovers over the paper.

"No feces. No piss."

"What?!"

"That's not on your contract, but I'm not into that stuff."

"Neither am I. *Sign it.*"

I know she'll make a good submissive because if nothing else, Latrice is obedient. At least when it comes to me. She signs her name. I exhale with relief and hurriedly sign mine with a flourish.

"There. It's done," I say, giddy and trying to maintain stern, dominant calm. I have her now. And I'm going to do so many filthy things with her.

"You're not going to bend me over the counter and ravish me, are you?"

"That doesn't sound like a lot of fun," I tell her, running my hand over her shoulder, "I prefer teasing you. The first time you take my cock, Latrice... you'll beg for it."

"I doubt that..."

"Careful, Latrice."

I put my hand on her thigh and squeeze it gently, giving her a warning that because this is her first night under my care, I will go easy on her. Unless she pushes me. If Latrice pushes me, I don't know what will happen.

Maybe I overestimated Latrice's innocence. Despite her inexperience with men, maybe my best friend has a dirty mind. Maybe that's why we were drawn together in the first place.

"Yes, Gal?"

My grasp on her thigh tightens.

"That's it," I whisper, "You're toying with me. Testing me to see if I'm serious?"

I lean forward and kiss her on the lips, surprising her with my gentleness. When I pull away, I whisper, "Is that what this is? A test?"

"I don't think you'll do it," she whispers, "I don't think you'll spank me."

I grin.

"Oh, I'll spank you. And then for your smart mouth, you'll spend the rest of the night servicing my cock."

I reach behind Latrice's head for a handful of her hair and guide her lips to mine, firmly moving her head so I can kiss her the way I like it. She melts when I kiss her.

It terrifies me how quickly her hands rush to my chest, how eager she is to touch the physique she's spent the entire summer scoffing at. I worry that I'll hurt her and my heart beats faster.

She belongs to me. I won't let anyone hurt her. Not anymore.

Teasing her will be a treat, but every moment I spend away from the wet center of Latrice's thighs is a moment I've spent depriving myself the euphoria of her sex.

Her hands travel down my chest to the top of my trousers.

"Not without permission, kitten," I whisper, "take your hand away."

Obediently, her hands return to her lap. Progress. Finally.

SEVENTEEN
100% SERIOUS

"Before any of that, you'll receive a spanking. Because this is your first time, I'll go easy on you. I'll use my hand."

"Will it hurt?"

She sounds so perfectly innocent as she asks that I nearly feel like a scumbag for what I'm going to inflict on her. I may not use my riding crop or a paddle, but my hands are well accustomed to spanking bottoms hard and it won't feel easy for Latrice. But I promised honesty and with Latrice, that means something.

"Yes."

She touches the contract on the counter again.

"And the money?"

Right. The money. I lick my lower lips remembering that I don't just have Latrice all to myself. I purchased her for seduction. My plan is simple: keep her close until she doesn't want to leave. Until she never wants to leave.

"You have my word, babe."

She bites her lower lip this time as I say the word babe. It's time to turn up the heat. To take control. I take her hand and pull her off her seat. I pull her toward my lap and issue a simple command.

"Bend over."

"You're serious."

"Yes," I say, "100% serious."

"Yes, sir."

Like every good submissive, as the threat of spanking draws closer, she suddenly finds the way and the means to behave more obediently. I love this part — watching her squirm and grapple with the fact that she's just as fucked up as I am for craving this. She wants me to command her over my lap, bent over as I plant firm slaps against her enormous bottom.

"Bend over. Now."

She sighs and bends over my lap. The first thing I notice as she leans over me is the weight of her breasts pressing into my thighs. Soft flesh from her stomach spills between my thighs and her breasts push together close to her face so her nose is practically buried beneath the enormous orbs.

My cock stiffens, and I know she feels it jutting into her belly. The act of having her bent over like this is more than I can handle. I need sex and sex with Latrice promises to reward me greatly as she trembles in fear.

I reach for her lower back and she flinches as I touch her. If she's this scared, she won't handle it well. I have to go at least a little easy on her.

"Are you afraid?"

"Yes, sir."

"You'll handle ten lashes tonight and then I want you to go to my bedroom and wait for me on your knees."

"Yes, sir."

"Are you wet?"

Her thighs squeeze together, but she doesn't answer. I know what that means. She's wet, but she's ashamed of it. She knows this is the last place she ought to be and the last situation that ought to make her wet.

She's submitted herself to my complete control and now, our

power dynamic has shifted in my favor, which is exactly what gets me stiff beyond reckoning. I lower my palm almost to her butt.

"Answer the question."

"I'm wet."

"Are you ashamed?"

She bites down on her lower lip hard. She really doesn't want to answer this one. But we promised each other honesty, so neither of us have a choice.

"Yes."

"There's nothing shameful about bending over a man's lap and awaiting your punishment. Now get your clothes off. I need your bottom bare."

She stammers like crazy, but I work her clothes off as she protests and she does nothing to stop me. Once I have her ass bare, I rest my hand on it and she gasps. Her ass is huge. Enormous. She has the biggest ass I've ever seen.

Normally, I'm holding onto maybe a tablespoon of flesh on each cheek with Latrice I have... so much ass I don't know what to do with it. Just my light stroking makes her flesh jiggle and the cheeks come together firmly.

And she's wet. Her juices drip down her thighs and I want to push my finger inside her before I spank her. But if I expect Latrice to behave with any manner of discipline, I can't let her sexy and immensely voluptuous body take control of me. I raise my hand and land a powerful smack on her ass that causes her to yelp out in pain.

"OUCH!"

"Nine more," I say firmly.

I hit her ass again. More juices trickle out of her, opening down the curves of her thighs. Her juices dribble tiny rivers of horniness through the dimples in her thighs and despite yelling in pain, she arches her back to give me greater access to her big sexy butt.

I hit her ass again. Seven more. She's shaking with pain but dripping with pleasure. I stop hitting her so she can recover. I touch my palm to her lower back again and murmur, "Seven more. Can you handle it?"

"Yes, sir," she says, lowering her head respectfully and preparing herself for the pain I'm eager to inflict on her large, protruding bottom.

"Good girl."

I'm more excited about getting Latrice naked and having sex with her than I am about spanking. But spanking her gets her so wet, and she hasn't even experienced my tongue between her legs yet.

I give her another hard slap on her bottom. Latrice whimpers and then makes a soft moaning sound. Really? She enjoys this more than any woman I've ever been with.

I should have known that I could never really make a woman like Latrice do something that she doesn't want to do. She wants this. Six more... I want to push her. I want to know how badly she wants this and how much she can take.

My next swat against her buttocks is much harder. Latrice cries out in pain this time, but she doesn't yell our safe word. She says one word that's music to my ears...

"More..."

Fuck. My dick is ready to burst out of my pants. I need her. I need to touch her and feel her. Latrice wriggles her thighs again, balancing in that precarious place between pleasure and pain. She loves this as much as I do.

"Five more," I say sternly, my voice achieving a bass I never thought possible.

Latrice gushes, "Yes, sir."

I spank her ass again twice in rapid succession. She cries out in pain again and I rush through the last three. I exhale once I'm finished. Relieved. Watching her butt move like that has done crazy things to my brain. I want to make love to Latrice more than anything right now. And now that she's been thoroughly spanked, she's exactly as compliant as I want.

"Get up, babe. I want your mouth around my cock."

"What about protection?"

We make serious eye contact and I sigh.

"We both went through the same horrors. It's a chance we're taking. I don't know if you want to take it. I won't force you."

Latrice shakes her head and whispers, "You don't get it. I'd do anything for you, Galanos."

"Why?"

"Because," she teases, "I signed a contract."

"So we risk it, then?"

"Even if it's incredibly stupid," she whispers, "And no one should ever do the same... yes. We're risking it."

"A body positive influencer promoting such risky behavior?"

"I'm not promoting it," she explains, "I'm held in a compromising position by a devilish Greek man."

"Devilish?"

"You're downright evil, Galanos, and I don't know why that turns me on."

Good girl...

EIGHTEEN
SHE'S A FIGHTER

atrice slides purposefully off my lap and onto her knees. She lowers her gaze, her eyes avoiding mine. The only distraction from the emotional tightening in my chest is the tent rising in my trousers.

"Take my cock out, kitten."

Latrice obediently reaches for my trousers.

"This really turns you on?"

"Spanking turned you on, kitten. So yes, it turns me on to see you on your knees like this."

She stops and bites her lower lip before looking up at me. Her painstaking pace forces me to wonder if Latrice is teasing me on purpose.

"You want honesty, right?"

"Yes, kitten."

"I'm scared. If you do this... I don't want you to think I'm... degrading myself."

"Do you normally find sucking cock degrading?"

"I don't *normally* suck cock," Latrice snaps, finally making brutal eye contact with me.

For a woman on her knees, she has far too much power to bring me to mine. I crouch down and reach behind her head, grabbing a handful of her hair before pressing her face to mine. She relents to the kiss and I enjoy tasting her lips. Fuck. It feels so good to have her finally, after a summer of dreaming and rejection.

I keep holding her head as I press my forehead to hers.

"I don't wish to degrade you, kitten. But I need a mouth around my cock tonight and I'd rather have yours. Plus... you signed a contract."

"Yes. I did."

"Is this where you draw the line? Sucking cock?"

Latrice double checks, "You want honesty, right?"

I nod slowly, my lips hovering over hers, ready to kiss her firmly or silence her complaints, depending on the next words out of her gorgeous mouth.

"Yes, kitten."

"I don't know if I can... please you."

That's it?

"That's the benefit of this, kitten. I will teach you exactly how to please me."

She doesn't move away from me, which is a good sign. I lean forward and kiss her firmly. I want to reassure her. If she'd been any other girl, I would have probably used... different methods. But Latrice... I have this fucked up desire to... well... to care about her. It only gets stronger the closer I get to penetrating her.

I wonder if I'll still want her when I've finally had what I want. Sex. Her sex specifically.

"Okay," Latrice whispers, her tongue jutting out to wet her lower lip, driving me crazy with the soft, slow movement.

I run my hand over her round cheek and whisper, "I'll teach you. So take my cock out and show me how badly you want to please me."

I return to my feet and glance down at Latrice, who shuffles across on her knees to my dick. I lift my shirt a little and she gasps. A tuft of dirty blond hair forms a happy trail from my navel to my cock.

Latrice unbuckles my belt and then unfastens the button. Her mouth is so close to my cock that I can feel the warmth of her breath against my underwear and my cock strains forward.

"It's huge," Latrice whispers.

My cock is larger than huge.

"Huge" describes these rabbit vibrators women love so much (especially Helen, I discovered after an ill-fated search for cigarettes amongst her personal effects). My dick ranks somewhere between unnatural and downright alien.

My doctor said, "I didn't know human penises got that big."

Then she wrote her phone number on the back of a prescription. Yiayia was furious. Apparently she moved away to Italy shortly afterward. Or Yiayia lied about what happened to her. Too bad. She was pretty. And she was right about my dick.

Latrice reaches for my underwear and pulls it down. She sinks into her kneeling position, getting as much distance as possible as she can from my cock once it springs into view.

"This is crazy," she whispers, breathless and melting at the sight of it.

The weight of the enormous hard member nearly drags it downward.

"Touch it," I command.

"Is this why girls put up with your personality," Latrice mutters.

I'm too high off my ego to bother with Latrice's manners.

"It's part of it."

She wraps her hand around it tighter and her fingers still can't reach around each other.

"It's huge," she whispers.

"Put your head on the tip," I whisper, "Take a little."

She slowly reaches out and tickles the tip of my cock with her tongue. I groan and Latrice reflexively pulls away from me.

"I didn't mess up already, did I?"

I shake my head.

"Wrap your mouth around with a bit of pressure and suck. Try it. Trust me, it'll take a lot to hurt him."

Latrice grasps the shaft of my cock and then her lips part again. She has to stretch her mouth to its widest capacity to fit the head between her lips. She manages a couple inches before she's practically choking on it.

She learns fast, bobbing her head along the inches of my shaft she can fit between her lips. It's plenty for me. I love the sensation of my cock sliding between her perfect lips. I squeeze my eyes shut and savor the feeling of her hands wrapped around my shaft as her tongue swivels masterfully around the head of my dick.

She pushes another inch into her mouth, and I groan in pleasure again.

"Keep going," I whisper, "keep taking my big white cock..."

When I say big white cock, something crazy happens. Latrice pushes even more inches of my dick between her lips. She's nearly halfway down the shaft which is impressive for her first time. She grabs my ass cheeks and leans into it, sucking me off as I touch her head, not guiding her but letting her know she lies just beneath my firm control.

"Deeper," I command.

Latrice squeezes my ass and takes me deeper, just as I command. My cock stiffens as she finally gets me deep.

"I need to cum," I gasp...

She takes more of me into her mouth, nearly getting my entire cock down her throat. It's too much for me to handle. She's too good at this for a first timer, and I can't hold myself back.

"I'm going to cum..."

She pulls away and before I can stop myself, my cum shoots out of my cock and splatters on her face. One spurt. Then three. I lose control as my orgasm sends my cum flying all over Latrice's face. I'm such an idiot.

I thought she'd keep my cock in her mouth and avoid this problem. Now there's semen all over Latrice's face. Latrice screams. Shit. This was an accident.

She gets off her knees and pushes me.

"Fuck you, Gal!"

I grab her wrist and drag her against me before she can run away. She has submitted to my control. She may not like my cum all over her face, but I can't allow her to talk like that.

I squeeze her wrist and keep her still.

"What did you say to me?"

"You degraded me on purpose," she hisses.

"It was an accident," I snarl, "And that's what you're for. You signed the contract. You're my sex slave. So serve me. Bend over and submit."

Latrice pushes my chest. Hard. I lunge for her and she throws the pen she used to sign the contract at my head. Some of the cum flies off her face, making the scene more grisly.

The worst part is — I'm still hard.

I like a woman who fights back. And fucking hell, Latrice is a fighter.

NINETEEN
SERIOUS PUNISHMENT

I take my hand and wipe my cum off her face.

"I'm sorry," I say, "But... we made an agreement. And pushing me, hitting me and carrying on is utterly unacceptable."

"You can always cum on my face again to punish me. Bastard," she hisses.

And then she says, "Or spank me."

"Spanking would let you off easy. I saw exactly how wet it makes you."

Latrice squirms. Good. She's realizing that she messed up. I hold my hand up, cum sliding down my palm.

"You can take your punishment or you can lick it up."

"It's cum," she hisses, "I'll take my punishment."

Poor Latrice does not know what's in store for her. I hold her wrist like a naughty little girl and drag her to my bedroom. I toss her onto the bed. She tries squirming away but I grab her and whip handcuffs — yes, real police handcuffs — out of my side table and hook one of her hands to the headboard.

"GALANOS!"

"I'm serious about punishing you."

She fights a bit more, but I already have one of her hands cuffed, so getting the other cuffed to the other side of the bed becomes much easier.

"You're crazy," she hisses.

I start working her quietly and the silence drives her mad.

"Why do you have two sets of handcuffs in your side table?!" Latrice panics, thrashing her legs about.

I don't mind if her legs are free. All the better for my punishment.

"Handcuffs come in handy," I tell her with a smirk, "Now... I am going to eat your pussy all night and you aren't allowed to cum."

"You can't forbid me from having an orgasm," she protests, "And you are not going to eat my pussy all night. There isn't a man alive capable of going down on a woman that long."

"You've seen my cock," I challenge her, "Do I look like I'm anything like other men?"

Latrice squeezes her legs shut and tests the handcuffs again with a huffy little grunt as she cannot break free. I don't know what she's expecting. I could leave her there for days and she'd never get free. I keep the key on my nightstand, a torturous four feet away from her where I know Latrice can't reach it.

"They're cuffs," I explain, kneeling at the foot of the bed, rolling my tongue around my mouth to prepare for a night of tormenting my latest find, "You can't break out of them."

"I could scream for help."

"And say what? A sexy blond man with a big cock is eating my pussy?"

"I hate you, sir," Latrice hisses.

She'll hate me so much more when I'm finished licking her cunt to my satisfaction. I ignore her protests and command, "Open your legs, kitten."

Latrice slowly parts her thighs, flesh parting around her mound as large lower lips spread apart to reveal a soaked pink center. It takes everything in my power not to press my cock between the soft folds of her pillowy cunt.

I examine her cunt visually first, inspecting her upkeep. I don't have much of a preference, but I like taking a good look. Latrice's inner lips protrude from her outer lips in a soft, dripping lily shape. I like pussy lips that pop out like that. Latrice's juices slide down those sexy inner lips and my cock nearly bursts out of my clothes.

I suppose my staring makes Latrice uncomfortable.

"Can you stop staring at my vagina?"

"Why?"

"It's weird," Latrice mutters, "Let's start there."

Unless she says *euthanasia,* I have no reason to stop.

She must be desperate to change my mind about the punishment. Too bad. I'll enjoy spending hours teasing her cunt with single-minded focus. That'll make finally piercing her that much better.

I reach my finger between the large spread lower lips and push her clit like a button. Latrice makes a sound between a moan and a yelp. I'm not exactly trying to please her. I've just been waiting too long to see her exactly like this, and I want to take my time with the exposed treasure between her thighs.

"Can I take a picture?"

"No!" She yells.

"Okay," I murmur, slowly stroking her outer lips with my finger. She squirms and makes a low whimpering sound.

It's not much, a small motion, but on a woman's sensitive spread cunt, these small slow motions amount to a torturous build to a climax that poor Latrice will never have until I decide it's time for her to cum.

"W-what are you doing?" She gasps, slowly losing herself but uncertain why such a subtle motion has this effect on her.

"I'm touching your cunt. It's soft. And wet."

I flick my finger over her clit and Latrice moans again, writhing and jerking her arms against the handcuffs again. I keep touching her clit as she squirms.

"You'll obey me," I murmur, "Or you'll never cum. I'll keep you here and make you wait days to cum."

"You can't keep me handcuffed to your bed," she says in an aroused, whimpering tone, "24 hours. We only have... twenty-four hours."

"I can do whatever I want with my pets."

That earns me another stiff glare from Latrice. What is it, then? Does she want to become more than a pet to me? I move my finger slowly around her outer lips. Tasting her will be even better than touching her.

Latrice is wet enough and I'm close enough that I can smell that magnificent pussy smell between her legs. Guys don't talk about it enough, but the smell drives any sane man wild. When it's a woman you want, she smells sweeter.

Latrice's perfect pussy has spent the past day simmering between her thighs. I need to have her. Tasting her becomes my only reason to exist. The intoxicating smell causes me to salivate with desire for the perfect black pussy ensconced between her thick fleshy thighs.

I crouch between her legs and kiss the tops of her knees first. She's still firmly fixed to my bed. I have plenty of time to explore every inch of her body and despite Latrice's desperate squirming, I'm in no hurry for her to climax.

There's plenty of pleasure before climax, especially if you take your time...

I kiss the tops of her thighs, taking a large handful of her flesh in my palm. Damn. She has such nice, juicy thighs and ass for days. Every bit of Latrice's body is perfectly voluptuous.

I lick the top of her thighs and she whimpers. I kiss the spot I've just licked and then blow cool air on the same spot. Latrice emits another agonized moan and not-so-subtly spreads her legs wider apart.

Fuck. I love this moment. I love turning women into sex-hungry, desperate messes, unraveling at the seams just to have my tongue between her legs. She wants my tongue in her cunt so badly. And the ache between my legs to have her only grows.

I may tease Latrice, but I'm torturing myself with this denial. It's worse than staring at a plate of Fallon's fried chicken and knowing I can only eat a piece of the chicken breast if I pull the breading off.

I kiss Latrice's inner thighs. She bends her legs at the knees and keeps her legs perfectly spread apart. I nearly burst. Her pussy isn't the only part of her on full display now. I can see her tiny puckered asshole too, and holy fuck... I want to plunge my tongue inside all of her.

TWENTY
LATRICE'S BACKDOOR

Latrice's backdoor will have to wait its turn. There's a dripping pussy with lips folded neatly as juices gush, and it's begging for my attention. I drive my tongue deep between her lips. Latrice moans with pleasure and thrashes. I push her thighs back and use my tongue to taste the length of her wetness, from her tiny backdoor all the way to her clit.

She cries out louder. Fuck. She's already about to cum. She wants me this badly that she'll cum from only a few licks of my tongue if I'm not careful. I pull my lips away from her wetness and kiss her inner thighs instead. She moans but she's still not worked up enough to beg.

I need to break her down until she admits what we both know. She wants my cock. My tongue isn't enough. Once I've eaten her to a climax, she'll want my dick between her legs.

Her whimpers cool to shallow breaths and I spread her lower lips apart again, running my tongue along the length of her wetness and then sliding my tongue right inside her as deep as I can go. Latrice moans as my agile tongue curves and explores her spongy inner walls. I have my nose buried between her legs as I lick her pussy clean and she smells even better up close.

She clenches her thighs together around my head so I'm nearly buried between thighs and pussy. I remove my tongue and work my way between her lips again to focus attention on her clit.

Latrice moans weekly, "Oh God…"

Her back arches and I know she's close again. I pull my lips away from her and this time, she can't stop herself from emitting a frustrated huff.

I kiss her inner thighs and lick them. She makes a mewling whining sound and spreads her legs wider. I make a play of moving closer to her pussy lips. She eagerly scoots her butt, hoping I'll lick her.

I grab a bit of her thighs between my teeth and press down. Hard. She yelps in pain next.

"What was that for?"

"I told you. This was a punishment."

"It hurts," she complains, "There's this… ache."

"Your body wants to cum more than anything," I whisper, kissing her outer mound and then Latrice's womanly soft stomach, "You would do almost anything for an orgasm, wouldn't you?"

"Shut up," she hisses, breathless as my tongue approaches her mound again.

Will I lick her or will I tease her more? I decide on another bite to her thighs. This time as Latrice yelps, I suck her flesh hard until I leave a mark on her inner thigh. Her legs tremble and her pussy dribbles more juices than before as I rub my thumb along the mark and press down.

"That hurt," she whispers.

I give her another matching mark on her other thigh as she moans. The wet spot on my bed is practically an ocean. She's soaking wet, trembling with desire and she still won't beg me to make her cum.

When I push, she pushes back harder. Latrice is the perfect submissive for me. Intense. Gorgeous. Strong.

I kiss her lower lips and then slowly open them again with my tongue. This time I'm French kissing her lower lips romantically instead of licking her. It's like I'm making out with her cunt and occasionally flicking her clit so she cries out.

Finally, I hear the words I've waited so long for.

"P-please…"

I pull my mouth away and she whimpers, "No… Don't stop."

"What do you want?" I say, sticking my finger against her entrance and taking some of her juices onto my hand before licking her off my palm with a flattened tongue. I stick my tongue between my fingers for any drops I might have missed and Latrice huffs again.

"Please… Galanos…I've learned my lesson."

"Have you?"

She gasps, "I've learned my lesson, sir. I want to cum. Please. Please let me cum."

"No."

I grin as Latrice's face hardens into her angry beaver scowl and then melts. I've finally broken her. She's a mewling mess of a woman enslaved by her desire for me. Right now, it's only the two of us. She'd never run off for an oaf like Loukas or fall for a head-case like Stavros.

Her pleasure belongs to me and the power brings me to the edge of cumming in my pants.

"Please," she whimpers, "I'm so wet. I need to cum."

"You are wet," I murmur, gathering more of her juices on my fingers before licking them off again, "Why should I care?"

"B-because. I'm going to burst."

"Beg me," I say, keeping a safe distance so she's not sure if I'll walk off and leave her handcuffed to my bed unsatisfied. The anticipation is… titillating. Isn't it always?

"I won't," she pleads, "Please…"

She can't help herself. Her pussy wants to cum so badly that it's actually taken over Latrice's rational brain. My mind churns with the things I could do to her right now. The things I could make her say just because she wants to orgasm.

"Beg," I snarl, instead.

"Please. Please eat my pussy."

"Why do you want me to eat your pussy... kitten?"

I smirk at her and Latrice squelches another angry beaver expression before saying, "Please... I'm begging you."

"Answer me honestly, Latrice. Why?"

"Because," she whimpers, "You are really good at eating pussy and I need to cum. So please... Please let me cum."

"I should walk off and jack off in the other room," I say.

"PLEASE. PLEASE DON'T. I NEED TO CUM."

She squeezes her eyes shut and I lunge between her legs, pressing my tongue to her cunt. I French kiss her slowly and then I use my fingers inside her, pushing deeper as I run my tongue along the length of her cunt.

"Oh God," she whimpers, tugging at her handcuffs.

I spread her thighs apart and force my fingers deeper, massaging her clit from inside her pussy as my tongue teases her clit and lower lips. Latrice arches her back and then finally succumbs to her desires. She cums *hard* all over my tongue. I pull my fingers out of her pussy and suck them clean before I clean her messy pussy and thighs with my tongue.

She cums several more times before I finish "cleaning" her off with my tongue. Latrice can't move by the time my tongue has ravaged every inch of her sensitive black pussy.

The color, the shape, the fullness of her lips, the thickness of her thighs and the tightness of her hole make Latrice the best I've ever tasted. If I'd known she'd taste that good, I would have pounced earlier.

Now, Latrice can only whimper and shudder as pleasure surges through every inch of her. This is a bad time for Latrice to zone out in a cock-crazed orgasmic haze. Luckily for me, my cock springs to full attention, catching Latrice's attention because my hard cock tends to garner the attention of a room.

It's freakishly huge and Latrice stares at the monster with the giant veins wrapping around the sides like she's not sure if she's aroused or scared.

"Now?" She whimpers.

"Yes," I murmur, "So keep your legs open, kitten."

She spreads her legs and her juices hang across in sticky string across her splayed lower lips. My cock jumps in anticipation of sliding into that soaking tightness.

TWENTY-ONE
PLANS FOR THOSE BREASTS

allow the head of my cock to pierce her entrance slowly. Latrice cries out and thrashes loudly, forcing me to hold her thighs spread apart so I can force the head of my giant cock between her legs.

"I'm going to cum," she gasps before I slide another inch inside. The ridge of my mushroom head massages her inner walls and the girth spreads her so wide that Latrice can't help but cum hard from the first contact with her tight inner walls. She's insanely tight. And watching her curves and folds of dark flesh surrounding my pale cock only makes sliding into her tightness better.

There's so much delicious goodness to hold on to. More thighs and ass everywhere I look. And her breasts... I have plans for those breasts.

I move another inch inside Latrice, and she cries out, orgasming again. Her pussy drips like a faucet as I get half of my cock inside her. I withdraw slowly and move just the first half inside her so she can adjust. The girth makes it easy for her to cum, but my length means we have to take this slow.

Tonight isn't a good night for painful entry. Although, like in all things, there's plenty of room for pain in good sex. She cries out as I plunge another inch deeper.

"It's too much," She gasps.

"Nearly there."

I thrust the rest of my length inside her. Latrice cries out in surprise.

"Holy fuck! You must be bigger than a horse!" She yells, arching her hips up, moving whatever she can to get her tight pussy to accommodate my enormous length. I just like being on top of her. Not just because I enjoy dominating her, but because I've wanted to be closer to Latrice's face since I ate her out.

But she's making that angry beaver face again, which is wrong because my cock is inside her. And I haven't moved yet. She should shake in terror.

"Your mouth smells like... vagina."

She whispers the word 'vagina' like it's a slur.

"I spent hours licking and sniffing your cunt. It's not bad. Taste it."

"No!"

"Taste it," I snarl, leaning forward and kissing her. She wants the kiss despite her protests. She lunges to grab my face, forgetting that she's handcuffed. I kiss her and press my weight against her breasts. I like how her large dark nipples feel against my chest. They're larger than four pepperonis arranged in a circle. My cock twitches between her legs as I think of her nipples and Latrice moans.

She reaches her lips for mine and kisses me again. I guess she doesn't mind the taste anymore.

"You won't make me beg, will you?" She whimpers, "Because I'll do it without asking, sir. I'll beg you to fuck me. Please. I am utterly shameless now. Please... fuck me Galanos Pagonis..."

I withdraw my hips slowly and then grind them against hers. Holy shit, she's tight. Re-entering her takes time, and she moans as I slide every inch into her tightness again.

I grab her hips and move slowly at first, taking my time to slide inside Latrice's perfectly tiny cunt before withdrawing. After a few strokes, she becomes an orgasm machine. When the tip of my cock touches her back walls, she climaxes, juices spilling from her cunt onto my cock.

I can no longer stand making love to her slowly. I need intense, hard fucking if I'm going to cum. But Latrice's tightness is perfect. I move faster and she cums as I fuck her harder, not caring for her pleasure as I usher myself toward a climax.

I groan as I finish. It feels amazing. The moment that I fall over the edge, my eyes meet hers and my cock spills into her, seed pumping out of my enormous dick as Latrice strains against her handcuffs.

She's mine and she can't leave. I lean forward with my cock buried between her legs and I whisper, "I love you."

She lunges for me, and then there's that angry beaver face again.

"What?" I whisper, kissing her lower lips lovingly and then her neck. Her neck tastes delicious. It's sweaty, but... I run my tongue along her neck and suck bits of flesh above her bared breasts.

"Don't say that," she gasps, "Don't joke..."

She whimpers as I run my tongue over her nipples. She squeals and my cum spills from her pussy. Fuck, that's hot. I run my tongue over her nipple again and more of my cum erupts from her pussy.

I can feel myself getting hard again. Latrice notices and her angry expression turns to panic.

"Again?"

"Yeah," I say, "I'm hard. Spread your legs."

I slide between her legs slowly again and Latrice moans as I bury my cock inside her. I kiss her neck as I make love to her again. Finishing inside her feels better the second time. I pull out of her and lavish her breasts with kisses before lying on my back next to her. She's still handcuffed, poor kitten, but I like her that way.

I don't like when women walk off after sex. I need...

"Galanos," Latrice says sharply, "Are you cuddling me?"

She's more surprised that I want to cuddle than she is that I'd want to tie her up.

"Hush," I murmur, "You have perfect breasts for cuddling."

I hold her close to me and press soft kisses into her shoulder. Latrice thrashes, nearly tossing me off her. What the hell was that for?

"It's like watching Satan pray the rosary," she hisses.

"Bit dramatic," I murmur, kissing her neck and nuzzling deeper, "It's called... love."

I kiss her hips and move my mouth between her legs again. Latrice squeezes her legs shut.

"No," she begs, "I can't cum anymore tonight. I can't stand it. I need to adjust to that... thing."

"Fine," I say, "I'll go get some strawberries and whipped cream. If you don't want to cum, I can arrange that."

I get off the bed and slide into a pair of black boxers, ignoring Latrice's screams.

"You can't just leave me here, Gal!"

"Oh, did I mention I don't have strawberries at home?" I call back, "I don't know how long I'll leave you handcuffed."

"Gal!"

I smirk. I enjoy knowing that I have her exactly where I want her. And I'm lying. There are strawberries in my fridge. And there's whipped cream. My cock aches as I walk into the kitchen, and I need to adjust my boxers. That was good. Better than good.

There's this weird warmth in my chest that makes me want to hold Latrice. Caress her. Treat her... kindly. It's amazing what an orgasm can do for you. I don't even crave cocaine.

But I crave a little more sadism. I take a strawberry out of the carton and rinse it, coating it with whipped cream before cleaning the cream off with my tongue and then slowly sucking and biting the strawberry. The fruit juice mixes with what's left of Latrice on my tongue.

Torturing her is torture for me too. That's the part they don't tell you about. I can hear her yelling at the top of her lungs and I chuckle at how desperate she sounds. Unfortunately, I miss a more important noise — the sound of my front door sliding open and my family pouring into my villa's foyer uninvited while I'm half-naked eating strawberries and my full-figured best friend is handcuffed naked to my bed.

Shit.

TWENTY-TWO
RESCUE MISSION

"HELP!" Latrice yells at the worst time.

"Oh my God!" Tisha screams, "That's Latrice!"

"He has Latrice back there!" She yells again, grabbing a gun from Loukas' holster before he can stop her and sprinting off to my bedroom with Fallon.

"You're pregnant, woman!" Loukas yells, tearing after her with Odin hot on his heels, barking madly after my brother.

I call Odin back to me, but the silly pup doesn't listen. I hear Loukas shrieking as Odin growls and pregnant Tisha escapes her husband, wielding his firearm as she enters the room where my new submissive lies handcuffed to my bed. Oops.

"Odin! Bite him! Bite him!" I scream as the dog bounds back into the kitchen and growls at Stavros, who growls right back.

My brothers don't take kindly to my attempts to sic my attack dog on them. Oops.

Before I can explain myself, Stavros pulls his gun out and sticks it in my face.

"Hands up, pervert."

"You're one to talk," I snarl, "I can hear you doing it while I tan."

"Shut the fuck up," Stavros says, "You ought to be ashamed of yourself. What are you doing to her back there?"

Odin scampers out the open door, oblivious to my pain, and jumps into the pool. Is this how my brothers felt when I lay by the pool while they worked? Odin might just be here to give me a taste of my medicine. I love the dog anyway.

My heart races with anger at first as my brother shoves the gun closer to my face. First anger, then delight. I smile and Stavros growls at me. Right. My brother has a gun in my face. I need to pay attention to that problem.

Loukas apparently catches up with Tisha because he re-emerges with his weapon and points it at me too. The only thing that would make this worse was Helen or Cass being here, and I'm thankfully spared that indignity.

"He has her naked and handcuffed," Loukas snarls, "Get him in the car. Another victim of Galanos Pagonis."

"I'm not going anywhere," I say, "You'll find that Latrice and I are engaging in consensual—

I groan as Stavros slams the butt of his gun into my face. He doesn't break skin, thankfully. I'm relieved he isn't hitting me that hard. Fatherhood must have softened him. I stumble over onto my counter and fumble around for the spare gun I keep in a drawer in case little family drop-ins like this turn sour. Yiayia wouldn't want me to hesitate to put a bullet in either of my brothers' enormous heads.

But I don't find a gun. I find... a sticky note? I pull it out, confused.

No more guns. ♡

— Latrice

She's written it in pink marker. Damn, I'm going to punish her for this.

"Latrice!" I yell, "Latrice, tell them the truth!"

I stumble backward, ready to fight my way out, but my older brothers grew up punching and kicking me around. I spent most of my life thinking my purpose was getting beat up by giant brunette lunkheads.

This isn't new to them. Before I can protest, they have me in the back of their car.

"What are you doing with Latrice?" I command, "I need to know. I'm in love with her and I won't let you hurt her."

"My wife and sister-in-law are rescuing her," Stavros said, "We need the truth about what you're doing to her. Tisha's had her suspicions for weeks and then Latrice goes radio-silent from the internet... We knew you were sick, Galanos. But this is too far."

"Your wife needs to stop watching true crime documentaries," I grumble. Both Fallon and Tisha spend a lot of their pregnant time watching one silly true crime series after another.

They're both married to bad guys, so I don't know who they root for.

"I love Latrice," I insist, "You can't take her away."

My stomach lurches at the thought of Latrice spending a night away from me. I don't want her to leave and I haven't wanted that since the attack. I failed to keep her safe once and here I am, failing again.

"I love her," I repeat.

Stavros and Loukas glance at each other in the front seat and snicker.

"There's no way you love anything," Loukas snickers, raking his fingers through his hair. He's been greying faster than usual lately. Idiot. Like I'm going to take romantic advice from a senior who was courting a teenager until recently.

Stavros taps his fingers impatiently on the steering wheel before booming, "Will you tell us the truth or will we have to play chicken again?"

"That game is stupid," I snap, "And I'm telling the truth. I love

Latrice. It took a tragedy to show me the truth and now... I'm sorting it."

"Sorting it?" Loukas snarls, "You had her tied up like a Thanksgiving dinner. The poor girl nearly lost her mind that I saw her naked."

"You saw her naked?!"

I lunge forward and wrap my hands around my brother's throat. Purposeful calm courses through me as I nearly squeeze the life out of him. I would have succeeded if Stavros hadn't pushed me off and threatened to shoot me again. One day, I ought to call his bluff. Not with Latrice's life on the line.

"I will kill you," I hiss.

"Big breasts," Loukas says, "Enormous."

He sounds more genuinely stunned than perverted in his intent.

Stavros glowers at him, "I'll tell Tisha on you."

"Sorry. But. They were out there."

"If you don't shoot him, I will," I say to Stavros, who isn't so quick to take my side, unfortunately.

Stavros casts a dark look in my direction.

"What on earth do you need handcuffs for to keep her in your bed if you love her, eh? Maybe she doesn't love you. Maybe she realizes you're a little sociopath and wants nothing to do with you."

Stavros has killed double the men I have. I don't need to listen to his stupid lectures.

"It's none of your business," I snarl, "Now tell me where she is."

"No," Loukas says, "We're still waiting to get her side of the story. Sit tight, little brother."

Stavros gets bored after three minutes without his bombshell wife at his side, so he drives us around Thessaloniki, singing sea shanties. I want to kill him. By the end, even Loukas agrees. His phone rings.

"That must be Tisha," he says, picking up without looking at it. He gets out of the vehicle and walks a few steps away from us so he can hear her better. Either that or he doesn't want me to hear what Tisha's saying either.

Have I mentioned yet that everyone in my family is insufferable?

Stavros turns around and scowls at me, "Love her? What do you love about her?"

"I don't know."

"Brilliant answer," he mutters, "Can you come up with anything better?"

"She's gorgeous."

"Hm. I didn't think she was your type."

"I don't have a type," I mutter. Except submissive. Except sexy. Except... big. I like girls like Latrice. I like women with more to love. My cheeks darken as my brother stares.

"What are you so embarrassed about," Stavros guffaws.

"I like big girls. Fine! I always knew you assholes would make fun of me."

That wipes the smile off Stavros' face. He tilts his head to the side, waiting for me to reveal that it's all a grand trick.

"I like women with giant tits, giant bums, soft stomachs, large stomachs, rolls in their thighs, round cheeks, nice pussy lips and... tight pussies."

I hang my head and Stavros clears his throat before announcing awkwardly, "Loukas is coming back."

Loukas slams his enormous frame into the front seat with an exasperated grunt.

"Tisha and Fallon have gone rogue."

"What?!"

"They claim Galanos has severely brainwashed Latrice and compromised her testimony. They've escaped on a boat. Fallon threw Tisha's phone overboard before she could tell me anymore."

"Fallon? What about our SON?!"

"He's *your* son," Loukas explains, "That makes him *your* responsibility."

"Where's *your* son?" Stavros snaps, exasperated with his brother's criticism of his parenting.

"Babysitting *your* son," Loukas shoots back raising a threatening brow at Stavros who leans back in the driver's seat.

I clear my throat and say, "Hello!? Brainwashing? What have your wives done with my girlfriend?"

"Right," Stavros mutters, "We ought to do something about that too."

TWENTY-THREE
NO CHOPPING OF COCKS

irlfriend. I've never used that word to describe anyone before but it slips out so easily that even my bull-headed brothers notice.

"GIRLFRIEND?!" Loukas roars.

"I told you," I grumble, "I love her."

Stavros snickers, "Let me guess, you had sex for the first time?"

"I've had sex before you idiot," I snarl, "And unlike you I didn't spread gonorrhea to half the girls in Thess."

"It was the aughts," Stavros says, "Gonorrhea was... what does your generation call it... *trending*?"

"Don't listen to him," Loukas says gruffly, "Gonorrhea wasn't trending, "AIDS was trending. And there's nothing funny about STDs."

"I didn't ask for a sex talk. I need to find Latrice. *Now.* Or when I get out of here, I'll behead you both."

Stavros and Loukas exchange glances and then look back at me.

"Promise us whatever was going on was consensual."

"Yes. Do you think I could have genuinely handcuffed Latrice to a bed without consent? She could kick my arse."

Loukas grins.

"And if we're lucky, we'll get to watch her do that one day. Stavros? Let's get your son and my son. They can't have gone far."

We drive back to the family villa. Antonio sits with Adrian on his lap, bouncing him and singing some Spanish song from the television. My nephew has a nice voice and wears his dark hair in a ponytail today. Antonio has new piercings from when I last saw him. Snake bites, which Loukas pretends not to hate.

"There they are. Antonio, I see you are getting along swimmingly with Adrian," Loukas says.

"Yes, papa. Carlotta went out."

"Again?!"

"She's with Tisha and Fallon."

"They came here?" Loukas asks furiously.

"Yes. Should I have stopped them?"

Stavros scoops Adrian away from Antonio and holds his son against his chest. Adrian gurgles and then clutches his father's chest, playing with a pendant shaped like a gun on his father's chest. Stavros murmurs something to him. Probably a prayer, superstitious bastard.

Antonio flips his sunglasses down and lounges in the chair with a yawn.

"They told me where they were headed but I'm not parting with that information for free."

"Well, Gal?" Stavros says, "It's your girlfriend. You cough up the cash."

"Your son is spoiled," I snarl at Loukas, before opening my wallet and flinging a couple hundred euros at Antonio.

"Thanks, Gal," he says, yawning, "They went to Albania. Tisha couldn't stop talking about this place Lou took her when they were on the run."

I glare at Loukas, ready to strangle him again. He gives me an unimpressed expression and sighs before turning to Antonio again, "Um... would you like to come with us?"

"Papa, no. I have a date tonight."

"Right."

"With a man."

Stavros looks up from his son and at Loukas. Antonio yawns again. This is the first time he's told his father and Loukas turns red and then he stammers, "I-I... I know. I mean... I... I knew... I always... Fuck..."

"Papa, stop," Antonio says, sitting up again, "I told you, okay? So stop acting strange and getting into my business. Leave. I'll look after everyone here."

"Can you feed my dog?" I ask him.

Antonio nods and waves me off, "Yes. I'll charge you by the hour now get out. I'm working on my tan."

Stavros packs a quick baby bag and we hurry out together. Stavros looks ridiculous with Adrian over his shoulder and a baby bag on his lap — while dressed like an angel of death. His black hair is slicked back against his head and his eyes stare brilliantly ahead at the ocean, reflecting the sea.

The only family boat ready for us is small.

"We should have a super-yacht," I complain.

"We can wait two days for a super-yacht," Loukas says gruffly, "Or we can find this woman you allegedly love."

"Question my love again and I'll chop your cock off."

"There will be no chopping of cocks," Stavros snarls, getting out of the car and kissing Adrian's head, "I need to change his diaper and I need you two to stop arguing. Come on. Loukas, you're driving. Galanos, make sure we have enough weapons."

Tisha's helped Loukas work out his nerves driving. I think he's scared to have her behind the wheel again after a pregnancy-hormone driving incident involving Avril Lavigne and an old man's farm. Long story.

"Weapons? Have things become that bad between you and Fallon already."

"We never know who else we may encounter on the water. It

doesn't hurt to be careful. I won't have anything happening to my family."

My heart lurches as he kisses Adrian's head again. His family. For all his flaws, Stavros loves his family more than any man I've known. Sometimes I even think he loves his family more than Loukas.

Loukas and I get guns onto the boat and Loukas punches in the coordinates. We have two bunk beds. I'll sleep on the top of one, Loukas on the bottom. Stavros plans to sleep on the bottom with Adrian on his belly. He's less furious than I expect about Fallon escaping without her son.

But after a while I realize he's not furious. He's brooding. And there's a reason my brother suggests guns.

Loukas pulls us away from the dock and starts our journey, the silent captain. I can tell he misses Tisha already. She brings the best out of him, really. He gets to dote on her and she's a girl who quite enjoys doting. Almost as much as she enjoys fast food and partying with Carlotta.

I sit across from Stavros and consider his facial expression. He looks like a younger version of Papa when he scowls.

"I can tell you're worrying," I say.

"Fallon wouldn't have left Adrian," he says, "Even if he was with Antonio. I... I don't know what she could be thinking. If she could believe Latrice needs her that much."

"She probably got swept up in Tisha's plans. That devious little wench can be compelling," I say in an attempt to comfort Stavros who shifts uncomfortably and appears suspicious of my intentions.

He answers gruffly, "Fallon is not one to get swept up. She's not swayed like other women."

Stavros, as usual, sounds defensive. He's the one who bought Fallon like a rump roast and treated her like an object in the first place. The baby hasn't helped with his guilt at all.

"Right," I say, "But who would take her without Antonio noticing."

Stavros raises an eyebrow that suggests he thinks I'm an idiot. A bad sign since Stavros is renowned more for his brutishness than wisdom.

"Yiayia," I whisper.

"Yes," he says with an icy tone, "Our grandmother."

"She doesn't know about Latrice," I say, "I'm not an idiot."

"We came over to talk to you," he says, "Yiayia may not know about Latrice...yet. But she knows we're up to something."

"What exactly are 'we' up to?"

"Tisha was making us tell you today. But... it's probably best we focus on getting your girlfriend back."

"I'm not a shit head kid anymore. I want to know."

"But you're still loyal to her, Galanos. I know she has a hold on you. I know our grandmother broke you. And for that, I'm sorry. But until I have more proof, I'm not sure I can trust you."

Hurt surges through my chest. I don't betray any of it to him. Maybe there's a twitch in my lip or a slight raising of my brow but aside from that, I only face Stavros with a cold smirk. My brother can't know I have feelings. He can't know how it hurt to grow up the shitty little outcast who didn't even look like the boys he looked up to.

"I understand."

"I need a nap," Stavros announces gruffly, "Make yourself useful on deck."

"Yes, brother."

Stavros grunts and I walk above deck to find Loukas gazing out at the ocean, a flask in his hand.

"I thought you quit drinking," I say.

He flinches like I've caught him in the act before he mutters, "It's only water."

I snatch it from him and taste it. He's right.

"Tisha wanted me to carry around one of those bottles for better hydration but... I prefer a flask."

"She's quite the little task master."

"Hm," Loukas grunts, "She's perfect. She's... gorgeous. I love her more than I've loved anyone."

Loukas quietly sips from his flask of water and then raises a curious brow as he asks, "What about you? Do you love Latrice?"

"Yes," I say without thinking. I don't need to think about it. I feel.

Loukas has an unexpected response. The flecks of grey on his head shimmer in the dimming sun.

"When was the last time you loved something, Galanos?"

"I am capable of it."

Loukas strokes his chin and shrugs, "Perhaps you are. But I think if you love Latrice, you'll always do what's best for her, even if it tears you to pieces."

"I don't remember asking for advice."

"It's not your job to ask for advice," He says, "I'm your older brother. It's just my job to provide it."

TWENTY-FOUR
ALBANIA

t's dark by the time we get to the Albanian shore. Stavros wants us to wait until morning so that Adrian can get a full night of sleep.

Loukas and I compromise with him by promising to head out alone on a scouting mission. The hotel stands right near the water. If it weren't dark, Tisha might be able to see us from whatever top floor pad she's probably rented out with Loukas' card.

He doesn't seem to care how much money she spends. I understand. If Latrice wanted to buy the last rhino, I'd capture the beast myself and hand it to her with a studded collar and a leather leash.

Loukas hesitantly arms me with a shitty pistol. I text Antonio asking for updates about Odin and he doesn't reply. It's Antonio, so he's probably having a sexy phone call with one of the several men he entertains.

My eldest brother stuffs his handgun into his jacket and we walk from the docks to the hotel lobby. The woman at the counter hurries over to Loukas a mixture of recognition and relief on her face. All the workers at Loukas' haunts know him well.

"Mister Pagonis!" She says, "You must hurry. We're too scared to go upstairs. Too scared to call the police."

He's serious now.

"What's going on?"

"Your wife was here but they took her. They took her and the fat girl. But there's still... We don't know if she's dead. They left the third upstairs. The one who looks like a model. Very sexy!"

Fallon.

Loukas runs. I run after him. My brother runs vigorously and he's faster than I am. I'm not far behind as we land on the eleventh floor of the hotel. I hear a scream from one of the rooms and Loukas shoots the keypad and handle with three bullets.

I push the door open while he reloads the barrel and hoist my gun, pulling the trigger without thinking. The man standing in the room had his gun pointed at Fallon's head and she screams as he slumps over and lands face-forward on the bed.

Fallon yells, "GAL!"

"Step back! Are there more of them?"

"No," Fallon says, "No."

She approaches the man, her face a sallow grayish brown as she stares at his corpse.

"Is he dead?"

Unlike Tisha, Fallon didn't enter our family with any blood lust of her own. Death makes her uncomfortable, especially because of the reaction it provokes in her husband. He hears voices when he kills and he sees visions.

"He's *extremely* dead," I tell her, "But that's not my concern. Who is he, and who is he working for and where on Earth is Latrice?"

Fallon can't keep her gaze off the man on the bed. Loukas approaches her and grabs her hand.

"Fallon. Don't look. Stavros has Adrian. We'll take you to him and then we'll clean this mess up."

"He's a Stathakis," she says, "By marriage. That's all I got out of him. I tried to keep him talking but—"

"What? That's impossible. I killed all of them."

"You missed a spot," Fallon says glumly, "I can't talk about this here. I'm not like the two of you."

Loukas and I exchange glances and make the decision not to let Fallon's comment get to us. Murder traumatizes normal people. For us, it's just another family outing. Fallon allows Loukas to guide her out of the room. In the hallway, Fallon turns to us and folds her arms.

"After you take me to Stavros, what are you going to do?"

"I'm going to find whoever took my wife and put a bullet in their head," Loukas says calmly.

Fallon's lips flatten into a thin, disapproving line but she doesn't say anything. Either Loukas takes care of the killing or the work will be left up to her husband, an unappealing prospect for Fallon Pagonis.

"You say he's a Stathakis?" I ask her, wanting to keep my head in the business of saving Latrice, "Then why didn't he kill all of you if he's here for revenge? Why take Tisha and Latrice?"

"They had their orders," she said, "They weren't all from the Stathakis family. One of them might have been Italian. I couldn't tell. Latrice was terrified. After all she's been through..."

My heart flutters at the mention of her name again. Nerves. The nerves are new. Since the incident with the men on the boat, I can feel them. Yiayia convinced me that part of my medical diagnosis was my lack of emotion. I shouldn't be able to feel nervous.

Fallon can't read my facial expressions. She always tries but I make her uncomfortable. Too bad, because I'm getting used to her. And I have to admit that her son is adorable.

"I will find Latrice and avenge her," I say, "I won't let them get away with this."

Fallon stops walking and raises an eyebrow as she stares at me and blurts out what she might have asked if a man wasn't just waving a gun near her head.

"Is this why you brainwashed her? You think you love her?"

"I love her," I snarl at Fallon, "And I don't need to explain myself to you."

"Speak to your elders with respect," Loukas grumbles.

"Hey!" Fallon says, "I'm not an *elder.*"

Loukas realizes he's shoved his foot in his mouth again and mutters something about us getting to Stavros quickly so we can figure out how to track the Stathakis bastard and crew who kidnapped Tisha and Latrice.

Loukas, for all his bluster, hardly seems worried that someone has kidnapped Tisha Pagonis. Has he forgotten the little imp is pregnant?

Before I can point out that Loukas is eerily calm, Fallon pinches my forearm.

"Ow!"

"Good," Fallon snaps, "Tell the truth. Did you brainwash Latrice?"

"No!" I snap, "I like her. I'm allowed to like women. I'm not *Antonio.*"

"Don't talk about my son," Loukas interrupts and then takes his phone out of his pocket to text Stavros.

"I'm serious, Gal. She's Tisha's cousin. She has people who care about her. If this is some twisted game—

"For fuck's sake, it's not a twisted game. I love Latrice. We were having sex when you lot barged in and—

"Sex? You were having sex with her handcuffed to the bed?" Fallon presses, like she's writing an investigative report.

I try to ignore the fact that my cheeks are turning red. The last thing I want to do is talk to my older brother's sexy thirty-something wife about my sexual practices.

"Is this *any* of your business?" I snap.

"I didn't know you were *Christian Grey,* that's all," Fallon teases with a smirk.

I have no idea what she's talking about.

"I love her," I insist, "I don't know why, but I love her."

Fallon makes a strange expression that I can't interpret. She tugs on Loukas' shirt and whispers, "Is it bad that I believe him?"

Loukas snorts, "I'm starting to believe him too. I've never seen him this focused on any woman."

"I can hear the two of you! Now can we hurry the hell up so I can find Latrice? Unlike Loukas, I worry about the woman I love."

Loukas' scowl finally cracks into a smile.

"Oh, Galanos. Anyone who kidnaps Tisha isn't doing themselves any favors. She can handle herself. Pregnant or not... that woman is wise beyond her years."

He can't help smiling whenever he mentions Tisha. He loves her so much more than he ever loved any of his other girlfriends. Matilda was by far the worst of them. Loukas doesn't even know she tried to sleep with me when I was seventeen.

"Let's hope she can keep Latrice out of trouble," I say to him.

We finally meet up with Stavros, who bounces a sleeping Adrian on his shoulder. Fallon rushes to her son and Stavros wraps his arms around both of them as Adrian snuggles against her chest.

"I'm sorry," Fallon whispers, half to Adrian and half to Stavros.

Stavros forgets he's angry with her for running off. Now that he has her back, it's all he cares about. Maybe it's all he ever cared about — keeping her safe.

TWENTY-FIVE
WHO COULD HE BE WORKING FOR?

After finishing our work — removing the body, paying the cleaning fee, disposing of the body, promising Fallon that everything is okay, we sit on the boat deck a few miles away from shore.

"All we know is this man was a Stathakis," Stavros says, "Who could he be working for?"

"An Italian, maybe?"

"Van?" Stavros suggests, referencing our Sicilian cousin who recently returned to his mother country after over a decade running away from the law. Van greeted his family with gunfire and stopped Loukas' daughter Carlotta from becoming a mafia child bride.

Loukas shakes his head.

"Not Van. I've been in touch with him recently and we have good relations."

"I have a problem with the Stathakis thing," Fallon says.

She has genuinely become an expert in psychiatry — the field she was in before her strange meeting with Stavros Pagonis — and Fallon always tries to ask *why*. This can be mostly infuriating but now, comes in handy.

She continued, "Why would the Stathakis brothers want to harm Latrice in the first place? And why would they keep wanting to harm her? She's not involved in family business. She's only involved with Galanos. It's like... they're following orders."

"Who the hell would give those kinds of orders?" I ask.

No one here knows what happened to me. I've kept that between me and Latrice. *My* rape. I don't want my family to know, even if this would add a valuable piece of the puzzle. The Stathakis men aren't after Latrice. *They're after me*. And Fallon's right to question their motivations.

I wait for someone to answer and then I notice they're all staring at me like I'm an idiot.

"What?" I snap.

The three of them say in unison, "Yiayia would give those orders."

My ears burn and my throat instantly fills with bile. What they're suggesting is beyond impossible. Yiayia wouldn't send anyone about Latrice because she doesn't know about Latrice. She was in a damned coma. Yiayia might be good but she's not superhuman. She has spies though. And she prepares for contingencies.

But we're talking about... *me*. I'm her favorite.

Yiayia would never have men do what they did to me. My cheeks turn red and rage courses through me. The three of them are allowing their biases to color the situation. They hate my grandmother so much that they can't see the truth.

"She would not," I insist, "Yiayia would never do this."

"You didn't see how she reacted to Tisha. They had to pump her full of Tramadol for three days."

"I don't need to explain myself."

"She had Cass raped," Fallon points out, referencing an incident with my slightly older sister and casually forgetting to point out that Cassia had a part to blame in all of it. YiaYia explained that very clearly to me.

"No," I say, "Yiayia wouldn't have done this."

"What makes you so sure?"

I clench my jaw. I don't want to tell them but blood rushes past my ears. Latrice thinks I keep too much bottled up. Latrice thinks I'm unemotional. Latrice thinks I'm just a wicked dominant who wants her for sex. But it's more than that. *She's* more than that.

The blood rushes faster and my head spins. I haven't had coke in so long thanks to Latrice. I'd never touch the stuff again if she asked. I'd do anything for her.

"My grandmother wouldn't have had a gang of men anally rape me," I say.

Two pairs of terrifying blue eyes gaze at me in shock. Fallon's face falls and I loathe the look of pity on her face. Her pity makes me want to hurt her. I scowl and lean back. Despite my urges, I am always in control. I am Galanos. I am my grandmother's favorite. I am dominant and possibly a little narcissistic. A sociopath, according to some doctors.

But I am in control.

I taste metal on my tongue and Fallon leans forward.

"Galanos. Is that what happened that night?" Fallon gasps.

My brothers are too stunned to speak. The blood pools in my mouth and I realize I've been biting my lip so hard it bleeds. I can't focus on Fallon's face and I bend over to vomit. I don't remember the next few minutes.

Fallon holds my hair back and strokes my head like I'm her son. Stavros puts a hand on my back and Loukas paces.

"We won't let her get away with this," Loukas snarls, "This time she's gone too far."

Stavros' hand moves along the length of my back. I want to fight him off but I'm too weak.

"She wouldn't," I murmur, "Not to me."

I still feel sick.

"If she found out about Latrice..." Fallon points out.

"If she found out about Latrice, she'll kill her," I snap, "She would. You all know it. So if she has Latrice, she's as good as dead."

"Galanos," Stavros says firmly, "You should have told us."

"Right," I scream, "So my older brothers who already think I'm a piece of shit will think so highly of me."

Fallon wraps her arms around me and I want to push her away from me but instead, I lean into her. And for once, I don't even think about fucking her. She's a person. My family.

"I'll go check on Adrian," Stavros says, "Loukas, get him some water. We'll get to the bottom of this."

I hear him whisper to Fallon, "He'll never believe it's her. He won't."

But my brother has me all wrong. I know exactly what Yiayia's capable of. I didn't want to admit the truth because I know what Yiayia's done will make me a dangerous man. I'll become the sociopath they think I am because if my grandmother did this, if I can prove that she did... I'll be the one to kill her.

I love her. I loved her the most. But I love Latrice more. And unlike my grandmother, Latrice is entirely innocent. I might have deserved what happened to me but Latrice didn't. It's what I always loved about her — the fact that my world never touched her.

And now it's my fault she's ruined. And Yiayia's. I thought I was being safe. I thought I was careful enough.

But this revelation has exposed a truth to me that I never thought I'd have to admit.

If I really love Latrice Boyd, I'll have to let her go. I'll have to rip up our contract and set the woman I love free. Because I can never let her get hurt like this again.

That is, if Latrice survives.

TWENTY-SIX
DIAGNOSED

Stavros returns with Adrian. Loukas cleans my vomit, with my help. Fallon paces for a bit and then whispers to Stavros. After a few more hours of heated discussion, we agree on a plan.

We take Fallon back to Thessaloniki with Adrian. Stavros will take a smaller boat to track whichever vessels Yiayia's using from the fleet. Loukas will call Papa and try to get him to reveal his mother's plans.

Papa is useless and he loathes me, but he likes Tisha enough to help Loukas save her. And he knows if he doesn't help, Loukas will finally bash his head in for all the times he's tried pinching Tisha's rump. (She's the only reason Papa hasn't suffered more for it yet.)

My job is to sit around and absorb my family's piteous looks. It's exactly why I didn't want them to know about what happened to me. I can't stand it.

Our return to Thessaloniki is boring and awkward. I tan for as much as possible and for once, my brothers leave me alone. I hate that I know it's only because they pity me. Fallon has a nice conversation with me. I know she's using her psychology witchcraft on me but I feel a little better.

Maybe talking through things is better than cocaine. But I'm not convinced entirely yet.

Antonio's gone when we get to Thessaloniki. Good thing. He *knew* someone was kidnapping Fallon, Tisha and Latrice. Yiayia might be paying him too. He at least left my puppy with someone responsible. Helen. She nearly didn't want me to take Odin back. She bought a diamond collar for Odin, who greets me with the excitement and unbridled love you can expect from a dog. Loukas agrees we can bring the dog to find our girls.

Helen hates me for taking Odin away.

Stavros leaves 24 hours after we arrive in Thessaloniki. I keep a low profile at Loukas' place. Carlotta's distraught over Tisha's absence and I spend time with her working on her applications to graduate school. She tells her father she wants to start a business and so he tells her to get an MBA. Loukas will allow his child to do whatever she wants., At least they fight less now.

Antonio plays video games with a 'friend' in the family room until the two of them fall asleep cuddling.

Loukas leaves for a late night run to Papa, who conveniently mentions that Yiayia's out of the hospital and has gone on a "retreat", all but confirming our suspicions. Papa is very smart not to get on his mother's bad side. Or perhaps he's stupid.

Like I was.

Stupid enough to think that my grandmother could have loved me enough not to have done this. I never expected Yiayia to change. I foolishly thought that I'd been more strategic than my brothers. *Smarter.*

The rage crushes me. It burns inside me. In the morning, Loukas prepares me to leave.

"Stavros went all the way to Italy last night. He's trailing them and he thinks we can find them somewhere off the coast."

"Great," I mutter sarcastically, "*Somewhere.*"

Loukas becomes instantly gruff and answers, "You need to improve your attitude if you plan on getting Latrice out of this alive."

"Yes."

"And you need to be careful with Yiayia."

I raise a single brow. I don't need to be *careful* with Yiayia at all. I'm working on other plans for her. But first... Latrice. She's more important to me than any family drama. I need to get her out of danger and then make sure my problems don't ruin her life even more than they already have.

"I can handle myself, Loukas. Let's go get your snack-obsessed wife and my... *Latrice*."

My kitten, I think privately. Loukas would never approve of such thoughts voiced aloud.

We get into the boat together. Odin "helps" by scampering around deck and tugging on the ropes until they're a tangled knot. Loukas teaches him to sit while I work through the ropes in the darkness before dawn. It takes a while to finish, but we have our guns, supplies and the fastest small ship we can find.

Odin scampers ahead onto the boat and I sail the ship away from the dock and toward the southwest.

I realize that I've never been alone with Loukas for this long. My now forty-two-year-old brother was always too much older than me to care. Or too drunk. Or involved in a screaming fight with some woman. And then there was Tisha...

He's never forgiven me for kissing her. And as for the other things... Well, I like to leave the past in the past. Loukas on the other hand seems to only have the past. He's turning grey. And it scares me. I've never considered that my strong brothers could get... *old.*

I turn the boat towards the open sea and Loukas sits with a wide stance, the grey in his hair glimmering in the early morning sun. He has coffee in his flask now. It smells like hazelnut. I don't know why he doesn't get a travel mug like a normal person. Then again, no one in my family is normal. Especially not me.

"Want some?"

"No. I'm fine."

"Are you using?" Loukas asks gruffly.

"I'm not."

Loukas grunts and takes a swig of coffee.

"Good," he says, "And how's your arse."

"Christ, Loukas. I'm not talking to you about this."

I killed the motherfuckers who did this to me. There's nothing to talk about. I sorted out my trauma on the correct end of a rifle and Loukas' son helped me. If he wants to know the gory details, he ought to ask Antonio what we did. He probably already knows *what* I did. Now he knows why.

Loukas' eyes are painful reminders that despite being *genetically* half-siblings, we are *brothers.* A bloody bond that can never break, no matter how horrible I am. My brothers have always been there. They're here now when I need them most. After all I've put them through.

"Take your health seriously," Loukas says, "Make sure you aren't sick. I can tell you from the wrong side of forty... you'll never have what you have now."

"You ran four miles this morning before I got up."

Loukas grins.

"I work very hard for this body. My wife is *twenty.* I've got to impress her before I shrivel up. Before I can't anymore."

Loukas really doesn't know how long Tisha loved him. I think she loved him the moment she first laid eyes on him. Before she knew what love was. Before she was adult enough for my brother to notice her. But he loves her back and he's scared of losing her. The way I love Latrice. I never understood what he felt. Why he was so angry with me.

But because of Latrice...

My cheeks darken and I nod respectfully.

"I will take care of myself. But I killed the men who hurt me. I don't need anything from you or Stavros. I don't need Fallon's curiosity."

"Fallon worries about you."

"Fallon loathes me," I remind him.

Loukas snickers.

"After all this time psychoanalyzing our family, you think she doesn't understand why you are the way you are?"

"I'm a sociopath."

Loukas' grin falls.

"Do you believe that?"

"I've been diagnosed."

Odin runs over to me and yaps, pushing his head against my shin, which is his way of begging for attention. I scratch between his ears and Loukas sighs.

"Yiayia has gone too far. Many times. But you are not a sociopath, Galanos Pagonis. Yiayia made up that diagnosis with that doctor because she wanted you. And the only reason she wanted you was to make Papa jealous and to get him to dump... I'm sorry, but I can't remember your mother's name. She wasn't around long."

My earns burn again. Rage. But there's no one for me to take my rage out on except Loukas. I freeze and my hands clench into foolish fists. Foolish, because my brother's hand moves instinctively to his holster.

I scream, louder than I've ever spoken before, "Why won't you fucking people stop *fucking me up?!*"

TWENTY-SEVEN
TISHA & LOUKAS

Loukas rises, startled and then moves his hand away from his gun.

"Galanos," he says slowly, "Fallon's been teaching me to resolve my family issues without violence. But if you make a sudden move, I will reach for my gun."

"I don't care! I don't care!"

I reach for my gun and shoot at my brother Loukas. Okay, not *at* Loukas. Past him. I empty every fucking bullet from my pistol and then in a rage fueled cry, I fling the gun into the ocean and fall to my knees. Anger. Rage. And then the only thing that could ever pierce through it.

The girl. The beautiful, full-figured brown-skinned girl who lay on my pool deck with a swimsuit that hugged her curves. I could see her smile so clearly, that through my meltdown, all I could do was laugh. And laugh.

Now Loukas thinks I've gone completely like Stavros. Mad. But I'm not hearing voices like my older brother.

"Thank you for not shooting me in the head," Loukas says in an eerily calm voice.

I'm good with my aim. Impeccable. *The perfect sociopath. The perfect killer.*

"If I wasn't a sociopath, I wouldn't have fired at you."

"If you were a sociopath, you wouldn't have missed someone standing three feet away from you. Galanos. You *love* Latrice. And deep down, you know you love more than her. You love Fallon. Stavros. Me."

He notably leaves out Tisha, but Loukas continues with the most sincerity in his voice I've heard from him, "You're the one who has been pulling away from our grandmother. You were 18 when you started to feel there was something wrong with her. You were still a *child* before. You were acting on instinct."

I don't remind him that I'm only a few months younger than his wife...

Loukas helps me to my feet and wraps his arms around me in a brotherly hug unlike anything I've ever felt.

"You've grown up. And you can choose what type of man you are. Not a sociopath. Not a killer. You can be something else. You can have a proper youth like Stavros and I never had. We will back you up."

"I hate her," I whisper.

And we both know I'm talking about Yiayia.

"And I love *her*," I whisper.

And then, we both know I'm talking about Latrice.

"You will know what to do," Loukas says, "Once we find her, you'll know."

We sail in silence for a few more hours. Loukas doesn't talk much. I catch him looking at pictures of Tisha on his phone. He has thousands of them. Tisha in cute little outfits. Tisha pregnant. Tisha eating fish. Tisha eating cupcakes. Tisha drinking boba tea. You get the point. He's obsessed.

I wish I had a picture of Latrice. There's always *social media* but now it puts a sour taste in my mouth. I don't want other girls anymore. I just want Latrice. I want to keep her safe.

We shelter from the sun during the day and emerge in the dusk when we're close to the Italian shore. Loukas calls Stavros immediately.

The last thing I hear him say is, "You take the Northern Cove and after, we'll go South. At least we know what boat we're looking for. The fucking Sicilians have their uses for once."

Loukas hangs up and turns to me, explaining the plan.

"So we need to go 3 miles South and—

HRRRRRNNNNNNNNNNGHHHHHHHHH! WHOOSH!

A boat speeds so close to us it nearly shaves some of hull.

"Motherfucker!" Loukas yells as the boat gets nearly tipped in the wake, "Go after them!"

"We don't know who they are! Shouldn't we *focus*?"

Loukas' face turns red and he snaps, "*My wife was behind the wheel of that boat and she's nine months pregnant! Go after her NOW!*"

Fuck.

Her boat is fast but Tisha isn't particularly skilled at boating. I can chase her and corner her somewhere until she runs out of gas. She won't outrun us and she doesn't know the water as well as I do. I get the boat up to speed with Loukas screaming at me like a madman.

I have no idea what he's saying. I go the opposite direction and then turn and point straight toward Tisha's boat, so we're aiming for a head-on collision. Never mind. My way will be *much* faster. Loukas pushes me out of the way.

"Are you fucking crazy?! MY WIFE IS PREGNANT. YOU CAN'T RUN THE BOAT INTO HER!"

"CALM DOWN!" I scream, shoving Loukas out of the way and nearly toppling his balance, "She'll stop! She's not going to win this game of chicken. Trust me, I know Tisha."

Odin barks and yaps, running fearlessly along the deck. Loukas yells at me even louder than before, "Oh I know you do, you perverted little shit!"

"Now really isn't the time, Loukas!" I scream and wobble the boat purposefully so he falls over onto his knees. We're 10 seconds away from a collision unless one of us pulls our motor to a sudden halt.

"GALANOS! GALANOS YOU'RE GOING TO KILL HER."

9

I have to know if Latrice is alive and it'll take over an hour if we have to chase Tisha's wild ass around the damn cove while she plays mob wife with a full womb.

This will be much more efficient.

5

Loukas pulls his gun out.

"STOP THE FUCKING BOAT."

"She'll get away!"

2

I kill the motor. Tisha kills hers at the same time. I wasn't sure if Loukas was leading me on a wild goose chase or not but as our boats slowly drift past each other, sure enough, Tisha Pagonis stands on the deck.

"GAL?!" She screams, "Are you crazy!?"

"Where's Latrice?!"

Sorry, I have to stay focused.

"She's below deck hiding out. What are you doing here?!"

Loukas regains his balance and emerges behind me, huffing like a dragon.

"ARE YOU OUT OF YOUR MIND, TISHA?!" He screams.

"Lou! Don't yell at me. *Rude.*"

"I swear I'm going to whoop your little behind..."

"Loukas! That's abuse! If you *whoop me,* I'll whoop your old ass right back."

Then Tisha screams and doubles over the railing. Latrice emerges from below deck and I'm ready to jump into the water to see her. She races over to Tisha instead of noticing me and glances at the ground.

"OH MY GOD!" Latrice screams.

"What is it?!" Loukas yells.

Neither of us can see clearly, but something is going on. Something scary judging by Latrice's face.

Then Latrice yells, "Her water broke!"

I'm already paddling our boat alongside theirs. We'll have to go back to shore. We're not close enough to Greece to make it back. Tisha lets out another yell. Latrice holds onto her.

"Breathe, Tisha! Breathe!"

Loukas scrambles over the railing with the speed and agility of Tarzan until he reaches her, stepping in the puddle of 'water' between Tisha's legs. He immediately springs into action.

"Tisha! Tisha, hold them in!"

"That's not how this works! AIIEEEEE!" Tisha screams.

I fasten our boats together and Loukas calms Tisha as he drives the boat back to the shore. Her yelling only gets louder and she starts freaking out.

"I'm going to die!" Tisha screams, "I'm going to die!"

We've already called for a car on shore. Van Doukas himself shows up with his fleet of Italian mobsters. I don't know him well. He brings Tisha and Loukas in his car to a hospital. His cousin, Eli takes me and Latrice in another car.

This is the first time we've seen each other since the fateful kidnapping. I've wanted so badly to see her again and now that I have Latrice close to me, I don't know what to do or say. Tisha's childbirth threw me straight into action and I feel... stupid.

Odin climbs into the back of the car with us, earning us a stern look from Eli who mutters something in bitter Italian under his breath. At least the pup sits still and he's still small enough that he doesn't have to shove his butt in my face.

I wonder how large the pup will grow and scratch between his ears as I slide into the seats next to Latrice Boyd.

Latrice tilts her head back, exhaling with relief. Eli turns up the radio and starts driving us to the hospital. Not the conversational sort, I suppose.

I turn to Latrice, examining her for damage. If I didn't know better, I'd say she seemed happy.

"Are you okay?" I ask.

"Oh. Yeah. I'm fine. Your grandmother on the other hand..."

"What the hell happened?"

Latrice looks over me and chuckles.

"Are you seriously worried?"

"Worried?! I've been *sick* with worry! I've spent every minute chasing you down. I *killed* someone."

Latrice's face grows temporarily solemn. Then she giggles again.

"Damn. You really went all alpha male, huh."

"I nearly watched my sister-in-law get shot."

"The Albania part was scary," Latrice says, "I'll admit. But once they left Fallon, Tisha knew Stavros would come for her. She let them take us. I thought she was crazy as hell but my cousin... I don't know what the hell y'all taught her because *damn*."

"You sound like you had *fun*," I sneer, furious that Latrice could be so casual about nearly losing her life.

"I told you Albania wasn't fun. We got kidnapped *again*. But when we got to Italy... Tisha pulled one stunt. She pretended to go into labor and then she pickpocketed this guy's pocket knife. Apparently her step-daughter taught her how."

Latrice laughs again.

"I'm going to keep you under lock and key once you're back home."

"Stop being so uptight, Gal. Tisha got us out pretty quick and then the rest was just stealing a few goats, trading them for a boat, seducing an Italian man to give us gas money."

"Seducing!?"

"Well... Tisha's married. So I had to seduce him."

"You *screwed* another man?"

Latrice has her angry beaver face again and she snaps, "No! Gal, can you chill?"

"Fine. Fine."

"He gave us what we needed and she was ready to take us back to Greece. I was fine, Gal. I appreciate you coming after me but..."

"It's my job to look after you," I say, "It's my promise."

Latrice puts her hand on my thigh and gazes up at me beyond long, dark lashes.

"I know that. And it's my job to always come back. So here I am."

"We can't exactly pick up where we've left off," I tell her, "Can we?"

"Nothing between us has changed. You haven't changed. It's just sex to you. Intense. Hardcore. Sex."

The driver clears his throat, but Latrice doesn't care.

"I *have* changed," I say, "Because I love you. I properly love you. And that makes everything between us completely different."

TWENTY-EIGHT
I WILL BURN

"I don't get it," she says, "I'm fine."

"You're not fine," I say, "And neither am I. Sleeping with you was dangerous. Everything I've done up until this point has put you in danger. My brother is right."

"Right about what?"

Now that I know Yiayia's responsible for this, I have to handle things. But before I do that, I have to do the responsible thing. I have to let Latrice Boyd go. I have to say goodbye to her and send her back to England. Or America.

"It's time you go home."

The words hurt her. I can see it written on her face. It's what she fears most from me. My rejection. She sees me as this statue of physical perfection and I know it hurts her to think I might be hiding evil behind the good looks.

"What? Are you crazy?" She asks. She's hoping I'm crazy.

We're at the hospital and there isn't any time to argue about this, which doesn't stop Latrice. If I thought she was angry with me before, nothing tops her mood now. Unfettered rage.

She follows me into the hospital, struggling to keep up with my stride and huffing as I move coolly ahead. I don't want to get emotional with her. I don't want to make this harder on her. She slams her fist into my back and screams.

"You are impossible!"

I turn around to face her again and wet my lower lips with my tongue. Cool air blows past us, blond hair whipping around my face.

"Latrice," I say calmly, "Tisha's giving birth. I know this isn't a great time but trust me, this is for the best."

She puts her hands on her hips and rolls her tongue around the front of her mouth. Frustration. Outrage. She's feeling a specific cocktail of emotions that only I can bring out of her.

"Don't I get a say?"

"You don't," I say stiffly, my jaw clenching.

It's time I prove to Latrice I love her by saying goodbye to her. By ending our relationship. I'll miss her, of course. Her warmth. Her laughter. The smile on her round face. The wide bridge of her nose wrinkled in disgust at something I've said.

"I'm not leaving."

"Let's go," I say firmly, "If you want to see my brother acting like a complete anxious idiot, we'd better head inside."

Latrice snakes her fingers with mine.

"I'm not letting you dump me."

"Dump you?"

"Whatever fucked up BDSM name you want to call it," she says, "But in my world, it's still called getting dumped."

I let her hold my hand. I enjoy it and then I squeeze her hand back. There's hope in her hands too. And in mine. Why doesn't she hear all the awful things that come out of my mouth and run away? Why does she stand next to me when she can't possibly love me.

"Do you think Tisha's big enough to give birth to twins?" I muse.

Latrice picks up the pace, eager to find out. We can hear Tisha wailing in a private hospital room while Loukas paces outside.

"She doesn't want me to see," he says, "I've asked her if she wants me to call anyone but she doesn't. I ought to have called her mother. I'm going to lose her..."

Loukas has already lost his mind, which I expected. He adores Tisha.

"Snap out of it," I snarl at him, "Go in there and support her."

"You're the expert now?" Loukas snarls.

"I'll go in," Latrice offers. Loukas nods at her and she pushes the door open. Tisha yells again and Loukas turns red.

"Relax," I tell him, "You're overrun with kids."

"Not Tisha's," he says, "Not with Yiayia around threatening to poison her food and have my wife raped."

"She said that?"

"Oh, she didn't take it well at all."

"You won't have to worry about that for long," I tell him.

My brother understands the insinuation and to my surprise, casts a disapproving look in my direction.

"She's an old woman, Galanos."

"You and I both know that Yiayia is not a regular old woman."

Loukas grunts disapprovingly but before he can chastise me more, a nurse comes to get him. Tisha's finally asking for him. I half expect him to come stumbling right back out of the room having fallen unconscious. Normally, I would have snuck off to another room to upload a surreptitious photo of my abs, but I just miss Latrice, even if she's on the other side of the door.

The nurses had me leave Odin in the car with the window cracked, so I don't even have my puppy's ears to scratch. And Latrice thinks I've given up on 'dumping' her. But I haven't. I need to get her to safety and if she won't go willingly, I'll get help.

Unlike *civilians*, you learn patience in the mafia. And if I have to wait a year to find my grandmother and make her pay for what she's done, I'll do it. But Latrice has to be safe until then. And I have to be safe too. I need to make sure I didn't hurt her with my recklessness. With *disease.*

She's so sure that we're not sick, but I'm already unlucky

enough to have a grandmother who will arrange my rape. I haven't exactly had the luckiest hand so far, despite the money. The abs. The pool.

Two painful hours pass and I have a plan. Three more nights with Latrice on my boat and then I take her to freedom. Three more nights of us indulging in all our kinky fantasies and then I will say goodbye to her forever and go on a suicide mission. Because to kill Yiayia, I may have to kill Papa.

No one in my family would approve of this plan. But this is what makes me different from them. I may have a fucked up way of showing it, but when I love people, I never stop. I can't. It's worse than being the sociopath I thought I was, indulging in violence for fun.

I will burn the entire world for this woman. I will burn the entire world for Latrice.

Loukas emerges with his hair stuck to his brow.

"She made it. They made it."

"Twin boys?"

"Twin boys," he says, "And they already look like her. I'm in trouble, aren't I? Stephanos & Stavros. She already has their names. Oh, I'm in so much trouble..."

"You were in trouble when you kissed a seventeen-year-old girl," I mutter.

Loukas raises an eyebrow and grumbles back, "She mentioned that?"

"Before her obsession with you, we were friends, you know."

"I'd feel sorry if you weren't a pervert too."

"Listen, Loukas. I'm sorry. For messing with her. For caring about her. I've changed. Once we're done here, I'm finally doing something that isn't selfish. I'm letting Latrice go."

"What?"

Now Loukas truly doesn't believe me. He's my older brother. I respect him and his advice and he makes an excellent point about Latrice.

"I have to keep her safe and she's not safe here. I have to accept that."

"Neither are you," Loukas says, "Why don't you go together?"

No. I can't leave with Latrice because I have business to take care of. I need answers and then I need revenge.

I explain my plan to Loukas. With newborns, I doubt he'll agree to it but he listens close.

At first, Latrice and I will leave Thessaloniki together. A three day sex romp on my boat with Odin in tow. Then, I'll sail her to Athens and put her on a plane back to London or wherever she wants to go. Loukas offers a wry half-smile.

"I hope she listens to reason."

"I will make her listen."

Loukas snorts.

"You're good with women, Gal," he says, "It runs in the family. But like your brothers, you seem to have fallen for another woman with a strong will. Making her listen won't be as easy as you think."

"Thank you for the advice," I answer, struggling not to sound both bitter and sarcastic.

Loukas is too excited about his new babies to care about my savage tone.

"Tisha's holding them. Would you like to meet the boys?"

"Yes. I must. Because you're naming one after me, right? It's not too late."

Loukas mutters something about me fist-fighting Stavros to determine who gets a child named after them. I follow Loukas. Tisha smiles at me and says my name in a soft, sleepy voice.

"Gal! I'm a mom..."

She starts crying with joy and clutches the babies to her tiny chest. I feel something strange in my chest. And then...

Latrice says, "Oh my goodness. Gal, are you crying?"

"I am *not* crying," I snarl.

Loukas takes one one of the boys from Tisha and hands him to me.

"Here," he whispers, "Hold your godson."

"Jaden and Brayden," Tisha says, "That's what I want to name them now."

"Tisha..." Loukas murmurs, "Because you just gave birth to my children... I'm going to avoid commenting on this *new* suggestion."

"Good," she says, "Now give him back."

Holding the child makes me feel something tender. Something raw. Latrice puts her arm around me and rests her head on my shoulder.

"Isn't he so cute?"

"Yeah," I murmur, "Adorable."

"Mixed kids are adorable," Latrice says.

I bite my lower lip and avoid blurting out that I'm wondering what our kids will look like. I really don't want to make things harder for her. We spend the night with family. In bliss. Fallon video-chats with Tisha and Stavros returns by midnight.

I take Latrice and Odin to Van Doukas' country villa for the night. Tisha and Loukas stay in the hospital. They'll be in Italy for a while, which means I can go back to Greece by plane with Latrice and get my boat for our trip. She thinks I've forgotten the properly dumping her part and that I've only ripped up the contract. Which I have... metaphorically.

I don't think I can properly rip it up. I'll want something to remember her by. On the flight home, Latrice sleeps on my shoulder and I stroke her hair, wishing that I could have her safely. I half expect Yiayia to shoot our plane down and by the time we arrive at my villa, I'm paranoid. Stavros levels of paranoid.

She could be here. She could kill us all. She could kill Latrice...

TWENTY-NINE
ANSWERS & REVENGE

atrice falls asleep readily once we're in the villa. I enjoy watching her bed down on my couch after I've suffered through one of those horrible romantic comedies she loves. When she falls asleep halfway through the movie, I rewind it back to the beginning and watch it again.

When Harry Met Sally. I wonder why Latrice likes it so much. The man doesn't even have a six-pack and the woman is much too pale, but her eyes are pretty.

I take Odin for a late night run to the docks — three fast miles with my pup and my pistol. 200 pushups, 300 squats, 100 pull-ups. Then bed. Odin rests his head on my chest and that makes it easy for me to fall asleep.

I wake up to Odin licking my face. And Latrice standing over me.

"Ugh. Go away..."

She giggles and pokes my side, "How late were you up?"

"Latrice... Beauty sleep... Please..."

"Okay. I answered your house phone. The boat's ready."

I open one lazy eye. Seeing Latrice wakes me up right away.

"Is it noon?"

"Twelve-thirty."

"Okay," I murmur, "Come to bed, kitten."

"Kitten? I thought we weren't still doing that."

"We're going on a boat trip. We can do anything we want on the boat trip."

"Right. And then we're taking a break from your family."

Yes... "We". Unfortunately, for my plan to work, I have to make Latrice think that I'm coming with her to America.

"I think you'll love America. We can visit Tisha's mom in Brooklyn. She's crazy as hell but... well... She's my aunt," Latrice says.

"What about your family?"

Latrice sighs.

"It's complicated."

"Come to bed and tell me."

"What about the boat, Gal?"

"They can wait," I tell her, "Please..."

I just want her close to me. I want to savor every moment of our last few days together. I want to savor every moment of having Latrice close to me. And more importantly, I want to *play* with her. I want to tease her and spank her. And lick her... you get the point.

Latrice slides into bed next to me and she tries not to only my abs. I stretch, making it very hard for her to ignore the chiseled body lying next to her. I tap my chest and she rests her head against it. Latrice...

I kiss the top of her forehead and she sighs.

"So. We're not together. But we're... doing this."

"You don't want a proper relationship with me, kitten."

"Right," she mutters, "I bet you tell all your cyber-slaves that."

Her accusation hurts. I know Latrice doesn't realize it but she has me utterly wrapped around her finger. Utterly tamed. But I have to ignore her little jabs. All I can afford to care about now is savoring her while I can.

"Listen," I whisper, "Tell me about your family."

"Okay," she says, "My mom put me on crazy diets when I was a kid and she completely hates what I do... so we don't really talk. And my dad... he's in the military. He left when I was a kid. He has a white wife somewhere and a bunch of mixed kids."

"Hm. So you aren't close?"

"My parents barely wanted me," Latrice says, "They're just happy I don't ask for any money."

"How can we be friends and I've never heard any of this?"

"You never asked," Latrice says and then the next words out of her mouth hurt ten times more, "You never *cared*."

"I care about other people," I whisper, "I know I do. At least... I care about you."

"Whatever. If you say so."

I wish she would say that she loves me. Latrice closes her eyes and nuzzles against my chest. Odin climbs onto the bed between us. Fuck. It's going to be impossible to let her go, isn't it? I'll have to become the sociopath Yiayia wanted.

"Come on," I whisper, "I need something to eat and then we'll set sail."

"No more mafia drama?"

"I can't promise that. I can promise that you'll have the time of your life, kitten."

At the docks, Latrice walks onto the boat with her bag and Odin runs after her, barking. The man at the docks gives me a stack of hundred Euro notes.

"From Stavros."

I nod and salute him. It's not like Stavros to be generous, so Loukas must have kept him informed of my plan. 72 hours from now, my relationship with Latrice will be finished and I'll leave her to hunt down the woman who hurt both of us. Answers and revenge. It's the mantra I repeat to myself while I work out.

There's still one thing I have to address with her. One scary, painful hurt that I don't want to talk about with anyone. I do what every Pagonis man does when we don't want to talk about our feelings. I sail the boat west out of the port and point to the skyline, describing the scenery, the blue, the houses and telling Latrice stories about my younger years.

Latrice has a degree from Oxford, so she spent most of her life studying and working toward her schooling. With her social media career (which I maybe ruined, oops), she has always focused on being the perfect role model. So stories of my less than chivalrous past both titillate and horrify her.

"You did *not* pull a teacher's pants down," Latrice chides in utter disbelief that Tiger and I might have gotten away with such a horrible thing.

"I did," I tell her, "He was a pervert. He totally deserved it."

Latrice sighs.

"Right," she says, "Your life is crazy, Gal. You don't know how lucky you are. Boats. Houses. Partying. It's… like I'm living in a dream world where money doesn't matter. Where everything comes easily. That's what it's like being around you. Completely… surreal."

I make an awkward grunting sound. Latrice won't have to worry about money for long. She doesn't know the extent of my plans but I *love* her. And even if I can't put her through the trouble of a Pagonis life, I will always take care of her. *My woman.*

We sail out a few hours until the sun has nearly set. I stop the boat and anchor down for the night. Latrice comes above deck, interrupting me before I have the surprise ready for her. I unfolded a snack table and Latrice emerges before I've set out a bottle of wine.

"Gal? What on earth are you doing?"

"I meant it as a surprise," I grumble.

"Please tell me you have more for dinner than just a bottle of wine…"

I turn red. Latrice only knows the worst parts of me. Somehow, she hasn't thrown me overboard. Yet.

"I brought more than wine. I prepared, you know."

"I have steaks."

"You're going to set out burners on your precious boat and grill steaks?"

"This kitchen isn't as big as the super yacht. I'm sorry."

Latrice laughs.

"You are the worst, you know that?"

Now, I'm really confused. I thought I was doing well. I thought I was showing Latrice my chivalrous side.

"Right. It was wrong of me not to bring the super-yacht."

"No!" Latrice says, laughing even harder at me, "You are such a freak. I mean... you realize most guys don't even have a car with half a tank of gas in it? And you're apologizing for taking me out on your less nice boat."

"Oh."

"You're not as bad as you think you are, Gal."

"Wait until you taste my steak. I'll have you worshipping my cock for more."

Latrice raises a suspicious eyebrow.

"*You* ripped our contract up," she reminds me, "So there won't be any cock-worship."

She hesitates around the phrase cock-worship, like she's wary of arousing me. *Oh, Latrice. There's nothing to worry about. I've been hard the entire time...*

"I know," I say, "I know. I'll... I'll start cooking."

"If I didn't know better, I'd say you were nervous."

Odin bounds upstairs and runs straight for Latrice, putting his head on her lap so she can scratch him behind the ears.

"I'm fine."

I take out my cooler and my gas burners. Cooking all rustic for Latrice probably doesn't compare to anything she deserves... but you're meant to cook for the woman you love. Especially when you'll never see her again.

The truth of the matter is, killing Yiayia might backfire. Killing Yiayia might end with Yiayia killing me.

THIRTY

WINE DRUNK WITH A CRAZY GUY

set the steak and potatoes in front of Latrice who glances up at me past long, curly lashes and lifts the round apples on her cheeks.

"Why does this steak look so good?"

"It'll be the best food you've ever tasted, babe," I say, faking confidence that I definitely don't feel.

She'll hate it. And then she'll toss me overboard and run off into the sunset with my dog and my boat.

At least she doesn't stop me from calling her babe. I sit across from her and stare. I'm too terrified to eat before I know how she'll respond. And I'm getting the urge to take my shirt off so she'll be too distracted by my incredible body to notice how shitty the food is.

How the hell is *Latrice* of all people the one person who can make me really feel insecure?

She cuts the meat and bites into it.

"Holy shit, Galanos. This is *amazing*."

"Are you serious?"

"You made this. In front of me. So I know you cooked it. But I don't believe *you* cooked."

"When Yiayia got angry with me, I followed around the maid. She put me to work and told me to imagine the tomatoes were heads of the boys at school."

"Okay," Latrice says, "A little disturbing. But damn... she taught you how to season meat?"

I don't know why it surprises Latrice that I know how to season meat. But for some reason, the comment amuses her. I can eat now. But more importantly, I can drink.

"Wine?"

"Hell yes."

"I was thinking," I say, as I pour her glass, "I shouldn't have had sex with you without protection. I know you agreed to it but... I don't think it's caring."

Latrice snorts.

"Since when do you do caring? I know what you're like Galanos."

"Since you."

"Right."

She sounds like she only half believes me. It hurts, but I know that I probably deserve her reluctance. I've hurt her. And I'm the reason she got hurt.

"You've made me realize that I need to stop being so selfish."

"How the hell have I done that?"

"Being here," I tell her, "I know you aren't selfish because you always cared about me. Even when I didn't deserve it. I wanted to sleep with you right away. But you were so... kind. I thought if we were just friends, it would go away. Like morning wood."

Uh oh. She's making that angry beaver face again. I am very ashamed that I always seem to incur her wrath.

"Are you comparing liking me to having morning wood?"

I bury my embarrassment in an enormous gulp of wine — directly from the bottle this time. Damn it. Does Latrice know how hard it is for me to voice this? The gentle smirk on her face betrays her intentions a little. But I can't really tell.

"Yes," I mutter, "But you don't understand. I've gone my entire life and slept with hundreds of women. None of them made me want to get to know them more."

"Glad to know that you finally scraped the bottom of the barrel."

"You know that's not what I mean," I explain to her, huffily.

Latrice says calmly, sipping her wine, "You treated me lower than dirt. For almost a year. I've seen how you treat everyone else. How can I believe that you suddenly woke up one day and started loving me?"

Now she has that angry beaver face. The face women have when you're definitely not getting laid tonight. But it's our last three days together and I plan on spending as much of that time as possible making love to Latrice. My heart races out of control because that's exactly how I feel with her. Out of control.

There isn't a contract or deal in the world that can make me get over the terror I feel over losing her the way I've lost every woman I've ever loved. The way I'll lose my grandmother soon. Latrice doesn't know the power she has and it makes me want to kiss her. And hurt her. And kiss her again.

"It's not sudden," my voice comes out icy and distant, "I hide my emotions to protect people close to me. I have to. And if I'd hid my emotions better, we wouldn't be in the position we're in now."

"And what position is that exactly?"

Fuck. I've nearly given away my intentions to make this my last weekend with Latrice. She wrinkles her brows and I mutter something about our position as survivors of trauma. That's something she keeps explaining to me, but I spice it up with some new vocabulary from Fallon.

I did most of my healing when I shot the Stathakis brothers. But there are more people I need to hurt. People I don't want to hurt.

"More wine?"

Latrice nods and waits for me to fill her glass. I tip the bottle into my mouth once I'm done and she watches me polish off the rest.

"Why did you take me out here, Galanos?"

Latrice suspects something. Shit. She's probably suspected

something the whole time. But I can't let her know that this is me saying goodbye. I don't want to poison our last few days together.

"Because," I say, thinking my excuse should at least be honest, "I love you. You were hurt. I want to look after you."

Odin barks and runs below deck. He probably wants Latrice to play tug-of-war with him. She never loses patience for the silly creature. Latrice sighs once he's gone.

"You know what's crazy, Gal? You're actually good for me."

"I don't believe that."

I open another bottle of wine because if we're talking feelings, I'll need to get properly drunk. Even Latrice is acting a little tipsy. And we're done eating, so our tummies are full. I've forgotten to count exactly how many calories I've consumed...

Latrice doesn't care about these kinds of things. She's not obsessive. She's... *happy*.

She'll be even happier when I've put her out of danger.

"You are good for me," she says, "Even with the social media thing... I don't want to be an influencer. I love my body. I love that people enjoy my badass attitude but no matter what, living for likes is nothing compared to just living. It's why I stuck around you so much. I thought the reason you were more successful than me at the whole influencer thing was because you lived a real life. A life people wanted to see."

"I think it's because I'm an insanely sexy blond white male with blue eyes, tattoos and a perfect body. And a big dick."

"Humble too..." she mutters.

Latrice makes her angry badger face again, but then she quickly softens to me. The way I soften to her.

"Maybe you are different," she says, "Maybe I can believe you love me. But even if you don't... you've taught me that the best way to love this life I live and this body I inhabit is to dive into the thick of it."

"This is your takeaway from getting kidnapped and shot at?"

"Oxford University, babe. They taught me how to think deep."

"I see... In your *Women's Studies* courses?"

"Yes, Gal. In my women's studies courses..."

"I've always wondered if I'd be good at women's studies," I muse, "I've always been very good at... women. I like studying... their *cunts*."

Latrice and I make eye contact. She laughs. I laugh. I don't really know what we're laughing at or if the sentence that just came out of my mouth even made sense.

"Why are you laughing?"

"Pass the wine," she wheezes, through more laughing.

"I asked you, Latrice... Why..."

She spills some of the wine on the table and I get up quickly so it doesn't dribble onto my clothes. Latrice squeals and drags me away from the wine, which now covers the table and some of our empty plates.

She's clutching my forearm and laughing still.

"Galanos. We are *drunk*."

THIRTY-ONE
ELEPHANT DICK

We are both properly drunk. The boat rocks and Odin barks, emerging from below deck.

"What's that in his mouth?" Latrice asks through drunken giggles.

Odin drops his prize before us.

"Oh my God!"

I lean forward, chuckling mischievously at the item that Odin must have wrested from deep within Latrice's weekend suitcase.

"Is that..." I ask...

"Odin!" Latrice screams, "How did you get that?"

"Is that a vibrator?!"

"No! It's not..."

I grab the item from the boat deck and lift it closer.

"It's like half the size of my cock," I complain.

Latrice snatches the item from me and hides it behind her back.

"Well, excuse me. They don't make vibrators in *elephant dick*."

"Elephant dick?"

"Your dick is enormous."

"Is that why you've been masturbating with this? To try to... simulate the effect? Where did you even get this..."

"None of your business! None of this is any of your business."

"You brought it on the trip. So now it is my business."

"I didn't bring it *up here*!" Latrice yells, "This is strictly for my *alone time.* Your dog stole it and... oh, never mind..."

She turns around and tries to throw the 8 inch vibrator into the ocean. I snatch it from her before she can fling it into the sea and then, I get a brilliant idea and press it to my nose.

"Don't smell my vibrator, Galanos!"

"You've *cleaned it,*" I mutter bitterly.

"Yes," I said, "I'm not going to pack something that smells like coochie along with my clothes."

"Coochie?"

"That sounds awful in your accent," she complains.

"Don't make fun of my accent, *American.*"

She lunges for the vibrator and I hold it over my head.

"Oh no, kitten. We aren't done with this..."

"Galanos! Give it back!"

I keep waving it over my head and then Odin, takes a running leap onto the table, flying our plates everywhere. With boundless energy, the dog bounces off the table and snatches Latrice's vibrator from my hands, foolishly attempting to balance himself on the railing.

I grab the insolent pup before he plunges into the dark sea and he lets go of the vibrator, which rolls off the ship's deck and careens into the Aegean Sea.

Latrice shrieks, "Odin!"

"If you want your cunt satisfied, all you had to do was ask," I tell her, scratching Odin between the ears and wondering if I'd finally found my right hand hell hound. He gives a satisfied little bark as Latrice gives him the angry beaver face instead of me.

"Thanks, Odin."

"If you want a proper cock, you can try mine again. But this time... I'll put your safety first. I brought condoms."

"How exactly do you find condoms for that thing?"

"Custom-made, babe," I tell her with an arrogant wink.

I mean, come on. Guys with dicks half my size brag about theirs. Why shouldn't I remind Latrice that I have the biggest dick she'll probably ever see in her entire life stuffed into my trousers. Not like she could ever forget.

"You're so annoying," she grumbles.

I set Odin down and he scurries off to the other side of the boat, wagging his tail and barking at nothing.

With my hands on my hips, I look at Latrice again. I properly look at her. When we're done, when I've finally said goodbye to the woman I love, I wonder what will happen to her. Outside of financially providing for her, it will be easier if I don't know. Loukas will help me set it all up. He'll help me with everything except killing Yiayia.

Well, he's helping me with that too. But he doesn't know it yet. He doesn't know my true plan because unlike my idiot brothers, I still only trust one person. Galanos Pagonis.

"Still drunk?" I ask her.

"Yes."

"Drunk enough to fuck me?"

"Definitely."

"Out here. In the open. This is where I want to make love to you."

"Galanos..."

"Listen, Latrice. I'm a passionate Greek man and if I can't make love to a woman on the deck of my boat, then I might as well never fire my gun again."

I stride across the deck and grab her hips, kissing her and dipping her. Her curves spill between my fingers as I hold her and she squeals in surprise as if she expects me to drop her. I'm strong. Strong enough for Latrice. And strong enough to do what it takes to protect her, even if it means breaking my heart in two. Forever.

I lift her easily off the ground. She squeals and jiggles in my grasp, nearly toppling over until I press her butt against the railing and spread her legs wide, sliding between them. I grab her lower lip between my lips and suck on it slowly before kissing Latrice properly, the way she wants to be kissed. I grab her cheeks and force her lips apart. When I pull away from her, my heart pounds and my need for her becomes *overwhelming*.

"I want you," I whisper, "I want to fuck you slowly."

Latrice grinds her hips forward and wraps her arms around me, leaning on my strength. My throat constricts and I want to rip her panties off and tease her entrance open with my fingers before plunging my member between her legs.

She moves one hand beneath her dress and eases her panties to the side. My hand meets hers beneath the dress and my fingers brush past hers. She's wet. Seriously wet. I groan as I touch her damp panties. I lean in and kiss her again, playing with her outer lips as our kissing gets more and more passionate. She rips at my shirt, tugging it off.

"Your body is so hard," she whispers, "So strong..."

My cock stiffens. Her admiration. Her desire for me. All of it awakens my urge to bury my cock inside her. Condoms... I promised her condoms. But now that I'm right here, all I want is to cum inside her.

She tears my shirt off finally and kisses my shoulders. My biceps bulge forward as Latrice greedily sucks on my neck and chest. Her head travels down to my nipples and I groan as she sucks on my nipple, flicking her tongue across my piercing.

"Gal..." she whispers, her kisses returning to my lips, "I *really* don't want you to use a condom."

"What about our safety?"

"With you, I want to be reckless."

"I could get you pregnant," I murmur, "Would you want to carry a murderer's baby?"

Latrice gazes away from me bashfully. I put my finger beneath her chin and lift her face to mine.

"Tell me what you want, Latrice."

"I want to feel you inside me. I want to risk it. I want to do something fucked up and terrifying just once. I want to stop being perfect."

"That's all well and good... but do you want a *baby*?"

"Why not now? Why not today? You're not going anywhere."

She runs her fingers over my chest and I dry swallow.

"I *fantasize* about it," I whisper, "Cumming inside you. Getting you pregnant. Sucking your tits. How could you possibly know that?"

THIRTY-TWO
PUPPY LOVE

’m Katie," Latrice says, and the secret rolls off her tongue like it's not earth shattering. Her worried expression causes her to grab onto my shoulders tighter, which is good because I've let go of her hips. They're perfect hips. Everything about Latrice's body is curvy, fluffy... just the way I like it.

But I can't ignore the significant information that Latrice has just revealed to me. My ears ring, like I've fired a shotgun. I don't understand what Latrice is saying to me. She can't be serious. She can't have been... *Katie*. No. Katie sent me pictures. Katie spoke with me for months. She obeyed all my filthy commands. She had her own ideas. Her own kinks about me, ropes and a paddle. Latrice couldn't have been Katie, though.

"Katie's white," I blurt out, which seems stupid. If I really think about it, the photos were horrible quality. I just liked Katie because she was obedient. Because she was... I meet Latrice's gaze again, anger coloring my cheeks.

"Katie's a *catfish*," Latrice says, "I'm a catfish. I was lying about my identity. I made her up and photoshopped pictures. I've been cat fishing you."

"We *sexted.*"

"Several times."

"You *lied to me.*"

I know I shouldn't get angry with her. I'm drunk. I'm holding her over the edge of my boat and I'm horny. Ridiculously horny. I made "Katie" do horrible things. Horribly sexy things. It's humiliating that Latrice knows this much about me. That's what made her want me... this secret she's been holding onto this entire time. But she rebuffed me. Several times. I feel stupidly drunk.

"She was white," I whisper, "I swear..."

"That was light and editing," she says, "I'm good with the apps. It was *me.*"

"How could you do something like this? *Why* would you do something like this? This is... this is *insane!*"

"I got caught up! I thought it was going to be this dumb joke, and we weren't even friends yet and then... everything escalated."

"I dumped you," I snarl.

"Well," she sighs, "I deserve that. For lying. Katie really misses you, though."

I lean forward, trying to kiss her, but accidentally nearly lose my grasp on Latrice. When I let go of her and she shrieks, nearly falling over the railing. I grab her by the waist again and pull her onto the deck, dragging her against my chest. She's shaking. She thought I'd let her fall overboard. Or worse... push her. Then she cries. Softly at first, but then she's sobbing as I clutch her against my chest. Did she think I wanted to kill her? That I'd let go of her at all?

. Latrice lied to me. She pretended to be another girl... a girl who I sexted... A girl who I dumped. But I can't bring myself to feel angry. Rage is normally simple for me. Rage has always been the simplest thing.

"I knew you'd think I was a freaky stalker," she whimpers.

But with Latrice, a warmth I'd forgotten how to feel easily replaces my rage.

My voice is soft and pleading, "Why on *earth* would you do something like this?"

"It started off as a joke. I wanted to prove to you that being a shallow prick on the internet would not get you anywhere. But then... I.... I started getting turned on. Not as a joke."

"I called Katie my *slave.*"

"It got out of hand," Latrice snaps, "Jeez! I wanted to tell you. Before asking about the sex thing. I had an entire plan. It had like a 0% chance of failing."

"Then I asked you to sell coke," I said, "Fucking everything up."

"You killed for me," she whispers, "You literally took someone's life."

She presses her hand to my chest. I know she can feel my heartbeat, pulsing slowly despite how nervous I feel. In that way, I'm exactly as reptilian as Yiayia raised me to be. I enjoy her fingers sliding over my skin.

"I protect the people I love," I murmur, wanting to kiss her again. Wanting to make love to her. And then tie her up for a few days, eating her pussy until I get bored. Or until she says the safe word.

"I feel safe with you, Galanos. Even if it's definitely the most dangerous place in the world to be by your side, I don't want to end up anywhere else."

Latrice is only right about one thing. By my side is the most dangerous place in the world.

"I love you, Galanos," Latrice says, "That's the only reason I did it. I never thought you'd fall for a girl like me. You made it pretty clear how you feel about people without perfect bodies."

"You *love* me?"

"That's the part you focus on?"

I grab Latrice's shoulders and kiss her. Yes. It's the part I focus on. Because it's the only part that matters. She pushes me away.

"Gal!"

"What?"

"I need to know if this is... if the only reason you like me is because this is your idea of a prank and it got out of hand."

"A prank?"

"You don't like fat girls."

I kiss her neck. Don't I? My cheeks are probably flushed with wine and embarrassment.

"Incorrect," I murmur, "I enjoy women. Women with bodies like yours. Women without them. My cock leads the way. I don't put a label on it."

"Why is that so hard for me to believe?"

"Because," I tell her, "You think I'm a shallow narcissist incapable of love, so when you see evidence to the opposite, you convince yourself it's all a lie. But this isn't a lie, Latrice."

"You lie all the time, though," she whispers, running her fingers over my liar's lips. She's right. Lying is a part of my family business. Selling drugs. Killing people. Stealing money. Buying boats. Procuring beautiful women. All of these things involve lying. I just have further limits with most people.

Latrice is the only person I've been entirely honest with. And I'm shocked not to see that angry expression crossing her round face.

"I wouldn't lie to you about this. We've spent so much time together. Friends. If I'm a shallow narcissist incapable of love, you're like... a fairy. Sweet. Innocent. Soft. I wouldn't hurt someone like that. I wouldn't want to make a woman become more like me."

"Gal..." she protests as I bend forward to kiss her neck. I'm ready to prove to Latrice exactly how much I love her.

"Don't stop me," I growl as I take some of her flesh between my lips, "I'm drunk enough to let this whole thing slide."

"I'm not drunk enough."

Our eyes meet again and we both giggle before saying together, "We're both drunk enough."

"Clothes off," I murmur, "I need you, kitten."

Latrice doesn't need me to issue another command. She's

completely naked on the deck of my boat within a few glorious minutes. I stare at her and she shyly tries to cover herself.

"Don't," I say firmly, "Take your hands away."

"I'm cold."

"I want to see your breasts. And then, kitten... I'm going to cum inside you."

Latrice nods and then moves her hands away. She squeezes her eyes shut, trembling from the cold but eager to show me how much she can endure on my behalf. A light-hearted smile crosses her face.

"I want you to be dirty about it," she breathes, "I want you to talk about how much you want to knock me up. I want to hear every filthy fetish of yours out loud, Galanos."

She's already *heard* my filthy fetishes. None of my dirty words scare her off. In fact... it's exactly what she wants. My cock stiffens and I lick my lower lips, ready to command her. Ready to enjoy the next three days and all the bliss they'll offer me.

"Get on your knees," I tell Latrice, "I need my cock sucked."

"Yes, sir," she breathes, dropping to her knees and dragging them slowly across the deck. She leans back slightly, showing me her breasts and watching my cock jut out further.

I groan as I watch her breasts sway and find my hand unconsciously moving to my cock. Latrice's round apple cheeks bulge in a sweet smile.

"Open wide," I whisper, pressing my hand to the top of her head and guiding her wide mouth around the head of my cock. Her mouth is perfect. Hot. Small. Delicate. And she wants to please me so badly, which makes feeling her mouth around my dick ten times better.

She stretches her lips to their capacity before the first two inches of my dick slide into her mouth. Latrice grabs my thighs and then her hands move to my ass. My flawless, muscular ass tenses as her hands brush against the most intimate part of my body as she slides her tongue along the underside of my head and struggles to take even more of me into her mouth.

"Latrice..." I gasp.

She lowers her head more and takes *the entire length* into her mouth. I want to ask her how she can even breathe, but she just looked up at me with soft brown eyes and I burst. Immediately. My cum shoots straight down her throat. She doesn't even have to swallow... I withdraw from her suddenly.

"I..."

I want to apologize, but Latrice has a dazzling smile on her face and she licks her lips.

"That tasted *amazing.*"

"It's cum," I say, "I don't think it's meant to taste amazing."

"Well, yours does. Like pineapple juice."

I take Latrice's hand and lift her to her knees, pressing her hands to my lips and then kissing her. This time, kissing her feels incredible. She pulls away from me, though, pressing her hands to my chest.

"This was way too easy," she whispers, "I lied to you. You just can't get over that. Aren't you going to take revenge? I've watched you take revenge on Tiger because he beat you at cards."

"Tiger always cheats at cards," I explain, "That's why I had to take revenge on him. And you... I love you. You're above revenge."

And this is the last time I'll get to hold her like this. I can't waste one second of our time together getting angry with Latrice.

"You peed in his carton of milk," Latrice says, "You're extreme."

"And he drank it," I reply, grinning, "Tiger's my *bitch.*"

"I thought I was your *bitch.*"

"Oh no," Gal murmurs, "I'd never call you that. You're my kitten... and I'm still ridiculously hard... so we need to stop talking. Now. Get your clothes off."

We're out in the open, but I know Latrice will obey me. My cock is harder than I've ever been, and I can hear a seam ripping in the crotch of my jeans.

"Here?" Latrice asks, but really, it's teasing. How much of her disobedience will I allow? Tonight I'm tolerant.

I turn her around and kiss her neck, forcing Latrice to gaze out at the open ocean over the railing. Here? Yes. Definitely here. I peel her out of her dress, slowly lowering it from her shoulder and rubbing her perfectly thick arms as I get her naked.

"I love your body," I whisper, "Have I ever mentioned? No Photoshop. Nothing fake about it. I love it."

"No one has ever said that to me before," she says.

"That's the difference between sex and rape, isn't it? A rapist doesn't like your body. They want you as an object. To remind you that you're worthless. But no matter what happened to us, Latrice, I love you. And I want you to know that to me, you aren't worthless."

If I don't tell her now, I'll never get a chance. My puppy love has metastasized into this monstrous romance that eats at me when I least expect it. It makes me sensitive. And hard. I'm more sensitive when I'm hard, really. Ironic.

A large black brassiere holds her breasts back, but I *need* to fill my hands with them. Lips around her neck, I unhook her bra and let Latrice's enormous breasts and large nipples fall into my hands. There's so *much* of her and even if she put her lips around my cock and I came within seconds... *I'm ridiculously hard and ready to cum again.*

THIRTY-THREE
GALANOS EATS

atrice moans as I pinch her nipples between my fingers. They're large nipples with soft bumps around them that get my cock extra stiff. I can already smell her pussy and it's making the hardness worse. Waiting even one more second is pure torture.

"Latrice," I whisper, "I want to enter you... But I can't until I've tasted you. Can you be patient, kitten?"

The real question is if I have the strength for patience. There's no more blood left in my brain for rational decision making. My desire compels all my subsequent actions. I nibble my way down her ass cheeks, lingering to smell her skin.

Latrice spreads her legs apart slightly, letting me know that patience is definitely part of the deal if it means having my tongue between the full, sopping lips of her cunt. I love her cunt. I dream about it. I close my eyes and think about the ways I want to lick and suck at her pussy lips.

I drop to my knees, ready to service Latrice's perfect cunt while she stares at the ocean. I can't wait to. When I love a woman, I become obsessed and right now I think I'll die if I don't immediately press my tongue between Latrice's legs. They're perfectly thick legs too, with texture and dimples and shape to them. The way her flesh sinks into my palm, making a soft pillow for my kisses and the rigid contours of my body never fails to turn me on.

As I grab Latrice's thighs, she moans, and I spread her ass and pussy lips apart. Her deliciously sweet smell is nearly enough to make me cum in my pants. I want to climax here. I want to put my cock between her legs and fill her with thick pumps of my cum and then watch my excess dribble down her perfect dark-brown thighs.

Fuck, she turns me into a pervert.

The fabric from her underwear gets stuck between her ass and pussy lips, totally soaked from her juices. My cock is definitely ready to *explode.* I pull her panties aside and press my nose right against her cunt. Latrice makes a sound halfway between a moan and a yelp.

Her scent hits me like a bump of coke, a jolt of energy rushing straight to my brain, and I grab the fabric of her panties between my teeth and easily rip them away from her pussy with one firm tug. Latrice squeals as the fabric rips, but before she can react, I force her to brace herself on the boat railing by driving my long tongue inside her. Fuck, patience. I want to eat some pussy.

I slide between her lips and easily find her clit. Her sexy jiggling and insanely voluptuous ass cheeks may suffocate me, but I don't care. I live for this. Most of the girls in our line of work have big fake butts, hard to the touch or silicon soft. Latrice's ass cheeks have all the signature features of an enormously perfect homegrown pair of ass cheeks. Her fullness matches the thickness of her thighs. The stretch marks, dimples and texture on her ass is like a giant highway sign telling me to cum inside her pussy.

She is every embodiment of my sexual fantasies. Loving her makes that better. Loving her makes this more real. It makes me want to take care of her. She moans as I rub her outer lips with soft kisses and saliva.

My tongue rubs against Latrice's clit, sliding along her perfect length and then returning to that hardened nub whenever her whimpering gets too loud. My attention makes her gasp, and then she moans as my tongue goes deeper. Her juices squirt out of her tightness onto my tongue and she's so ridiculously wet that I think there's no way in hell I deserve the pleasure of Latrice's cunt. It's perfect. And she has a large, soft mound surrounding it with bulging, sensitive outer lips that I want to fuck. Daily. All day, really.

I grab her thighs and lick her pussy until my tongue finds a sweeter, tighter hole...

Latrice cries out as my tongue tastes her backdoor.

"Gal!"

I pull away from her, dragging my teeth along her dimpled butt cheeks, growling. I don't want her to stop me from licking back there. I've dreamed about that backdoor more than anywhere else. But before you enter a woman, it's always a good idea to get a taste of where your cock will go. Kissing before blowjobs. It's an important rule.

"What?" I growl, licking her ass cheeks and preparing to dive back in to the hole I just dipped my tongue into. She won't stop me from having it, will she? It's the one hole I've never tried to touch like this, but tonight, I want to give her crazy pleasure Latrice will never forget.

"That's my butt hole," she says flatly, as if I accidentally stuck my tongue in her ass. Trust me, kitten, it was no accident. Since she already knows all my filthy fantasies, she might as well know that I dream of licking every inch of her from her clit to her tight ass. I don't even care if she stops shaving her cunt. I will lick and suck every inch between her thighs all day long if she'd allow it.

"I'm aware," I growl, spreading her cheeks again and running my tongue around the rim, readying myself to drive myself into Latrice's wet backdoor.

"You're *licking it*."

"Quiet," I murmur, "Enjoy it."

I lick her butt hole again and Latrice cries out, spreading her legs wider, showing that despite her protests, she enjoys a good tongue in her ass. I run my tongue in slow licks along the length of the hole, getting it nice and wet, watching my spit coat every inch of her ass cheeks. She's gasping and squirming, desperate to stifle the lusty little moans coming from her mouth.

"But Galanos... It's my *butt hole*. Who did you learn this from? Odin?"

I drive my tongue into Latrice's ass and she cries out louder than I've ever heard. I press two fingers against her pussy and with my tongue deep in her ass, I push my fingers inside her. Latrice cries out as she cums... *hard*.

I'm not done with that tasty thick ass. I let go of her ass cheeks and allow Latrice's enormous butt to squeeze my face deeper between her butt cheeks. She moans in pleasure, but she's still disturbed by my willingness to please her by sticking my tongue in her ass. Let go, kitten. If a man enjoys eating ass the way I do, there's only one way to stop him...

"Gal..." she moans as my fingers stroke her to the verge of another climax, "Galanos... I could *fart*."

"Please don't," I mutter... but I think her ass cheeks drown out the sound and I don't really care because I have two fingers in her pussy and a tongue on her ass and Latrice's moans have escalated to loud yelps as I push her over the edge to another climax. Juices and saliva drip down her thighs and I move away from her precious tight asshole and start cleaning Latrice's legs and cunt so I can finally give her my cock. I'll remember licking her ass in vivid detail for the rest of my life.

"I can't believe you ate my ass," she whimpers as my tongue runs back up her thighs and I gently nibble her outer lips before moving back to her ass cheeks and giving them a firm bite.

"I'm not done with it yet," I whisper, "But... I need you, Latrice. I can't wait anymore."

She turns to face me, but probably hesitates to kiss me because I had my tongue in her ass.

"You're all red," she says, giggling.

"Turn around," I gasp, "Give me your pussy, kitten."

Latrice turns around and I finish ripping her underwear off before dropping my pants and sliding a condom over my cock. No more risks. It doesn't matter how badly I want her. It doesn't matter how badly I want her pregnant. Considering I plan to never see her again, that one is a bad idea.

I press my cock against her entrance and Latrice shudders as her grasp on the railing tightens. She remembers what it was like fitting a cock as large as mine between her legs and at first, she's shaky.

I hold on to her, kissing her shoulders as I guide the first inch of my hardness between her legs. My mushroom head pierces her wetness and Latrice moans as the first inch of my dick slides inside her.

"Galanos..." she gasps, "It's so big... Give it to me... sir..."

Fuck... She knows exactly how to get me aroused. Her wet sloppy ass and pussy give me plenty of lubrication to enter her, but she's still so damn tight. This time, I can't enter her slowly. I can't make myself stop. Not as slowly as before. I push more of myself into her. She cries out, struggling to adjust to the first four inches of my cock. *The first four inches of my cock would be the entire cock of a typical man.*

Her ass cheeks jiggle around my cock as I press another bit inside her. She's soaking wet from arousal but still tight and as she wriggles her ass around my cock. Latrice cries out as I grab her hips and hold her still. My kitten's teasing me. She's begging me to slam my entire cock into her, but if I don't go a little slow, it'll hurt.

I'm done hurting her...

"Shhh," I whisper, rubbing her shoulders and kissing her neck as she whimpers for my cock. I never expected to have my best friend in this position.

"It's... big..." she whimpers.

"I know," I whisper, "And you like it, don't you? You like my big white cock."

Latrice groans as I slide more of myself inside her.

"Yes," she gasps, "I love your big white cock, sir."

"That's right," I growl, "You love my big white cock disappearing into your sexy black pussy."

"Yes, sir…"

I slide the rest of my dick between her legs and Latrice's pussy gets creamy wet now that she has my entire dick completely buried in her pussy. I pull out of her slightly, watching as her white cream coats the girth of my impressive cock.

Then I grab her hips again and slide all the way in. My dick caresses the most sensitive parts of her wetness, and I can't help but groan as I'm buried inside her again.

"I love black pussy," I whisper, "Have I ever told you that? I'm just like my brothers. Except… I enjoy it even more…"

I cup Latrice's breasts, massaging her nipples as I move into her pussy from behind. She moans as I thrust into her slowly. But I want more. *We both want more.*

With my lips on her neck, sucking bits of her between my teeth, Latrice is in no position to protest. And she's about to cum… *hard.*

I drive my cock into her deeper and Latrice moans, her juices now flowing rivers out of her pussy. She feels so good. I grab onto her hips and slowly withdraw while she cums. Her pussy vibrates and clamps around me harder. Her butt cheeks jiggle and I know I'm going to erupt.

I hold on to her as I cum between her legs and Latrice climaxes at the same time. We're both gasping for breath. Every muscle in my body is awake and throbbing with desire. My cock jerks inside her and she moans tenderly as I withdraw.

I am still rock hard, and I need to cum inside her again.

Latrice turns around, expecting that we've finished. She glances at my monstrous, drooling cock, still rigid and ready. A look of terror and intrigue crosses her face, and her mouth literally hangs open in surprise.

"You're still hard?"

I lift her onto the railing and spread her legs apart. Her butt barely rests on the metal as I hold her up. I love her body. How large it is. How soft her flesh feels against my stiff muscles as I press the head of my dick against her entrance.

I still have to go slowly… I still don't want to hurt her.

THIRTY-FOUR
TOYING WITH SUBMISSION

"Can you handle another round of my big white cock?" I whisper into her ear, pressing the head against Latrice's dripping cunt. One orgasm isn't enough for her, and it's not enough for me either. I could go another night. *I don't plan to stop until sunrise.*

Latrice grabs onto my hair, her soft hands parting the blond strands as she nods.

"Yeah. I can handle you. But please... don't drop me in the sea."

"I will never let go of you," I whisper, pulling her close to me and sliding my dick inside her one inch at a time.

She cries out and wriggles and nearly tosses herself out of my arms, but I keep her still so she can accept every inch of my thick, pulsing shaft. My cock still struggles to fit inside her tightness, but once I'm buried inside her, she moans and wraps her thick thighs around my torso.

"You're so deep," she gasps, grabbing onto my biceps, "It feels so good."

"Better," I murmur, "I belong here. Between your legs."

She nods and moans as she accommodates my gigantic cock.

"Your cunt will always be mine," I murmur, "Mine…"

I move my hips out slowly and then drive into her again. Latrice cries out and I spread her thighs even wider so I can take my pleasure between her legs. Within a few strokes, she cums hard again and gasps as she leans forward.

"I'm not finished…"

"Galanos… you already came… it's too big…"

I pull my cock out and put my hands on my hips as Latrice lands on her feet, gasping for breath.

"You can't breathe," I tell her.

She shakes her head.

"I'm not in great shape like you. Do you really have sex for *like… hours*?!"

"We're going to have sex until morning," I tell her, "If you'd like, I can use another hole."

Latrice's angry beaver face is back and my cock is stiffer than I ever remember seeing it. Fuck, she gets me so hard. It literally hurts to watch her like this and not have my cock inside her.

"I'm *tired,* Galanos. And we've both already finished. It's not like we'll never get to have sex again."

"Babe," I tell her, "I understand. But… I love you and my dick's hard. What do you want me to do? I have to try to fuck you."

"Well, you can't chase me down and ravish me just because you have an erection."

I wriggle my eyebrows suggestively and then lick my lips, "Is that what you want? Us running around the boat naked until I catch you. Then… I get to ravish you."

Latrice's angry beaver face turns into a "disturbed but maybe it's a little sexy" face. Trust me, I get that face a lot. She licks her lips and then flicks hair out of her face.

"Galanos," she says, "I can't handle another round of your monster dick."

"We'll see about that…"

"Gal!"

I lunge for her, and Latrice takes off for dear life. I didn't think she'd run that fast. She's screaming at me that she's 100% serious. Don't worry. I'm mostly trying to scare her...

We're running around the boat naked and screaming when I finally catch her. She turns to look over her shoulder and nearly trips over a few of my dumbbells I brought along for light lifting and toning when we weren't having hot kinky sex.

As she stumbles, I catch her, holding her waist before she hits the ground and urgently pulling her body against mine.

"I caught you," I murmur, "So now I get to fuck you."

Latrice scowls and says, "Ever heard of consent, Galanos?"

"Oh, I'll get consent."

"How do you plan on doing that?"

I drop to my knees, and then I look up at her. My blue eyes meet hers and I know she can't help but have them melt her.

"Begging," I say, keeping my gaze on hers before slowly licking my lips.

"And how do you plan on begging?"

I give her a pleading look with the blue eyes I know she can't help but love. They're as blue as the Aegean Sea, eyes that hold our family's history alongside the bloodlust and desire. I wet my lips and keep my gaze fixed on Latrice as she stares down at me. She has all the power now. The power to deny me. The power to put her foot on my head and push me to the ground. I maintain what little control I have.

"Spread your legs," I tell her, dragging my knees across the deck and wincing as my cock weighed down by its own stiffness touches the ground for a moment, "Let me show you how I beg."

Latrice gently parts her legs. My fingers sink into her thighs like I'm clawing at prey. I push her thighs further apart. I only break eye contact with her as my tongue sinks deep into Latrice's cunt. She moans and nearly stumbles backward again. But I'm holding onto her protectively, pulling her body against me as my tongue wraps around her clit and I suck it like a fresh summer raspberry.

Latrice cries out as I move my tongue between her legs and then refocus my attention on sucking on her perfect clit. She responds to my tongue now that she's had several orgasms and I use that to my advantage, teasing her close to the edge of orgasm and then moving to kissing her outer lips when she gets close.

Her moans and pants get more high-pitched as the teasing goes on. Just because I want to fuck her again doesn't mean I can't be patient. Being in the mafia is mostly waiting to fuck someone or fuck someone up. I'm very good at both...

"Galanos..." she gasps, "Stop..."

"Okay."

I sit back on my heels, gazing up at her still. She can command me any way she likes. She can have my cock or my tongue or send me away. I will do anything she wants. I will do anything for her... even if it kills me.

"No... I meant... Stop teasing me," she protests, blissfully unaware of the fires of doubt brewing inside me. Why don't I want to let her go? Is it just my selfishness or do I love her too much to set her free? My head hurts when I think of morality.

I grin.

"Okay. Spread them wider."

I move between her legs again and she moans with desire and relief as my tongue finds her clit again. She wants more, and I spread her juicy lower lips and give it to her. Latrice climaxes and then she pushes my head away. The rejection sends a pulse of desire through me. I ignore the panic in my racing heart because I know I can retake control.

Latrice protests, "Damn it, Galanos!"

I lick her juices off my lips and lower my gaze respectfully before asking, "Changed your mind?"

"Yes," she says, "I've changed my mind. But can we at least do it in a bed like normal people?"

"I'm not normal, babe. I'm a fucking freak."

She pats me on the head and lean forward to grab her nipples between my lips and suck. She squeals and I wrap my arms around her.

"I love you," I whisper, kissing her again before rising to my feet, "So... we will fuck on the bed *until morning*."

I don't have a problem with compromise. She wants to be angry with me, angry that I've convinced her, angry that she *really wants this*. But Latrice can't wipe the smile off her face because she knows she's going to cum again and again...

THIRTY-FIVE
FIXATION

We fall asleep at four in the morning and I don't wake up until I hear Odin and Latrice thumping overhead. *Christos, what are they doing...*

I roll out of bed and salute the stack of used condoms on the ground. I think I came ten times. Half of those times, I came inside her. I watched my seed spill from between her legs and even if it was foolish and stupid, we were both drunk and enjoying the way my cum dripped from her soaked black pussy.

Poor Latrice lost track of her own orgasms. I fell asleep with my tongue in her pussy, I think. I stumble above deck and she's wearing this cute lace robe and staring out at the ocean with Odin by her side, barking at sea birds.

"Good morning," I grunt.

"It's 4 p.m."

"Is it really?"

"I finally realized why you wake up so late."

"Fucking all night will do that to you," I murmur, "Do you have a cigarette?"

"No," she says, "And you don't need a damn cigarette. Now come."

She opens her arms and I go in for a hug. *I fucking love this woman.* She's so soft when she hugs me and I kiss the top of her head as I grasp her sweet, plump shoulders.

"Are you horny?"

"Boy, HAVE YOU LOST YOUR DAMNED MIND?"

"Huh? I said are you *hungry?*"

"No. You didn't."

"Oh. I meant to say hungry. I mean... I'm both..."

I flash her an impish grin and she gives me her little angry beaver face again. I like that face. I kiss her cheek and say, "Come on. Let's get food."

"I already raided your stash," Latrice says.

"Good. I nearly wore you out."

"You didn't *wear me out.* You destroyed me. I don't think I can walk and you... *licked my butt hole.*"

"It was delicious."

I slide cream cheese over a bagel from our food stash and lean against the railing as I enjoy the taste. Latrice introduced me to bagels when we first met. I'm too hungry to bother counting how many calories are in it. I think I burned more than I ever had before from a night of intense sex with Latrice.

"I don't know how you can say a butt hole is delicious."

"Not just any butt hole. Your butt hole is tasty. It's soft too."

"Okay, that's enough."

"I'd like to fuck you back there."

"Gal!"

"Sorry. Was that too much?"

Latrice folds her arms and pretends to be all angry, "Do you always have to be so blunt about everything?"

She's smiling and doesn't have her usual angry face.

"Yes. Well. Only with you," I explain.

I grin and have another bite. Latrice scratches Odin between the ears and he rolls out in front of her on his back, expecting a more intense tummy rub.

"I can't imagine having that big thing up there."

"Unfortunately, I can say from experience that a cock up the ass hurts like hell. When done wrong."

She hates that I can talk about my rape so casually while tonguing the cream cheese off a bagel. Even if I'm not completely broken in this way, I'm an utter freak. I wish I could change it. But I'll save the personal growth for after I've killed my grandmother in cold blood. I don't want to get too soft.

Latrice reaches for my free hand and squeezes it.

"I'm sorry for what happened to us."

"It was my fault," I say, "I deserve it for what happened to you."

"You shouldn't look at it that way. I don't blame you. I truly don't..."

"You're too angelic for me, Latrice. What on earth do you see in a demon?"

Latrice protests readily, "You're not a demon."

"I kill people. I've lied to you. I've done other horrible things. I'm the reason you got raped. What more would it take to be a demon?"

"That's not the way I see things," Latrice says sweetly, "You always make sure I orgasm. You say the kindest things about me when you know I'm insecure. You lavish me with attention and kisses and adventure. You may not love the way other people love, Galanos Pagonis. But I know that you love."

We look at each other and for the first time, I feel properly seen. Like she gets it. Odin whines between us, but neither of us pays him any mind. I don't want to seem soft in front of Latrice, but I can't stop my jaw from moving nervously back and forth.

"I see," I say, "I'm no good at playing tough around you then?"

"Oh, no. You still scare the shit out of me. But I know beneath all that, there's just a little boy who wanted someone to love him."

"I think you've been spending too much time with Fallon."

"I love you, Galanos," Latrice says, "I'm sorry I lied about anything and I'm sorry any time I wasn't a good friend or if I acted jealous about you and other girls. I don't know how or when it happened, but I've fallen for you. Hard. And I don't want to lose you."

"Listen. Nothing could make me stop loving you. Now come."

I polish off the bagel and hold her in my arms. Her closeness makes me stiffen again. Two more days. If we have sex at 7 p.m., I might make love to her until 2 a.m. or even 3 a.m. I'm going to need a lot more food and a lot more wine to do that.

"Are you hungover?"

Latrice shakes her head.

"Good. Because I'm not either and I want to open our tequila."

"Oh hell no, you can't get me tequila drunk," Latrice says urgently.

Oh, Latrice. When will she learn the trouble with bad boys? We *love* corrupting good girls like her. We live for it.

"Why not? It's a party, Latrice. And trust me, my tongue in your pussy while you are tequila drunk will be quite the experience."

The thought of having my tongue between her legs again clearly affects her, even if she wants to pretend it doesn't.

"Okay. Tequila. What's the worst that could happen? Drinking tequila with a crazy mobster and his giant dick."

I lean over and elbow her, teasing mercilessly, "Can I do a shot out of your butt hole?"

"Galanos... NO!"

THIRTY-SIX
START WITH THE TEASING

Latrice was right. Tequila was a crazy idea. By the time I wake up from the haze, I have a sunburn all over my ass and legs. Latrice lies on her back with chocolate sauce covering every bare inch of her skin.

Somehow, we have Mardi gras beads around our necks, pink and purple, and I remember us taking the boat on a joy ride with Odin barking his ass off. Fuck, that was a crazy joy ride. I don't remember the last time I had this much fun. When I say goodbye to Latrice, my fun will officially be over. We're close to Athens. Close to goodbye. We only have a few hours left and I'm more hungover than I've ever been before.

Latrice groans and sits up. I coated her thighs in a mixture of her juices and possibly mine. I love cumming inside her. There's something incredible about watching her voluptuous ass cheeks jiggle as I cream deep inside her pussy. She always moans when she cums and I love it. I love her face now, too.

We exchange a grim expression and say at once, "What the hell happened to us?"

"We had sex," Latrice says, "I think."

"I don't remember everything."

"You licked chocolate sauce off my ass cheeks."

I grin and assure her, "I remember *that*."

"Great."

"We need to get to Athens in a few hours. Want to jump into the water?"

"It'll be cold, Gal."

"I'll be right there with you. Come. We need to get cleaned up and my ass has a sunburn."

I stand up and Latrice follows suit, staring at my body like she usually does. I'm staring at hers too.

"I've got chocolate sauce *everywhere*."

"Take my hand."

She takes my hand and we jump off the back of the boat together. Latrice holds onto the stairs once she resurfaces and I swim out a few feet, hollering from pain and relief.

"I told you it was cold!"

"Odin, come on!"

Odin does a running leap into the ocean and swims next to me. Latrice sits on the stairs and rubs chocolate sauce off her nude body. Once she's clean, she climbs out of the water and gets a towel. I follow and Odin climbs behind me. We get toweled off and I sigh, taking her in.

This is almost it.

"Athens for the night," I tell her, "Are you ready?"

"Yeah. Sure. But... you're hiding something from me."

"Am I?"

"Don't bullshit me, Galanos."

"I don't want to," I tell her, "But Latrice, I've made promises to you I intend to keep."

"Okay. Don't be all mysterious about it."

"Please. I don't want you to worry. It would break me if you worried."

"You're *so* dramatic," she complains. But I know she loves it. And

I know that what I'm about to do to her will break her. Saying goodbye to Latrice will *break her.*

I take the boat to port in Athens and we take a taxi to a nice hotel close to the airport. Executive suite, free once I flash my Pagonis ring to the manager at the front desk. I'm charmed. Latrice doesn't understand enough Greek to know exactly what happened, but she's always suspicious of me.

"Are we going to do any sightseeing?"

"What sights are there in Athens?" I scoff, "American tourists and worse, the British. No, thank you. I prefer Thessaloniki."

"You're so arrogant."

"I'm not arrogant. I'm literally better than most people. More attractive, richer, bigger cock..."

"Better personality?" Latrice mutters under her breath. I take it as a compliment.

Odin barks and I assume the pup agrees with me. He walks alongside Latrice the entire way, as if he isn't sure who his proper owner is. Silly pup.

We enter the executive suite, and suddenly, Latrice stops arguing with me and she's gasping. This place is incredible. Large windows overlooking the city, modern furnishings, an enormous bed and an infinity pool on the balcony. I shut the door into the hallway behind me.

"For the night, it's ours. And then tomorrow, we leave Greece."

"Right."

"I want room service and then... I want to service you."

She prances back over to me and tiptoes to kiss me on the lips.

"Is this how you get when you really love someone? Is this your natural state beneath the psycho killer?"

"Believe me," I whisper, "The killer inside me isn't far off. He's just distracted by an exquisite woman..."

"No more tequila," she whispers.

"No more," I agree, although I remember our tequila sex being kinky. I remember saying filthy things that made Latrice cum hard. If she doesn't remember that, I won't remind her.

I want to remember our last night together. So I've arranged a surprise... something that neither of us will forget. Especially not Latrice.

"I'm going to tie you up tonight," I tell her, "And I'm going to spend our last hours before the flight eating your pussy, so you're guaranteed to sleep the entire way."

"Is this your idea of looking after me?"

"Yes," I tell her, "A man's job is to keep his woman's pussy wet... always."

"I've never heard that in marriage vows," Latrice mutters.

And I have to stop myself from promising her I'll put those words in our marriage vows. We won't have any marriage vows and although I know saying goodbye to Latrice will break her heart, I don't want to shatter her. I want to save her life after all.

I want to save her from Galanos Pagonis, the psycho killer she can't help but feel raw animal attraction to.

I touch her cheek, drawing her face to mine. The doorbell rings and its room service. Special room service, armed with my surprise. I open the door and grab the brown paper bag before shutting it in the man's face and sliding a €50 tip beneath the door, which disappears promptly.

"What's in the bag?"

"Ropes. A feather duster. Lots of whipped cream."

"Are you joking?"

I reach into the bag and pull out the "surprise gift". Latrice gasps and I have to look at her face to determine that her gasping isn't out of dismay, but excitement.

"A butt plug?"

"For the best butt I've ever tasted."

I take her hand and guide her to the bed, kissing her with each step back as my impressive height looms over hers. We're nearly at the finish line. Her last submission to me before I let her go forever.

Odin lies curled up on the hotel balcony, sleeping away in the cool breeze.

She grabs my face and kisses me madly. I like when she unwinds like this, when she releases every inhibition to allow her most forbidden desire for me to jump out. Her fingers claw along the sharp angle of my jawline and I feel my cock getting stiff.

"Hands behind your back, kitten. I need to get you ready for the night."

"Ropes. Feathers. Whipped cream. Butt plug."

"Oral. Sex. Teasing. Ass eating. Do I have your consent?"

"Yes, sir," Latrice eagerly breathes and my cock nearly bursts again. I kiss her and push her slowly onto the bed. I never said what order I'd start with. Now that I have her here, I think I'll start with teasing...

THIRTY-SEVEN
THE PLAN TO KILL

hate goodbyes. They're always painful. This goodbye is worse because when Latrice figures out I've betrayed her, she doesn't seem angry.

"Why aren't you coming?" She asks, like she expects a reasonable answer from me.

I'm blunt about everything else, but this is the one part of my life I promised I would truly protect her from. I won't let her get raped again and I won't see her until I am certain that the people I love won't get their hands on her again.

"I'm sorry. I can't," I explain, "I know it was a ruse. But I need you to leave."

"You lied... again."

The betrayal in her voice hurts. We have minutes. Seconds.

"I have to send you away," I say stiffly, "It's not a choice."

"You've been lying for days, maybe even weeks," she says, resigned to the fact that the man she loves is a failure. I'm garbage. Less than nothing. I am worthless because of how I'm hurting her.

Good. I hope she uses this icy indifference to forget me. To forget the mafia monster she once loved. The best-case scenario is I'll become a nana-killer and the worst-case scenario, I'll end up dead or raped again by a man who works for Yiayia. I can't let Latrice be a part of that, and I can't let her worry about what awaits me. A man accepts his fate with a loaded gun.

All I can manage is 8 letters and 3 words, spoken barely above a whisper, "I love you."

"I *loved* you too," she whispers, using the past tense to twist the knife in, when it's clear that she still loves me, "Which makes this hurt ten times more."

"I wish I wasn't like this."

"But you are," she snarls, "You're an entitled, spoiled, cruel beast who wouldn't know what to do with genuine love if it followed you halfway across the world."

Her words cut me, but I saw nothing, pursing my lips into a fine line and letting every ounce of hurt wash over me.

"Find a better man than me, Latrice. Please."

"How dare you," she hisses, "How dare you, Galanos."

And then she flounces off. Latrice doesn't want me to see her hurt. She knows that I've broken hearts before and she's seen me revel in it. Now, it's her heart's turn to be broken, and it's over far too quickly. Her shoulders slump as she walks away and I fight back tears. I want to call out to her, but my voice only comes out a whisper.

"Latrice..."

She doesn't turn around and the last view I have of her imprinted in my mind is her perfect butt, walking away. Odin whines miserably, aware that something's going terribly wrong, but he's only a pup and as much as he tugs on his leash, I can't let him chase after her and take her back to us.

"It's only us now," I tell him, and Odin lets out a protest-bark. We return to the docks and once I'm on my boat again, and I realize how messy it is, the realization hurts me even more. She's gone. Latrice

Boyd is gone and the way I've broken her heart, I'll never see her again. I can feel it. I'll never forget her. I'll never have another lover. She was the one.

I fall to my knees on the boat and Odin comes up to me with an eagerly sniffing nose and a tongue lolling out of his mouth. I wrap my arms around his neck and I want to cry and shoot something at the same time.

"I miss her," I murmur into Odin's neck, "I'm always going to miss her…"

Odin barks and I imagine he's saying "man up, you pussy ass blond". I still cry as I get ready to sail. I start my boat for a much faster journey towards Thessaloniki. Loukas and Stavros are at the dock waiting for me when I return. I'm instantly suspicious as I leap off the boat and Odin follows.

"What are you idiots doing here?" I grumble.

"Here to stop you from doing something stupid," Stavros replies, lighting a cigarette as Loukas swigs water from his stupid flask.

"She's gone," I tell them, "I'm not doing anything stupid."

They both know I'm obviously lying. I always lie to Loukas and Stavros because usually these idiots trying to figure it out gives me time to hatch a better plan to avoid them. Loukas and Stavros exchange glances. They're one step ahead of me this time. Stavros shrugs and tells him, "I'm not doing the brotherly advice. You're the eldest. You do it."

"Galanos never listens to me," Loukas hisses, "Never!"

"I'm standing right here, imbeciles."

Stavros clears his throat and puts a "warm" hand on my shoulder. I don't think he can help how threatening his hand feels.

"We need to discuss your plans with you," Stavros says urgently, "Loukas told me you have every intention of running off half-cocked to… eliminate… Yiayia."

"Loukas ought to keep my business to himself," I say scowling, "He wouldn't like it if I probed into the details of his attraction to a teenager."

"Quiet, you little shit!" Loukas snarls, losing his cool. I have this effect on my brothers and in a time like this, I'll do whatever it takes to keep a smile on my face. I spent so much time crying into the Aegean Sea, I'm surprised my tears didn't drown me. But Latrice is gone forever now, and the time for crying is over.

Stavros puts a hand on Lou's back, successfully calming our bulldog of an older brother. He's getting grumpier in his old age. I will remind the twins that their father is crazy once they're old enough to understand.

Stavros, the middle child, is used to being the peacemaker, that is when he's not cavorting around speaking to invisible people.

"Listen. What Loukas means to say is that even if he firmly disagrees with this murder and Fallon has instructed us not to take part in your hair-brained assassination plot... I will help you."

"This is not what we discussed!" Loukas snarls.

Stavros musses Lou's hair, which really annoys him. Stavros is nearly as good at that as I am.

"Plans change," Stavros says, "And if she'll have her precious Galanos raped, what will she do to my black son? I'm sorry. Fallon will learn that sometimes a man needs to handle his business the old-fashioned way."

"I should have never let Tisha convince you to watch mob wives with her..."

"If I have to spend an entire weekend guarding your crazy young wife, I need her entertained," Stavros says, "Plus... the show is very insightful. Italian Americans are fucking crazy."

"We already knew that," Lou grumbles.

I bring them back to the matter at hand, "Will you really help me?"

Stavros nods and answers, "Yes."

"I'll help you too," Loukas says, "By punishing my son for accepting a bribe from Yiayia to lie to us. But I won't be murdering anyone. Not even her."

"Are you too much of a pussy to kill your own grandmother?" Stavros says, laughing a little too hard at his own joke.

Loukas snarls, "Murder isn't funny. I kill when necessary, but I don't enjoy it."

"Neither do I," Stavros says, getting serious again, "But our brother... He's young. I won't let him do this alone."

I feel warmth from Stavros Pagonis that I've never felt before. And all I can offer him is an earnest thanks. Maybe Fallon has had an excellent influence on him.

"Don't thank me too soon," He warns, "We need a plan, brother. A plan with no room for error."

"I'll take you monsters back to the family villa," Loukas snarls, "Odin, come."

The dog responds well to Lou. He has a way with animals and with younger brothers. I half expect him to do the work of convincing us out of murder on the drive back to the villa, but Lou is conspicuously quiet.

"Tisha's sleeping upstairs and Fallon's laying by the pool with Adrian," he says once we arrive, "Helen, Cass and Sandros are out for a fishing trip with Sandros' parents. They'll return in the morning. Antonio's grounded."

"Ouch."

Loukas snorts, "It's what he deserves. He's far too casual about the danger he put our family in. He needs hard discipline."

Stavros offers Loukas a bleak, but understanding expression. We stand outside the car next to each other. The angels of death. We look as dangerous as we are. Tall, looming... icy blue eyes.

We walk into the house together, the three Pagonis brothers finally united and finally ready to plan an assassination we should have completed years ago.

If any of the women know what we're doing, they keep their distance from us. Antonio eventually goes upstairs to help Tisha, working off his debts to his father by taking care of his half-siblings. He's probably convincing Tisha to put on more reality television or watch music videos.

We barricade ourselves in the kitchen, talking in hushed voices and preparing to rain hellfire on the woman who gave us all life, the woman who hurt us all, the woman who tried to take something from each of us.

Our grandmother. Yiayia.

THIRTY-EIGHT
A VERY PAGONIS ROAD TRIP

'm drunk and high by the time I careen into my bed, early by my standards. Fallon and Stavros are arguing upstairs while Adrian sleeps next door to them. Loukas and Tisha have the twins, and they're singing to them together in the living room. Loukas has his arm around Tisha and I know he doesn't want to let her go. He doesn't want to risk this going wrong and losing his fresh start.

Just like that, Fallon and Stavros aren't arguing anymore. I hear moaning. It gets louder. We all have our own villas, but when there's work, it's better to stay here. Yiayia and papa haven't been here in a while. I wonder what papa will do to me when I kill his mother. If I have to kill him too, I'll shoulder that burden alone. My brothers are doing enough to help me.

Odin climbs on my back and rests his head on my shoulder blade. I'm so alone without Latrice. And I miss her already. I chase an urge I haven't felt in a while, and I look her up on social media. As I scroll through her account, I hear Cass and Sandros coming in downstairs.

I can never talk to Cass about feelings now that she spends all her time with that idiot boyfriend. I suppose he's nicer than I am. I keep looking at Latrice's page.

There's a picture of the sea from my villa with a caption that reads:

Not every fresh start feels right.

I want to comment, but I make a post of my own. A picture of my face, blue eyes tilted toward my lamp, so they reflect nicely in the square frame and the caption.

Missing a girl.

The photo gets 45,000 likes in an hour, but none of the likes are from Latrice Boyd. I don't want it to hurt as much as it does. I don't want to miss her like this, even if it's for our own good.

I turn my phone off and try to fall asleep, hating myself for pushing her away for good.

I wake up only a few hours later, expecting Latrice's gentle nudges but getting a face full of Stavros' exhausted mug. His breath smells like coffee and Fallon's perfume.

"GET UP!"

"Leave me alone..." I murmur, stretching like a cat until Stavros barks at me like a feral coyote.

"You imbecile... if we want to have any hope of tracking her, we need to get started early. So get your lazy behind out of bed."

"Do you kiss Fallon with such horrible breath?"

Stavros grabs my ears and I push him off as I scramble out of bed. I'm red-faced and looking to Odin to protect me, but he's eating a piece of meat that Stavros is feeding him out of his other hand. That traitorous pup doesn't know what's good for him.

"I'm up!"

"Here's your weapon. Six bullets. We're moving incognito. Cars without plates. Minimal weapons and cash only. Lou is loading the car downstairs."

"He's coming after all?"

"Tisha convinced him. Her bloodlust and her sex drive basically amount to mind control."

Stavros grins and then sobers up.

"I told Fallon the truth," he said, "She understands, but... she's scared. I don't mean to hurt her."

"Sometimes you hurt the people you love," I say, wistfully, and even if I know he has marked disrespect for what he views as puppy love, Stavros doesn't dispute my statement. He tosses me a silk shirt and trousers.

"Hurry," he says, "I want to leave here before dawn."

I can't remember the last time I got up before noon. It's still before sunrise, so I must be wrong about how long I've slept. Not enough sleep for this.

I like nighttime. I feel safer at night. Stavros enjoys dawn for the same reason. I plead with him for a bump of coke, but he mutters something about responsible fatherhood and refuses me. Unfortunately, we need to leave Antonio out of our plans, so I can't ask him.

I walk to the car, surprised to find Cassia leaning against it with a gun at her waist. Her brown hair is in a single braid down to her waist and she has skinny black jeans tucked into heeled boots that look like Antonio's.

"Hello, shit," she says when she notices me. I didn't remember cluing Cassia into my plans.

I ask her, "What are you doing here?"

"Fallon told me you bastards were killing Yiayia. Remember my husband, Ofek? I believe I owe her something special for that."

Cassia's coldness probably means she's definitely working for the Italians. I notice that her lap dog isn't here, which probably means he doesn't know what his crazy Pagonis woman is up to, or Cassia uses mind control of her own with him. She's a Pagonis too, but I shudder to think what powers Pagonis women have.

"Come," Cass says, "Give me a hug. I know how much it must have hurt you to let Latrice go."

"This family is full of gossips," I mutter, but I hug Cass and even let her ruffle my hair. She understands that even if I'm an idiot, beneath it all, there's a heart. We don't fight as much anymore, especially not since Carlotta went blind. Where was Carlotta? I forgot to ask Lou.

Cass sighs and says, "She made you kinder, you know. Latrice Boyd. She's a strange girl, but... I liked her for you. You're a strange man, Gal."

I don't like the idea of leaving Odin behind, but I don't want him getting hurt or worse, giving us away and leading all of us to our deaths. Cass hits my shoulder and says, "Cheer up. You might not even have to take the shot."

"We aren't shooting her," I say, "We have to make this painless."

Cass shrugs.

"Trust me," she says, her voice crisp and cruel, "Having a fat Israeli man trying to enter me was anything but painless. I don't worry about her pain."

I feel no regret at her words. Cassia's honest.

"As long as we get it done," I say coldly, and Cassia's expression matches my own as she nods. Cass and I sit in the backseat next to each other, and she leans her head on my shoulder.

"Pretty Galanos," she whispers, "How could Yiayia lose your heart..."

"Pretty?"

Cass giggles and hushes me, "Crazy brother. Let's get some sleep before we get there."

"Do you know where we're going?"

I close my eyes, wishing that Latrice were on the other side of me. Cass sighs.

"Oh, who knows? We leave it all to Loukas and Stavros, right? They're the older ones."

Loukas makes an underwhelmed grunt, but I know he's secretly proud whenever we openly look up to him. He needs to look after people. He's always been as much of an older brother as he's been a father. Stavros gets in the car and leans back.

"Well, we are all going to hell," he says, "Killing our own grand-mother. How are we going to explain that at the pearly gates?"

"Luckily Loukas will die first," I point out, "You know, since he's old. He can explain, and if it doesn't work, he'll send us a sign. A boiling summer."

"42 is not old," Loukas snarls, "And watch your mouth before I make *you* drive."

Cass sits up straight.

"NO!" She pleads, "The last time I got in the car with Galanos he ran over a sheep!"

"That was hilarious," I say, laughing and yawning sleepily. Cass nuzzles against my arm like a cat.

"It was cruel," Cass says, elbowing me hard, and lifting me out of my near-sleep, "Would you like it if someone ran over Odin?"

My stomach flips uneasily. If anyone hurt Odin, I'd kill them. But I love Odin. He's not a stupid sheep. He's my dog, and that makes him special and important.

I'm not as comfortable being calloused and cruel anymore. Not since Latrice, and not since Odin too. I wanted us all three to be a family. But our hope of that has been squashed completely.

"Buckle up, kids," Stavros says as Loukas starts the car, "We're off to kill the Wicked Witch of the West."

I don't know what I've gotten myself into on this little road trip, but I'm trying to ignore the pit in my stomach that tells me Yiayia already knows.

She's been one step ahead of me the entire time. Getting rid of her may not be as easy as we think. She's fooled us all before several times. We could be riding along, letting Loukas drive us to our deaths.

Latrice is safe, though. That's all that matters. She's thousands of miles away from here and no matter how stupid it gets in Thessaloniki, I at least have the promise of her safety.

THIRTY-NINE
UNBLOCK KATIE

Two hours out from Thessaloniki and Loukas needs to take a piss. I make a quip about his aging bladder and he gives me a look like he wants to tie me to train tracks and run me over. Cass sits on top the Jeep with a cigarette between her lips and Stavros does pushups on the ground outside. Not one to be outdone, I join my brother.

Stavros snorts at me, unimpressed that I've joined him, "You think you're tough, eh?"

"Men..." Cass snickers and flicks some of her ash on my back. But I don't stop, because Stavros claps between pushups and counts us off. No problem, I can keep up. Sweat drips off our toned shoulders and Cass laughs.

"18... 19..."

She's keeping count for us and we make it until 1,000 before Stavros "pretends" he's tired to "let me win". He also claims that there was never any contest. We're both covered in sweat and Loukas is still red in the face. He didn't take that long to piss, but he's above our "silly contest" which Stavros insists isn't a contest.

"Tisha called. Sandros brought over a plate of focaccia bread and fried fish so they hardly even miss us."

Stavros grunts and wipes sweat off his brow.

"Sandros fits right in with them," Stavros grumbles.

Cass rolls her eyes and comments, "He's so sensitive. He's been stress baking for days since Van and I..."

"Since you and Van, what? We all know you're working for the Italian bastards," Stavros presses.

Cass rolls her eyes at him. They have a complicated relationship. Before Fallon got his ass on the straight and narrow, Stavros was perfectly willing to sell our dear sister off to an Israeli more than twice her age. Cass hops off the vehicle and gets in the back seat.

"Whatever," she says as she slides into the Jeep, "I don't have to answer to you punks. If you want me to stop working for Van Doukas, buy my time. It isn't cheap."

There's not a Pagonis alive I'd describe as cheap. We pile back into the Jeep and Lou cranks the A/C. Stavros gives in to ragged breathing and leans his red face out the window. He's definitely tired from our contest and he's also avoiding eye contact with me since I definitely won.

I poke Cass in the stomach.

"Van. Tell us what you're doing. Murder? Theft? *Prostitution?*"

Cass elbows me hard because of the way I say *prostitution*.

"I'm helping him get a girlfriend, okay?" she whispers, but my brothers still hear her.

I scoff, unimpressed. "That's it?"

Stavros laughs, "Why can't he get a girlfriend? Is his cock too small."

"All Italians have small cocks," Loukas answers solemnly.

"How would you know? Do you see many Italian cocks?" I ask.

Loukas slams on the gas and peals us away from our resting spot. More driving, less talking. Cassie screams with delight at his sudden increase in speed and hangs her head out the window, yelling. When was the last time we were all together...

Except, we aren't all together. We're missing Helen. Ah, we're always missing Helen, aren't we? Cassia's phone buzzes. She wrinkles her nose.

"What is this? Some idiot has sent me a strange message. Galanos, one of your internet sluts is on the loose."

"What?"

I grab her phone. It's a message from an account I don't recognize. The message means nothing to my sister, Cassia, but it means everything to me.

Tell Galanos to unblock Katie. Urgent.

It's Latrice.

I take Cassia's phone and try to throw it in her lap, but it flies out the window.

"GAL!"

"What's going on back there?" Stavros snarls, "I'm SLEEPING."

"Loukas, stop the car!" Cassia screams, "That idiot threw my phone out the window!"

"SERIOUSLY?!" Loukas yells.

Cassie out-screams him, "TURN THE CAR AROUND, *IDIOTA!* I NEED MY CELL PHONE TO CALL SANDROS!"

She punctures her demands with a high-pitched scream — Cassia's usual call to arms when I would fight her as a toddler. Don't be fooled by her size now. When we were kids, she could kick my ass. Loukas, still cowed into place by Pagonis women, slams on the brakes and turns the car around.

Stavros grumbles, "We're going to be on the road for hours if you idiots can't figure out how to keep your hands inside the car."

"It's not my fault!" Cassie yells.

"It's not mine either," I say calmly. "I threw it, I missed. It's up to fate."

I furrow my brow and open my account. 75k new followers. 80k likes on my latest picture. 20k comments. Nice. *WAIT. Focus, Galanos.*

I unblock Katie and the messages pour in.

Katie: Your grandmother knows you're coming.
Katie: The Jeep has a bomb
Katie: 12:38 p.m.

The car screeches to a halt and Cassia leaps out. My heart pulses madly. What time is it? 12:36 p.m. *We are completely fucked.*

"EVERYONE GET OUT OF THE CAR! EVERYONE GET OUT NOW!"

"What?!"

"OUT OF THE CAR. TRUST ME," I scream.

Blood rushes past my ears and adrenaline pumps through me as all the information in those three simple text messages courses through me at once. I don't have time to wonder how the hell Latrice knows this. I have to get my siblings as far away from the car as possible.

"COME ON!" I scream, throwing my door open. Loukas and Stavros mirror my actions, throwing their doors open and gently lowering themselves onto the ground as if we have time to stand here and argue. Two minutes. We can't get away fast enough.

"If this is some kind of game..." Loukas snarls.

"THERE'S A BOMB IN THE CAR. RUN. RUN!"

I assume that the information is good. But that means that my grandmother has Latrice. I failed to send her to safety. I assumed her posts on social media meant she'd arrived far away from me and that she'd finally reached safety.

Latrice isn't safe. I run away from the Jeep. I don't have time to think. All my body can do is exactly what I train for. Running like hell when someone straps a bomb to the bottom of your car.

"What the hell are you talking about?" Stavros snaps, getting more gruff when he notices how fast I'm moving away from him.

Listen, I don't care enough about my siblings to stand around and get blown up with them. If they want to stand around like a typical loud Greek family, arguing over every detail, that's their choice. We're parked overlooking some farmland, and I take off down a rolling green hill as fast as my legs can take me.

Cassia's smarter than my older brothers, so with her phone in hand she follows me, screaming back at them, "He wouldn't be running if he was lying!"

Stavros and Loukas catch on, and we run for as long as we can. We don't know how big the bomb is, but judging by the ones we typically use for *family business,* we have very little time unless we want to be blown to smithereens. I can't imagine my chiseled jawline going out like that.

I push my body to its limit, keeping Cassia's hand in mine so she doesn't fall behind. Then I feel the warmth on my back before I hear the boom. My ears ring. Cassia screams and I grab her hand as the blast throws the four of us forward. *Far.* I cover my hands over my head and gasp as we lay there, waiting in silence to make sure the explosion's finished. The ringing keeps pulsing long after the explosion ends, and I can smell the burning from the car.

We've lost half our arsenal and our only vehicle. Not to mention, we nearly got blown the fuck up by our grandmother. Not exactly a good day.

"We're safe..." Loukas growls after a few minutes, "Let's brush this off quickly and survey the damage."

I forget how good Loukas can be at conducting the family business. Unfortunately, even my eldest brother can't provide for unforeseen circumstances like this one.

We hear a gun cock and I don't have to look up to know that even if we've just narrowly escaped a bomb, we are definitely not safe.

FORTY

AS LONG AS I GET TO KISS THE GIRL

"Shoot us, then!" Cass says, "If you're such a fucking badass."

"CASS!" the three of us scream.

Maybe she's picked up such horrible practices from the Italians.

"Cassia," the Sicilian-accented voice growls, "You damned fool."

We all recognize the voice. But what on earth is he doing here... Van Doukas, our Sicilian cousin, typically has no business in Greece. He sheaths his gun and my brothers stand up, following Cassia's lead.

We're all humiliated that they scared us shitless and our little sister was cool as a cucumber. Van gives me a cool once over.

"Little Galanos. Well... You aren't so little anymore."

I tower over Van Doukas, even if he's well over six-feet tall. He grins as we make eye contact, and then he turns attention to my brothers, who he knows far better than he knows me.

"Stavros. Loukas. My pleasure to make your acquaintance," he says, pulling them both in for a tight hug. Lou mutters something about his joke and Stavros gives a blessing to his family back in Italy.

Loukas put Van's brother in the ground, an incident they're both grateful for.

Cass smiles as Stavros turns to her with a glare and says, "Sorry, boys. I had no plans to leave my life up to chance."

"You call *us* chance?" Stavros snarls, "We've been killing since Van was in diapers. No offense."

"None taken. I owe Cassia a favor. I'm getting married soon," Van says, "Thanks to Cass."

Lou mutters in surprise, "Seriously?"

"Thank you, cousin. For everything... I owe you one, which is why I have gone above and beyond what you've asked of me."

"You got the message out about the bomb," Cass says, relief flooding her face. We were all scared, but Cass is the only one who shows it now. Van looks at me before he speaks next.

"Yes. And I got the hostage from your grandmother," he says, "But... we still have a problem."

"The hostage?"

Van grins as he gives me another smile that looks warm, except for when I stare into his cold, dead eyes. The Sicilians are more fucked up than we are. *Someone should write a book about the Doukas family.*

"Latrice speaks highly of you," He says, "And we have her. Unfortunately, in commandeering this old woman's farmhouse, we had to take some measures that Latrice did not take kindly to... she's barricaded with the old lady in the bathroom and they've made several demands for civil rights... I don't really understand."

"Take me to her," I say, "Please. Is she hurt?"

"Not as such," Van says, "But I have to warn you... our methods did not please Yiayia very much. She won't be where you expected to find her. Judging by my conversation with Latrice, she suspects your plan. Tread lightly, Galanos. An outraged woman can be difficult to subdue."

"Like you know anything about subduing women," Cass mutters, earning her a fierce glare from Van that might have put the fear of

God into anyone but my mischievous sister, who appears to have the Pagonis charm when it's required of her.

"I just want to see her," I say, my heart pumping blood into every part of me, including parts of me that definitely don't need any blood. I can't be blamed, can I? Latrice is here. And if my first plan to keep her safe didn't work, then I might as well have her... if she'll still have me.

I need Van Doukas to let me at her. He might not have the gift of inspiring submission from women, but if I can make love to a chocolate sauce covered Latrice Boyd, I can do anything, right? We all follow Van Doukas down the hill toward the farmhouse. He brought a battalion of Italians, all suave and dark-haired, sucking back cigarillos and speaking in their rough, Sicilian tongue.

He walks us through the house and then to the upstairs bathroom. Three men guard the door with AK-47s.

"Is this really necessary?"

Van pauses and sighs, rolling up his sleeve. I wince as I see the nasty open wound on his forearm.

"Your girlfriend bit me," he says, "For my personal safety, the AK-47s are necessary. But you are family, Pagonis. I haven't harmed a hair on her head, despite *many* a temptation."

I nod solemnly. I love Latrice, but I have faced those temptations myself. It isn't my fault I was born to love stubborn women. The question now is, what will happen when I see her again? Will she forgive me?

Van claims he hasn't harmed her, but my grandmother must have harmed her. How the hell did she get kidnapped from *the airport...*

My heart quickens, and I don't think I can see her. Van puts a hand on my back.

"Girlfriend, you say?"

I nod.

"I can see why you like her. Whatever happened between you, remember. Apologize."

"Apologize?"

Van nods.

"Men never apologize. But remember that whatever's wrong... it's probably all your fault so you should admit to it. This never fails."

It's better advice than anything my idiot brothers have told me.

"Thanks," I whisper.

"Twenty-years-old and you're about to have your hands full."

"What?"

"The baby," Van says calmly, as if I ought to know what he's talking about, "Latrice told me about the baby."

"Ah," I say, nodding with understanding, "Tisha's babies. I still hope to change the birth certificates and name them after me."

"No..." Van says slowly, "Your baby. With Latrice. The one she's pregnant with."

Perhaps I prematurely diagnosed Van as a smarter man than my brothers because he's being idiotic now. What baby? Latrice and I don't have a baby.

Van's voice sounds like ringing in my ears. I don't want to believe what this idiot is saying to me. I knock on the door and hear Latrice's musical American voice yell back, "Go away! I don't care what false promises you make, I won't negotiate with terrorists. HELP! HELP ME!"

"So the father of your child is a terrorist now?" I snarl. She's quiet. I press my forehead against the door, my chest heaving as I wait for her to say something. Say anything, Latrice. Please.

But Latrice says nothing. She flings the door open and rushes me, wrapping her arms around me. I'm too surprised to hug her back. Pregnant. Latrice Boyd is pregnant. She grabs my face and kisses me before I can protest. Well, there's nothing to protest now.

She's *kissing me.* I wrap my arms around her waist and pick her up, pressing her against the door frame as I kiss her. Van clears his throat. But I don't care. I hike my hands up her thighs and press my hips against Latrice's crotch as I kiss her. This is a reunion I thought I'd never get.

I don't care who watches, as long as I get to kiss the girl.

I know we have to stop, but I don't want to. Latrice pulls away from me and my hunger for her is stronger than any drug.

"You survived," she whispers.

"I'm sorry," I say, "I'm sorry for thinking it was smart to let you go."

Van pries me off her and clears his throat, more loudly this time. I'm beginning to see the family resemblance between him and my annoying brothers.

"We need to move, Galanos. I have no intentions of impeding your reunion, but... *business comes first.*"

Unfortunately, I must admit, idiotic Van Doukas is right.

FORTY-ONE

BABIES, WIVES, REVENGE & MURDER

5 WEEKS LATER

Tisha holds Stephanos on one hip, and Carlotta holds Stavros Jr. They both look more like Tisha than Lou. Except for the eyes. Despite their mixed-race heritage, they have Pagonis eyes. Lou paces the kitchen with a "virgin mojito" that Tisha concocted for him. When I point out that her mojito is just water with a hint of lime, she sticks her tongue out at me.

Stavros (not the baby) cleans his gun with Adrian on his lap. Fallon's not thrilled about having her baby near guns, but she's helping Helen brew coffee for all of us, trusting Stavros' questionable parenting. That's what I'll have soon. Babies. I haven't told my siblings yet, but now I notice how many damn babies have filled this house in the past few years.

Soon, I'll add more to the mix. We will. It makes me nervous to think about becoming a father. I'm not as young as Lou was, but I'm twice as vain at least.

Latrice and I sit at the kitchen counter with stools nearly fastened. I haven't let her out of my sight since Italy. Five weeks and we haven't had a sign of Yiayia or Papa. Five weeks of negotiating business with Van Doukas and the Sicilians with no luck. I want vengeance for Latrice. I need to find Yiayia. Until I do... Latrice won't be leaving my sight, and she knows it. As long as I give her back massages, I can quiet her down about leaving Greece.

Antonio tried to win his way back into Loukas' good graces by tracing down their location, but we hit a wall and we're still there. Yiayia's lost.

Loukas is angrier than any of us and thrice as angry as he needs to be since he quit drinking. We're practically a sober house thanks to the women. Tisha plops her tit out and starts feeding Stephanos, distracting Lou from his rambling about our grandmother to watch her hold the babe to her breasts.

Helen and Fallon bustle out toward the kitchen counters with trays of food and coffee.

"There's more in the main kitchen," Fallon says. I rush to my feet to help the women out. Fallon takes my seat next to Latrice with relief as I scurry off to help Helen bring in more food.

Helen has a cigarette in each of the ash trays flanking the stove and we haven't been alone together in... ages. My eldest sister hates men, and she doesn't mince words. She grabs a knife from the block and turns it on me. Suddenly.

"Helen!"

She rushes forward and presses it beneath my shirt, scowling with those blue eyes that look so very much like our grandmothers.

"Don't lie to me," she snarls. "Where is she?"

"Do you think I know?"

"You always know, Galanos. You're her lap dog. She's not running from you. She's running from Loukas. She's running from Stavros."

"I'm the one who wants to kill her," I say, stiffening my back as my sister presses the knife against one of the ridged muscles on my stomach. My crazy sister will cut me if given the chance.

"Don't lie."

"I'm not lying."

"Five fucking weeks I've had this house packed with my brothers and more children than I know what to do with. I want you all back in your villas and arguing with each other so I can..."

Helen trails off and presses the knife harder. I wince.

"OW!"

"Tell me!"

"What? Do you have a boyfriend or something?"

Helen's cheeks turn red. I thought she hated men. Something about us all being rapists and killers. I am unclear about Helen's problem, but holding a knife, she terrifies me. She's too much of a Pagonis with a knife.

"Shut up, shit," she snarls. "You know where she is. Maybe you're honest now, but somewhere in the back of your mind, you know where Yiayia is. Maybe you're not ready to kill her... I would understand that. But don't make the work harder for your brothers."

"I won't."

"Take the food out," Helen answers sharply, returning her attention to more pressing matters, "And come back when you have another cigarette for me."

I walk out with the tray of food, and Fallon gets out of my seat so I can be close to Latrice again. She grabs Adrian from Stavros and takes him upstairs to put him down for a nap. I can't stop thinking about Helen's words.

My older sister might be disturbingly cold, but it's only because we've made her cold. I return to a kitchen with a cigarette, which Helen snatches without thanks. We can hear Cass and Sandros arguing from the villa gates. They're late.

I stumble out of the kitchen by the pool while everyone pitches their ideas for our weekly meeting where we all waste time brainstorming what part of the world my grandmother could be. She could be anywhere. With all the money in the world and family connections that are deeper than we imagine, where the hell could Yiayia have ended up?

Is Helen right?

Latrice approaches on the deck, padding across in her kaftan to sit at the edge of the pool with me. She's beautiful. Five weeks of having sex with her every day and I haven't stopped loving her or wanting her. I know I never will.

She reaches for my hand.

"What did Helen say to you?"

"How did you know?"

"Whenever you talk to Helen, you look like you had an encounter with a ghost."

"Helen..." I grumble, hating how obvious my emotions are to Latrice.

Latrice kisses my shoulder. And it feels amazing.

"Tell me," she whispers.

I glance at Latrice. How can she still care about my plans after what my brilliant ideas put her through? I guess it's different for her now. She's pregnant. None of my siblings know. Tisha and Fallon don't know either. But I know the secret presses on Latrice. We haven't spoken about the pregnancy since Italy.

I answer Latrice's question, even if I'd rather talk about our child.

"She thinks I know where yiayia is."

"Maybe you can't find her. Maybe she'll never come back."

"She'll come back," I whisper. "That's what we can guarantee about her. She always comes back."

Latrice sighs.

"Is that why you want me to have an abortion?"

"What?!"

"We haven't spoken. I thought... I thought you might not want a kid. I mean... we're only twenty."

"Age doesn't matter," I say, "A man never abandons his children."

"Don't get all old-school about this one thing. We don't have to have a baby together, Gal."

"Stop it, Latrice," I snarl. "We're having the baby. If you talk about murdering my child again... I'll punish you."

At first she's scared, but then she sees the corners of my mouth turning up into a smile.

"Why can't we talk about it then," Latrice whispers, the joy fading from her voice. "I thought you didn't want a kid. I just…"

"I want children. I want children with you."

Her body gets closer to mine, which feels like a good thing. I shrug and continue. "I ought to marry you. I want to marry you. But… me? I can't ask you to marry me."

"Why not?"

"I believe I would be a disappointing husband."

"So you're never going to ask?"

"We've only dated a short time."

Latrice rolls her eyes.

"I once watched you propose to an Icelandic D.J. because Tiger told you she had a coke hook-up in Amsterdam."

"You know *way* too much about me."

"Let me get this straight, you'll marry a D.J. with a drug problem, but make excuses about us."

"It's not an excuse," I snarl. "I love you. I love you so much that I might have to do what's best for you even if it kills me."

We look at each other, and Latrice's face softens.

"You don't get people at all, do you?" She whispers.

I shake my head, wishing that I was different. Why is it like she's the only one who can understand me? Is it because she loves me, she understands me, or the other way around?

"Ask me," she says, "When you're ready, ask me. My answer might surprise you."

I lean over and kiss her. Kissing her feels so good. Her lips are warm and soft and her body… I pull away from her before I try to get her clothes off with my family arguing within earshot.

"I want us to have a baby," I whisper, my forehead pressed to hers. "I'm scared, Latrice. The thought of having a kid scares me out of my mind."

"So am I," she whispers. "I'm scared of twenty million things, but when you're here, I feel safe. You may be blunt and terrifying, but you've always protected me. I know you'll never abandon me, Galanos. You're as loyal as Odin."

"Hopefully, I'm more loyal..." I mutter, considering Odin now prefers Latrice over me.

She giggles and brushes her finger over my lips.

"I love you," she says, "You're not too dark or too fucked up for me. Trust me, I never wanted to live a boring life."

"Is that what the pink wigs are all about?"

"Hell yes. And everything else. It's why Tisha and I are so close. You only live once. I want to make the best of it."

We kiss by the pool until supper at 9 p.m. Helen's lecture has so far yielded no insights about Yiayia. I fall asleep dreaming of babies, wives... revenge and murder.

FORTY-TWO
A WHITE BOY'S PROPOSAL

2 WEEKS LATER

I propose to Latrice. By "propose" I mean I can't decide between four rings so I accidentally spend €145,769 getting all of them. I threaten Stavros, Loukas and Antonio with the dirt I have on them to help me plan the proposal.

The accountant is furious with me, so I ask Stavros to spot me the helicopter rental. He reluctantly pays in cash for the experience. But I know my brothers, so I double check the parachute myself.

Latrice agrees to my proposal and then I whisk her off her feet to my bigger surprise celebration: engagement sky-diving. Unfortunately, she doesn't know about the sky-diving until she says "Yes". Then she says "NO!" until I drag her out of the plane myself. I point out that it's perfectly safe and only fifteen people have ever died sky-diving here. She screams all the way down.

But we're still engaged and alive in the end. I'm very pleased.

Latrice unfortunately makes the angry beaver face at me for the rest of the afternoon and complains that "only a white boy" would make her jump out of a plane.

We have the best sex *ever* that night, so I think my proposal went very well. I lick and suck every inch of her until she forgives me for the sky-diving.

We have no news about Yiayia, but a suggestion from our contacts in Ethiopia that she may be somewhere along the East African coast. Helen still thinks I know where she is, but our search turns up nothing.

None of us like when Yiayia is quiet, especially now we have to plan a wedding.

FORTY-THREE

IT'S ONE CHICKEN

2 MONTHS LATER

"Let me get this straight," Cass says, messing with her hair, "the sickest sociopath in the family is the only one to get married in a church? Not even religious Stavros?"

"Stavros isn't religious," I grumble, "he's deranged."

I'm gazing mercilessly at my body in the mirror and I snarl at my reflection, "I look fat."

"You don't look fat, *idiota*. You're wearing a suit. You look fine."

"I should go shirtless. You can't see any of my muscles in this."

Cass rolls her eyes and mutters, "Scorpio men…"

"What did you say?"

"With a moon in Virgo!"

"Shut up, Cass and tell me something useful."

"You smell like a butt," Cass says.

I glare at her, and she laughs at me. Stupid Cassia.

"Is she there yet?" I ask her, since she refuses to be useful.

"Stop worrying about Latrice," Cass says. "She has Fallon and Tisha. Do you really think they'd let anything happen to her?"

A mix of wedding planning, newborns and toddlers has filled the Pagonis family villa with such an overload of hormones that I had to beg Helen to return from Albania for my wedding. She's officially given up on getting all of us to move out and we're all losing steam when it comes to Yiayia.

Well, my brothers are losing steam. I work my angle... but more on that later because right now, Galanos Pagonis is marrying his best friend.

"Like my suit?" Cass says.

"Is Sandros okay with you dressing like a lesbian?"

"Shut up," Cass snarls, "I work now. I can't chase after bad guys in a dress."

"It's like you're forgetting that we are the bad guys."

"Are we? I can't keep track. But that's not my job. My job is point and shoot."

I brush off my lapel for the third time and pretend to be casual about what I'm asking her, "Is that what you did for Van?"

"Mind your business, fatty."

"I knew it," I grumble. "I *do* look fat."

"Latrice needs to work some of her self-esteem magic on you," Cass says. "You are far too vain..."

Before I can do the opposite of minding my business. Stavros comes in, holding a caged chicken and looking completely dumbfounded.

"Why are you holding a chicken!? Don't let that thing shit in here!" I yell.

Cass screams with delight and takes out her phone to snap a picture of the offending bird, now clucking dramatically as Stavros glowers at both of us.

Odin awakens from his spot in the room's corner and races at the cage, barking madly at the chicken who fluffs itself out and sends a spattering of feathers everywhere.

"Odin!" I call to him.

The dog heels, and Stavros continues looking flustered.

"How many people did you invite to this wedding?" Stavros roars, "Why couldn't you be smart like the rest of us and have a small *private* affair?"

"I'm Greek."

"You're GREEK?!" Stavros roars, "Then you should know exactly how crazy we are about weddings!"

"Relax, it's one chicken. Just get it out of here before Odin snaps its neck between his teeth."

Stavros blusters, turning seventeen shades of copper before he yells, "We have ten goats, fifteen chickens, four cows, six horses, a bull, five kittens, an Alsatian puppy, a receipt for four Bitcoin from Tiger and enough food to feed every cursed bastard in your bloodline! Those are just the *minor* guests. The Stathakis family's rivals sent you *three* new Porsche sedans now parked in *my* driveway."

I roll my eyes at Stavros as he continues listing excessive or irritating gifts. Whatever, brother... I have my own problems.

My brothers still don't know Latrice is pregnant... Stavros is furious now, and I understand why as one of the offending goats pushes the door open and waltzes straight up to Cass with an annoying bleat. She laughs with glee and bends down to pet the goat.

"Relax, Stavros. These are wedding gifts. Simply have someone else look after the problem."

"Only you could say that with six horses standing outside! We need to do something with the animals..."

Cass puts her hand on Stavros' back and guides him out of the dressing room. I add more gel to my hair and unbutton another button on my shirt. No. It looks stupid. I button it back up. I wonder if Latrice is nervous.

I'm not nervous about marrying her. I'm nervous about being good enough after we're married. The door to my dressing room pushes open again and I'm ready to tell off Cass and Stavros again, but they aren't the ones who enter.

Loukas cleans up nicely for an old man. He comes over to me and hugs me.

"You look fantastic. And if you're curious, so does she."

"So she hasn't run off?"

"If she tried, we'd have to catch her," Loukas says with a serious tone.

I nod solemnly, although I privately hope he's joking. I don't plan on pushing any of my wives to run off. Odin barks and runs up to Loukas, who gives him a dutiful pat on the head.

"My latest contact found this. I wondered if you could tell me anything about it."

"Is it about her?"

He nods, because we both know that right now at least, there's only one possible 'her' we could be talking about. I put the folded paper in my breast pocket.

"After. I want to wait. I want to get married."

Loukas nods.

"Yes. I've had my fair share of marriages. Make this one last, Galanos. Keep her safe. From us most of all."

Funnily enough, I think Latrice can handle herself with us. If she couldn't before, she can now. Still, I appreciate my brother's advice and he gets me to the church on time so I can see my beautiful Latrice and make her mine... with the best contract anyone could hope for. Marriage.

I wait nervously at the altar for the music to start so I can see her. I don't know what Latrice's dress looks like and I don't know what I'm expecting. Latrice likes glitz and glamor, and she's anything but boring. The music starts.

Stavros gives me an approving nod, even if he's dripping with sweat from his afternoon spent as a goatherd. Fallon sits with the kids in the front pew. Latrice's bridesmaids include a couple social media friends, Tisha, and Carlotta. Cass's suit matches Stavros, Sandros and Loukas's.

Helen sparks up a cigarette as Latrice floats down the aisle, holding Antonio's arm. We negotiated Antonio down to a suit with kitten heels, which click loudly as veiled Latrice glides up the aisle.

I can't wait to see her. My bride. *My pregnant wife.*

It's about to be a very Pagonis wedding.

FORTY-FOUR
GET INTO POSITION

The moment I see Latrice Boyd for the first time on our wedding day, I cry. Yes, I'll admit it. I'm the only one of my brothers to cry at my wedding and they're all surprised. Everyone in the church is too terrified to comment on it, but Latrice cries too once she sees me crying. And we don't wait for permission to have a long kiss.

Yes, I use tongue. No, I don't stop until the preacher clears his throat loudly. Several times. Okay, I may have been groping Latrice's bum too. But in my defense, it's a nice bum and there's a lot to grab, so I had to give her a very thorough touch.

We ride horses back to my villa for the party. The villagers throw flowers at us as we pass and a child slips a little bracelet on Latrice's wrist. We get to the villa and it's a Galanos party through and through. Since Latrice can't drink, I won't either. But for once, I actually care if other people have fun... not just myself.

I will remember to ask Latrice if she always feels this way... if she's always... *cared*.

Loukas takes the twins home early so Tisha can have a night to herself and Stavros eventually does the same with Adrian. Fallon has a little champagne for the first time in ages, and it gets her tipsy right away.

"Gal! You've grown up so much..." Fallon says, wrapping her arms around me. I almost suspect she will stab me in the back, but it's a genuine hug. My throat tightens nervously as she pulls away, grinning.

"I don't know how Latrice got to you... it's a medical marvel."

"Is that a compliment, sister-in-law?"

"Oops," Fallon giggles, "I haven't had anything to drink in a *long* time. One sip and I'm gone. If it makes a difference, Stavros is proud of the man you're turning out to be. We love you, Galanos."

I groan.

"Love? Fallon... please. We don't have that kind of relationship."

Fallon giggles and rolls her eyes.

"Sure we don't, Gal. You're just like them, you know. Convinced that you have to be all tough, all the time. Maybe Yiayia's never coming back. Maybe for once, the three of you can get to know each other. Relax. Put the family business aside."

"That's a charming sentiment, Fallon."

My back stiffens, and I push my hands into my pockets. I forget she understands Pagonis men too well.

"You're never going to give up on revenge, are you?" She sighs.

"When a Pagonis gives up on revenge, Greece will have sunk into the sea."

"See what I mean? You're just like them. Protective. Stubborn..."

"Victorious," I finish, "Not yet. But soon."

Fallon nods and finishes her drink.

"This may be the champagne talking... but I don't even blame you. If I were in your shoes, I would have considered this a long time ago."

I've never heard Fallon say anything so coldly. But she stumbles off and I recall the time my grandmother made her lick coffee off the dirty floor. Humiliation worsened by the time she spent as my brother's captive. How they ended up married is... confusing. I will ask Latrice about this as well.

Speaking of Latrice, she swoops in behind me and clasps her hand in mine. She's still wearing that gorgeous white dress and I am desperate to take it off her. The bodice hugs every inch of her curves, presenting her breasts pushed together like a wrapped chocolate delicacy. I can't help but staring at her breasts... even now.

She nibbles on my earlobe as she wraps her arms around me and whispers something magical into my ear.

"Should we disappear into the dungeon, *Sir?*"

I hold on to her, inhaling her perfume and letting myself feel the longing that's pulsed beneath the surface all day as I've watched my *wife* prance about enjoying herself. I want to fuck her. I want to claim her.

"Yes," I murmur, "That sounds like a lovely idea."

We face each other and Latrice pushes hair away from my face daringly.

"The wedding was perfect."

"Only because you're perfect," I murmur. "I love you with my entire heart."

"I love you too, *sir.*"

I love it when she calls me sir. The word gets me instantly hard and I clear my throat nervously as she presses against me, her crotch nestling against my body like she's compelling me to feel her warmth.

I yearn for her warmth. I *need* it. My hands tighten against her waist and I ask her the second most important question I'll ask her that day.

"Pain or pleasure?"

"Both," she whispers. "Tonight I want both, *sir.*"

My breathing quickens as my hardness threatens to rip the seams of my trousers. I want to give her both too. But there's something I've been saving for a special occasion. Something I know Latrice wants while desperately fearing.

She doesn't shy away from my desire to inflict pain, from the way it arouses me to watch her squirm, but tonight, I worry about going too far...

"Do you trust me, kitten?"

She nods and kisses me, affectionately rubbing my chest through my shirt. Yes, she trusts me. Yes, I can have her. Yes, tonight is all about 'I do'.

"You're hard," she murmurs, struggling with her instinct to reach for my cock in public. We're in the center of a room, surrounded by people dancing and chatting, but the moment a cock becomes part of the equation, we'll definitely attract even more attention, so Latrice only holds my gaze and trusts that I know what she's thinking. Intimately.

I wet my lower lips and nod.

"I'm incredibly hard," I say, "And I need your cunt."

"But..." Latrice whispers, tugging at my collar, "You need to hurt me first."

I almost think she's judging me, but then she smiles and a flurry of warmth and desire settles me. Latrice slips her hand in mine and we slip away from the center of attention to the private place I promised to show her the first time we sat at my kitchen counter and discussed our first contract.

Things are different now. We have a new contract. One that's even more detailed than our marriage contract. One that serves our complete pleasure and satisfaction. The rules begin in the dungeon.

At the end of the longest hallway in the basement — unusual in our part of Greece — I outfitted a soundproof door with keypad entry. Yes, it cost several million dollars, and I was drunk when I had it installed.

Latrice presses the numbers and the doors open. Red velvet covers the soundproof walls. She can scream as loud as she wants in here and believe me, she usually does. I close the door behind me and turn the lock.

"We're alone," I say.

That means our ritual begins. Latrice lowers her gaze and whispers, "I submit myself to your will, Galanos. Tonight my body belongs to you."

The ritual of those words gets me hard. Our brief signal to each other so we know we're playing a very important and very exciting game.

"Lift your dress," I command.

Latrice slowly grabs the white hem of her long dress and lifts it. I can smell her as I drop to my knees.

"I want you wet before I hurt you," I say, "So bring me your cunt."

"I haven't showered since this morning, sir."

"Don't fight me, Latrice. Bring me your cunt," I command.

She steps forward, and I grab her thighs, greedily kissing the tops as she whimpers. My tongue finds the garter wrapped around Latrice's thick thighs and I push it between my teeth, slipping it off and letting it fall to the ground as I push my head beneath her dress again, and she lets the skirt fall.

Now I can smell her cunt much better. *Much* better. The scent gets me even harder. I grab her panties and push them over her hips. Latrice makes a little whimpering noise as my hand grazes the top of her mound. She's sensitive and willing. *She needs this as much as I do.*

I pull her panties away from her pussy with my teeth and she whimpers as a gush of wetness makes peeling the fabric away from her cunt even more difficult. Her dark pussy lips conceal the delectable pink flesh between, and I want my tongue on all of it. I want her pussy to coat my face by the end of the night.

My tongue slides over Latrice's clit, and she emits the most magnificent moan. I grab her hips and push my tongue deeper, sliding along the tasty slit and licking up every drop of her juices before I press my tongue into the crease of her thighs and lick up any part of her I can get into my mouth before returning to her throbbing clit.

She cries out again and I push my fingers into her pussy, taking her by surprise as I feel around her cunt. *My cunt.* Latrice moans as I finger her while eating her pussy with an agile tongue. I can feel her climax getting closer. Her body throbs and squirms with desire as I hold her firm and lick her folds until she can't take it anymore.

"I'm cumming..."

I hold her firmly and make her cum. Hard. She backs away from me, and I watch the anguished look on her face as she realizes this is the last orgasm she'll have for several hours.

"Galanos..."

"Pain," I say, rising to my feet and staring at my beautiful wife with a glint in my eyes. "A little pain..."

"Just remember," she whispers, "I'm pregnant. Sir."

"Get on the bed, kitten. Get into position."

She gets into position, leaning forward and arching her back and letting me fasten her arms to her lower legs so she's in the perfect position for fucking and completely immobilized.

Latrice is shuddering and whimpering in her wedding gown, which I never asked her to remove. The poor girl thinks I'm going to spank her, but I wasn't talking about *that* kind of pain.

FORTY-FIVE
A THUMB IN THE _______

reach into one of my pleasure drawers and take out a bottle of lubricant. Latrice doesn't know what's coming, and she's completely silent. Patient.

I take a healthy dose of the lubricant and slide it on Latrice's butt hole, pressing some of it in with my thumb. She moans, partly in surprise and partly because it's a well-lubricated thumb in her sensitive ass.

"I promised you pain," I whisper, "But only because I can't do this in a way that doesn't hurt you. *My dick is too big.*"

Goosebumps prickle across her large butt. Her cute butt. I want to bite into the cheeks, but I rub the lube over her tight backdoor.

"Do you know what I'm going to do to you, kitten."

Latrice whispers, "You're going to fuck my ass, sir."

"I'm going to make love to your ass. Then I'm going to make love to your cunt. I'll cum inside you and keep fucking you until you're satisfied. When I pull my cock out, I'll watch the cum dripping out of your cunt and then... I will release you."

"Yes, sir."

Music. Those two words are music. I put my thumb against her backdoor and slowly massage it open. I can tell this hurts her a little as Latrice has a very tight asshole. I ease her ass open and put my tongue against her exposed cunt, lifting her dress so I can access both.

Lube drips from her ass to her pussy as I lick her close to another orgasm while getting her ass used to my thumb. I pull my finger out and although it might not make much of a difference, I hope it will be easier for her to take my cock.

She squirms as I rest the condom-covered tip of my cock against her backdoor. I hold on to her ass and spread her cheeks a little wider as I press the head inside her. It hurts. She cries out, but she can't thrash. I take a nice toy and set it buzzing on her clit.

Now she likes it. A lot. I push another inch inside her and make the toy vibrate even more. She likes a nice big cock sliding into her ass while I make sure her tender clit gets attention from her vibrator. I push another inch inside her, and she moans in pleasure and pain.

Some nights, you need both.

"Yes, sir," she whimpers, "More sir…"

I grunt and push inside her.

"Your ass is tight…" I grunt.

Latrice cries out and cums as the vibrator pushes her over the edge. As she climaxes, her body convulses and her ass tightens around my cock. I lose control. I'm halfway in an extremely tight ass that just got even tighter.

I need to fuck it.

I slide the rest of my cock deep inside Latrice's insanely tight ass and Latrice screams. Without the soundproof dungeon, Fallon and Tisha may have made another rescue attempt. Latrice's ass cheeks are like two giant bubbles splayed open as my dick disappears into her tight asshole.

I keep the vibrator on her clit because I can feel it moving against my dick, buried in her ass deeply. I move my hips slowly and then thrust the rest of my dick back in. Fuck. I've never had an ass this tight. And it's mine… I drive my cock into her again as she moans.

Cum for me... cum...

If she cums again, I know her ass will squeeze my cock like a vice and I can cum deep inside her sexy ass. I massage her clit and push in deeper, enjoying the sensation of her tight ass wrapped around my cock, when she finally cums hard. I grab her hips and make love to Latrice's gorgeous, sexy ass as her bubble butt bounces around my cock.

"Oh yes, kitten... enjoy my big white cock up your ass..."

Latrice moans as I swirl the vibrator around her clit and fuck her nice and hard in the ass. I pull out of her and drop to my knees, licking at her cunt as she squirms and moans.

It's too much pleasure for her, and she wants my cock in her pussy *badly.* I grab her hips and push my tongue inside her deeper, enjoying Latrice's restraints and enjoying the way her juices gush onto my tongue. I never want to stop licking her juicy black pussy.

But Latrice moans for me to stop. Begs for it. So I stop. And then I press my cock against her pussy.

"Yes," she whispers, "Please..."

I slide into her dripping pussy slowly, and she moans as she takes every inch. I need to cum inside of her pussy... *now.* She's tight and dripping wet and the *heat...*

I press the vibrator to her clit and slowly withdraw my hips from Latrice's dripping wetness. Her butt cheek jiggles as dimples form across her ass. I grab onto her hips and move faster, making her cum as I take her as urgently as I need to.

Her moans get louder as she cums, and I feel the tightening and then the release. My cock spasms as thick bursts of my seed enter Latrice, coating her walls as she orgasms loudly. I bend over and bite her ass cheeks.

"I'm not done," I growl, grabbing her hips and continuing to take her from behind, pumping into her deeper and slower as she moans. Her juices and my cum coat my cock and the thick sticky fluid makes fucking her pussy even better.

"Yes..." she cries out. "Yes, sir... I want more..."

I take my thumb and press it against her asshole as I fuck her pussy from behind and keep her vibrator on her clit. Latrice cums again, her pussy grabbing onto my cock with insanely tight grip. I push my finger deeper into her ass as I fuck her. Hard. When she cums three more times, I'm finally ready. I groan and release inside Latrice again, adding to my first load with more thick spurts of cum.

When I pull my cock out of her, the creamy liquid drips out of her tightness, dribbling down her thighs as she moans and catches her breath. I gently slap her butt, and more of my cum spills out of her. I kiss her thighs and then her butt and find myself tempted to put my tongue in her ass again.

Not yet.

Maybe later, but not yet.

I remove her harness and Latrice sits up on her knees, her breasts hanging like gorgeous melons as she glances at me excitedly.

"That was... wow."

"You liked my dick in your ass?"

She nods with greater enthusiasm than even I expected.

"We're married," she says gleefully, "I enjoy having your dick everywhere."

"Everywhere?"

"Don't get any sick ideas," Latrice says, "I want a kiss... sir."

I lean over and give my perfect woman a kiss. She grabs my hair and rubs her tongue against mine as she kisses me back. When she pulls away, I'm grinning at her madly.

"What?" Latrice whispers.

"I need to tell you a secret."

"Okay..."

"You're not going to like it. But you're my wife. So you *will* obey me."

Latrice gives me that angry beaver face again. But I know she will obey me, anyway.

"Tell me."

"I solved the case. I know where Yiayia is."

"What? How?"

"Sex cleared my head, and I remembered. Helen's right. I know her better than anyone, and I know where she runs when she doesn't want anyone to find her. She probably thinks I forgot. She probably thinks I want to forget. Yiayia knows my mother. If she wanted to go one place, she knows I wouldn't even want to look, she'd go there."

Latrice grabs my hand and squeezes.

"You're going to kill her."

"Don't ask me," I say sternly, "Because I won't do it tonight. Tonight, we're going to have sex several more times. I'll plan my journey for a few more weeks. I won't bother my brothers with this. When I leave, you will tell everyone I've gone back to London. Understand?"

"I will keep your secret, but you have to make me a promise, Galanos. And you have to mean it."

"What's that?"

"Promise you won't die."

"I—

"Don't tell me you can't," she snaps, "You know it's not the answer I want.":

"I won't die."

"Say it again. Say it like you mean it."

"I won't die, kitten," I say, meaning every word of it for her.

FORTY-SIX
WASHED UP EMINEM WANNABE

2 months later

My mother. Why the fuck does everyone always want me to think about my mother? She is young. She *was* young. She's a whore. I know I shouldn't say my mother is a whore, but she really is.

She doesn't want me, and she never did. She tried to sell me to a man when I was three. Papa dragged her back to the villa by her hair, beating her the entire way, and locked her up for a week. She was only seventeen, and he was too old to have a girl like her. She was too young to have me — the baby she never wanted from him.

Yiayia carried me home and bought me ice-cream.

I never said Papa was perfect. They were two demons who should have never found each other's corners of hell. If my mother was a succubus, my father was a spoiled prince. Yiayia pushed them together.

And what do you expect when two demons have a child? You get me.

And aside from Latrice, I haven't done much good. She's the best thing I have right now.

I deserve my mother's hate now, anyway. I sent my mother dog shit in the mail. Guilty as charged. But I can safely say she started it.

She cut my first line of coke for me when I spent a weekend with her at twelve. Her boyfriend touched my cock when I was fourteen. Stavros handled that one, and he roamed around Thessaloniki yelling at no one for weeks afterward. Loukas was busy failing as a parent and never knew.

Whenever I visited her, she'd get me drunk or give me coke. She would sometimes try to get me to sleep with men and women for money so we could get high together.

I lost my virginity that summer to my mother's best friend. She was older. Thirty-five, I think. Yiayia handled that one. The woman survived the attack, but she never spoke to my mother again. Yiayia didn't like me going there for weekends anymore. Papa didn't even know I was going. He had a new girlfriend.

My mother and I hate each other really. But Yiayia always tried to put us together, just long enough so she could remind me all the ways my grandmother was better.

I don't want to see my mother. *Talia Voulgaropoulos.*

I've spent months planning the visit and even now, I'm not ready. My brothers don't know what I'm doing. I've told them I've given up and I'm pursuing boring marital bliss with Latrice. It's a half-truth. She's still pregnant and we're thinking about getting another dog.

It's not like Odin isn't enough, but we don't want him to eat the baby out of envy. Latrice read an article about it on social media and now that she's pregnant I do whatever she says like I'm the submissive.

Back to the matter at hand. My mother. I'm on a boat, sailing to the isle of Lemnos in the Aegean Sea, the town where my mother lives, retired from her life of prostitution because of the hefty divorce settlement from my father. She tricked him into marrying her, which was impressive.

I dock the boat in Myrina, near the rocks beneath the castle overlooking the Aegean. The sea will always look better from Thessaloniki. I have to step into the icy water to make it to shore. Pagonis arrival on this island would cause a stir and I would obliterate my advantage.

For as much as I've underestimated her, Yiayia underestimates me as well. She set up our rape. I know without a doubt that there are no lengths she wouldn't go to. She'd even make me interact with my mother. After everything she knows. Yiayia isn't aging well. It's time someone put her out of my misery.

I load my gun and walk up the beach, a cool breeze blowing my hair back. I can still smell Latrice's perfume on my shirt. Oh, Latrice. I'm happy she doesn't ask me more about what I'm doing here. I don't want her to know this side of me. I like the side of me I have with her.

Latrice makes me feel... normal. I've lived an extraordinary life, and all I wanted was a beautiful girl who lived a normal life. Who wants a normal life. A child. Hopefully four. Two dogs. I might even want a second home in Sicily or America.

I want a life with her. A life without fear. A life without my grandmother. I have made things right with my brothers, but I still have work to do. Thank goodness they don't know I'm here.

I walk Northeast along the Navarchou Kountourioti, attracting the attention of barking stray dogs and desperate stray cats. The faint sound of electronic music pulses down the dark streets and the fried seafood smell is everywhere.

I stride purposefully past all the overpriced restaurants until I get to the place my mother owns. Cavo Del Mare. The little sea café attracts many important visitors, most of them hoping to score more than extra-strong espresso.

She still works on her back when she needs to, but she mostly hires other girls too. Or has her men kidnap them. The scumbag who sold Fallon to Stavros? Yeah, she dated him for a 15% off discount.

Talia isn't a normal mother.

It's dark and all the lights are off in the building. There aren't even any street lights outside. My breath puffs out of my mouth in a small white cloud and my slow breathing brings in an unfortunately deep inhalation of urine and dog shit.

I watch the café from the street, standing on the stones like a ghost, watching the home that ought to have been mine. The mother who ought to have loved me probably sleeps inside with another boyfriend. She always had a boyfriend that I needed protecting from.

Latrice doesn't know about that either. How often I've been hurt that way... in a way none of my brothers experienced because they were wanted.

My fists clench unconsciously, and I know what Latrice would want. She'd want me to take deep breaths and suppress all thoughts of murder.

I swallow slowly and imagine killing my mother too, but I know doing that would be too reckless. I know Latrice wouldn't want me to go that far. And I can't kill my mother now, anyway. I need her to tell me where Yiayia is.

First, I need to watch and establish how many people are in the house. Then, I need to watch her movements. I need to hunt her and make sure that Yiayia doesn't find out I'm here. I walk back to my boat and flick the light on below deck, staring at an older face that I don't recognize.

"Latrice, I'm sorry," I whisper as I pull out the shaver and give myself a buzz cut. The blond hair drops into the sink and I hate myself for wanting to cry.

I look like a washed up Eminem wannabe.

The thought runs a chill down my spine. That's scarier than killing someone.

I take out the box of dye and color my hair black, apologizing to

Latrice again. I didn't warn her about the "getting rid of the blond" part of the plan. I was in denial.

But I need to get rid of my most defining features. Sunglasses for the eye color. Ducking behind alleyways during the day ought to handle the rest of it. I don't plan on spending much time where anyone could recognize me, so I have minimal other ways to disguise myself. I have to reject fashion in favor of subtlety for once. And I have to be patient.

I hope Latrice can be patient too. I text her a picture of my new hair and then turn my phone off. *Sorry, kitten.*

FORTY-SEVEN
TALIA VOULGAROPOULOS

watch the café for a painful week. My mother has a boyfriend, but he's even more of a junkie than the men she usually goes for. And he's around my age. Thankfully, he's smaller than Sandros, otherwise he would have been a real brute to take down.

She has five girls working for her, but they leave at 3 p.m. after servicing clients in the back for the day. (They speak loudly, like most Greek women from the island...) They go to work for the big spenders at night and then the boyfriend comes.

I think I'll have it easy until the seventh day. A car I don't recognize approaches the café, and I assume it's Yiayia. But then a man gets out of the backseat, holding onto a little blond boy's hand and he runs toward her screaming, "Mama!"

His voice sounds like mine. He sounds innocent. I storm back to the dock, feeling reckless and angry. How could she have another child? How could she do this? I want to call Latrice. I want to talk to her... but I'm too hot-headed to sit still.

I fume silently for hours, simmering in my rage the way only a Pagonis could. As my rage burns, I feel my heart getting colder. I wait until midnight and walk back to the house. Her boyfriend leaves at one in the morning.

I don't wait as long as I should before I find a weakness in her back door and slip into the house. I need to find the little boy first. I need to handle him before I go upstairs and finish the job with my mother... a job that's been twenty years unfinished.

I hear little footsteps touching the ground and I creep down the hall, flicking on the child's bedroom light as he eases out of bed. When he sees me, his immediate reaction is terror. His wide, blue eyes meet mine and despite his fear, the little boy holds his ground.

"What are you doing in my bedroom?" He asks, "Are you with mama?"

"I'm your brother. Galanos."

"I don't have a brother," he says, frowning.

This is what I must have looked like to Loukas and Stavros. So small... innocent... weak. I crouch down and fold my arms.

"If I weren't your brother, don't you think I would have done something incredibly scary by now. Like kidnapped you."

"You could still kidnap me," he snaps.

"How is mama?"

"She's sleeping," the boy whispers.

"Are you going to tell me your name?"

The boy shakes his head. I can't win every battle. I nod and tell him, "That's okay. I know you probably don't believe me, but I am your brother. I haven't come to hurt you. I've come to take you to my family."

"To my papa?"

"To a place where no one will hurt you the way mama does."

He glances away from me. Ashamed. But now he knows, on some deep level at least, that I'm telling the truth.

"She won't let you take me. She says never again, not after what they did to..."

"Gal?" I finish.

He nods and then whispers, "Adam."

"Okay, Adam. Pack a bag and wait for me here. No matter what you hear, don't open this door until you hear three knocks."

He nods.

"Repeat it."

"Don't open the door until I hear three knocks."

"Good," I whisper. Then I ask him a question that I don't think anyone should have to ask a child.

"Have any of her boyfriends hurt you?"

He nods and I want to break my mother in half. I want to kill her. But I can't now, can I? Not with him in the house. Not with him needing her. He at least needs to know the truth. She would have never chosen him. He can't know that for sure if I kill her.

"Pack your things," I answer and I close the door, sticking a chair under the handle just in case. Listen, it's not the most ethical thing, but I don't want the boy seeing worse than what he's already seen.

I walk up the stairs slowly, but not too carefully. If she hasn't heard us by now, it's because she's drunk. Or high. Thankfully, that will make my job easier. I know which bedroom's hers immediately. The largest one with the ocean view and the balcony.

I push the door open and she doesn't move from the center of her king-sized bed. Definitely passed out. I watch her for a few moments, her chest rising and her sleeping body looking uncharacteristically innocent. She knows where Yiayia is. She must.

Well, I'm not one for subtlety and I have a gun. I flick the lights on.

"Wake up, mama. Galanos is home."

She groans, "Take him if you want..."

Okay, I'm not bulletproof. That hurt. But at least it made my job easier. I stride over to the bed and wrap her hair around my hands, pulling her face up.

"Wake up," I snarl, "Wake up and tell me where my grandmother is."

Her eyes snap open and now, no drug or drink she's taken is strong enough to stop the adrenaline coursing through her body, willing her to survive because her adult son just broke into her house and he's ready to kill her.

Her instinct is to fight. She scratches at me like a drunk chicken and I throw her back onto the bed, pulling my gun out and pointing it at her head.

"Don't make me kill you with Adam in the house," I whisper. "Don't do it. Make this easy on me, mama."

"You're a fucking thug. A fucking mafia thug," she hisses.

We haven't seen each other in ages, but as Pagonis family reunions go, it's on the friendly side. Only one of us has a gun.

"It doesn't matter what I am," I say. "All that matters is the information I need. And the conversation we need to have. But unfortunately, I need to take care of Adam first. Good night, mama."

I'll spare you the details, but I get her unconscious and then tie her up. Ropes. Handcuffs. Zip ties. Duct Tape. A proper gag. I keep her seated upright. I'll be back for her soon. I return downstairs to Adam who waits with his bags packed.

I crouch down to him again.

"When was the last time she hit you," I whisper.

He lifts his pajama top, and the welts are fresh. I nod and tell him, "Do you trust me?"

His voice drips with skepticism that reminds me of Loukas when he grumbles, "Not really."

"Okay. Well. I am your brother and I promise you safety. If I break that promise, my life belongs to you."

He stares at me wide-eyed, but a thrill crosses his face.

"Like the mafia."

"Yes, Adam. Exactly like the mafia. Will you come with me even if you don't trust me?"

"Yes."

"I'm taking you to my boat."

He takes my hand. It's eerily silent upstairs, but I walk through the streets with him toward the boat. It's a long walk for a kid and it's the middle of the night. Fuck. I need to be a proper big brother.

Maybe I ought to teach him how to clean a gun? No. I don't have time for that.

"Uh... how's school?"

That's what Latrice would say.

"Stupid," Adam says, wiping his nose.

I couldn't agree more with the child. He gets a little tired and snappy, reminding me of myself at that age.

"Are we there yet, Galanos? I'm tired and it stinks like fish."

"We're close."

"Mama will be really angry with you."

"Don't worry about her."

"Did you hurt her?"

"No."

And finally, we're there. I put him up onto the boat and sigh. I don't want to leave him here alone, but until I get back, this is the safest place for him. Especially considering what I'm going to do to our mother next.

"Will you listen to me, Adam?"

He nods.

"I'm going back to the café to talk to mama. You must stay here. Do not come above deck until you hear me knocking at the side of the boat."

The kid learns fast because he says, "Three knocks?"

Exactly. Three knocks. I leave him there and instruct him to go straight to sleep. I doubt he sleeps. He must be around five years old. I never knew I had a brother. A little brother with an age difference similar to mine and Loukas'.

I'm hot with rage when I return to the café. My mother is still tied up, but now she's awake.

FORTY-EIGHT

NOT YOUR TYPICAL MOTHER-SON REUNION

She can only stare at me, trying to find what angle she'll use to manipulate me emotionally. It's her special talent. I approach her and rip the tape off her mouth, removing the gag as she coughs and retches. I roll my sleeves up and pull my kit out of my pocket.

I talk to her like any problem I handle. "Hello, mama. We're going to have a conversation. It's been too long."

She goes straight for the jugular because I haven't left her much choice. There's no fighting back from her anymore. I'm not the little kid she pushed around anymore. I'm a sick fuck who could kill his own mother without flinching. Who might kill his mother.

"You're sick in the head. Your grandmother's right about you."

"Probably," I say, "But if I were you, I wouldn't have admitted to knowing where she was."

"I admitted to nothing. You won't find her unless she wants to be found."

I take out a small scalpel and grin.

"Are you sure?"

"You don't scare me. Come. Be a man. Cut me."

I let the scalpel fall to my side. I'm not against the idea, but I need to start slowly and get the most important answers first.

"Who is the boy's father?"

"None of your business."

"It is my business. I'm taking him back to Thessaloniki."

"Do whatever you want with him," she says, "I don't care. He's at that age where all they do is cry and ask for things."

"How could you say that about your own son?"

She tosses her head of hair back, the only thing she can do to look haughty in her restraints.

"Men are shit," she snarls, "Sons are shit."

"Men are shit? You didn't believe that about Viktor."

She smirks, and I want to do worse than stabbing her. She knows what he did to me. Stavros killed her boyfriend several years ago when he found out what happened. How Viktor hurt me.

Talia smiles on purpose. Not because she's thrilled that her boyfriend touched me and my brother killed him. This is her game. She wants to get me angry because if I'm angry, I'm out of control. Men are unstable. Men are violent. And because of that, we're easier to manipulate.

I know that's how she thinks.

"Who is his father, or I will cut off your pinky toe."

"Fuck you."

I crouch down. She can't move her legs, but her body stiffens because she desperately wants to. I press the scalpel to the top of her pinky toe, assessing quietly how much force I'd need to slice it off.

It's not your typical mother-son reunion.

"Okay!" she shrieks because my mother is predictably cowardly.

"His father is Italian. He's a Doukas."

"Seriously?"

I can't hide my disgust. I hope it isn't Van.

"I don't know which one," she says, "I was working a party."

"That's great. Classy."

"I don't need your judgment," she hisses, "You're privileged."

I stop pressing the scalpel against her toe and move away, sitting against the wall and considering her. She doesn't scream. She looks at me, waiting for me to say something. But I want her to say the next words. I want her to realize that her life is in my hands — and that won't change.

"Tell me where my grandmother is."

"You won't like my answer."

"Will it be the truth?"

"I lost touch with her two days ago."

"I was watching you. When did you lose touch."

I want to hear her lie to my face. But she surprises me by telling the truth for once.

"Then you'll know that I was home early two days ago. I was waiting for her, but she never showed up. Maybe she guessed you'd be here."

"Where was she staying?"

"The place is empty. I went there yesterday, and they must have new tenants already. She skipped town, Galanos. You missed her. So take Adam away and leave me alone."

She doesn't even care about Adam. That makes me sick. I scan her face and then her arms for track marks. No track marks, but there are other ways for her to get her fix.

"New tenants?" I question her, struggling to focus. There's always unfinished business between me and Talia. Killing her would be easiest. Killing her would be cathartic. But I have to focus on Yiayia.

"There were three black Jeeps in the driveway. Not her style," Talia continues.

"Where," I hiss.

"Promise me you'll look after him."

"Do you care about that?"

"I care about you," she lies.

I rise to my feet, towering over her and gazing down at her with a loathing that I ought to conceal. She'll use everything against me, even that.

"You don't want me to kill you."

"Will you?"

"I want to, Talia. I want to kill you. But you aren't worth killing. And Adam deserves to know how shitty you are first hand. I don't need to tell you not to come back to Thessaloniki for him. They'll rip you apart."

"Her villa's near Gomati beach. You'll know the one."

"You've made my job easy."

She snorts, "And you've sentenced me to death. You might not pull the trigger, but she'll kill me for telling you."

"Well, you're very brave," I snarl sarcastically.

"I did what I had to so I could look after myself. You're a pig, just like your father."

"And what are you, Talia? A pig-fucker?"

I think that's a pleasant note to leave her on. I put my kit away and shove my gun in my pocket. I can take the boat up to Gomati beach and make sure Adam gets some food. I'll need time to stake out Yiayia's place.

"Goodbye, Talia. If we're lucky, we'll never see each other again."

I cross the room and kiss her on her forehead, surprised she doesn't head butt or spit on me. My mother's shaking when I kiss her. For all her bluster, she knows that I could have killed her if I wanted to.

I'm too calm around her. It's the mistake they all make in my family. They think I'll always be a little boy. But I won't be. I have Latrice to thank for that. My mother doesn't even know I'm married. I don't want to tell her.

I walk toward the door and she screams, "Aren't you going to untie me!?"

"No."

I leave the house as she screams and begs me to untie her. I walk away, thinking that her shouts and cries sound like music. When I get back to the boat, my heart tightens nervously. I fear the boy has wandered off or drowned. I knock three times and he doesn't answer, so I climb onto the boat and find him. Sleeping.

Adam Voulgaropoulos. I'll make a Pagonis out of him. I stroke his hair and whisper, "I won't let anyone else hurt you. Not just for you, but for me."

Latrice may eventually tire of me adopting a living thing every time I work. But I can't help it if I'm a killer with a soft side. She ought to be proud of me. I mean to sleep, but I end up watching Adam. His chest rises and falls and I think of my future son.

I don't know if I'll have a boy, but all my brothers have sons, so I expect to end up just like them. I'm more like them than I wanted to admit for years. Adam wakes up with the sun and he crawls out of bed with a groan.

"Where are we?"

"Lemnos. Near the shore."

"It wasn't a dream," Adam whispers.

"No," I tell him, "It wasn't."

"Where's mama?"

"Alive. If that's what you're asking."

He looks a little scared, so probably wasn't what he was asking. I change the subject.

"Hungry?"

He nods.

"How do you like energy bars?"

Adam wrinkles his nose and shrugs. I hand him one from the little room in the boat. We need to get going soon, and I don't want to risk anyone seeing us in the daylight. They're rather sweet. I think he might enjoy them, given the chance.

Adam's hungry because he polishes it off and gasps, "Water."

I get him some water and he finishes as much as he likes before handing it off to me.

"Are you taking me somewhere?"

"Yes," I tell him, "The beach. Have you ever sailed before?"

"With mama's boyfriend. Not the fat one."

"The fat one?"

"Mr. Pagonis."

"What?"

"He comes every month. She says he pays well."

Every month. How long has this been going on? I quietly fume about this revelation as I sail Adam around the island. I try to act as normal as possible around him, talking about the water and the jellyfish and the different sea creatures in the Aegean Sea. He wants to try fishing.

I tell him about Odin and the villa, hoping that maybe he can forget his mother. I know it won't work. I never forgot her and even now... I can't bring myself to kill her.

How will I make myself kill Yiayia...

Sigh...

FORTY-NINE
100% CHANCE

The moment we approach the villa from the sea, I know something's wrong. All the glass windows facing the ocean are broken. I don't want Adam to know how rattled I am, or that I'm even doing things like noticing broken windows on hilltop villas. If I run, I can make it up the hill in 5 minutes, 6 minutes if I bring a weapon and it looks like I need more than a weapon.

If there's already a gunfight happening up there, I'll need backup.

I glance at Adam, ready to give him his instructions, when several rounds of rifle fire blare across the sea. Okay, there's no hiding it. I adopted my five-year-old half-brother and five minutes later, immediately brought him into the line of rifle fire. I may have to pray before my son is born if I'm going to be such a horrible father already.

"Below deck," I tell him, "Hurry."

The boy's Greek and he knows mafia families, so my guess is he understands gunfire. I grab a shitty revolver for my pocket and a sawn-off shotgun I got during our last weapons run in Ethiopia. It's a beauty, but I don't have time to admire the gun... I race toward the house.

Six minutes… five minutes…

Twenty-million thoughts race through my head. I have no plan. I meant to do this with a plan. But now I'm heading into danger. And if Latrice knew what the hell I was doing, she definitely wouldn't approve. I hop the fence…

Three minutes…

My heart beats so loudly that I can't hear my breath. I can't hear anything at all. Instinct courses through me when I push the front door of the house open. I hear an argument, but I don't register all the faces in the room, although every face surprises me. I fire four shots from my revolver into the air and they all scream.

My entire family is brawling in the center of the living room. Odin has his mouth wrapped around Yiayia's leg. Fallon and Stavros are holding back Tisha. Latrice is holding back Loukas — rather miserably — with Antonio's help. Papa's desperately attempting to drag Odin off Yiayia and none of these people should be here. I made this plan in secret?!

Now that I've stopped them from all brawling and given them more than a moment to react, there's a wave of clicking as we all draw our weapons and my grandmother's assassination attempt becomes another family argument where we all point our guns at each other.

"You shoot that damn dog and I will pop you," Latrice yells at Papa, who lowers his gun because Tisha has her gun pressed into his head.

"Yeah," Tisha says. "And say sorry for pinching my ass, you stinky old pervert!"

Fallon and Stavros have given up on holding back Tisha, but they keep their weapons pointed at Yiayia, who screams loudly after Tisha's comment.

"I'M DYING! THAT DOG WON'T LET GO! AHHHHHH!"

"MAMA!" Papa yells, but Tisha cocks her gun and Loukas joins her on the other side of his father, pressing a revolver to Papa's head.

"Fuck with my wife, you fuck with me."

"You'd kill your own father, eh?" Papa says, resigned. He blubbers and then wails, "I'm sorry, mama! I will pray for you every day. I will pray at your grave."

"I'M NOT DEAD," Yiayia protests.

She turns desperately to me, ignoring my blank face, "GALANOS. YOUR HAIR! IT'S HIDEOUS. BUT HELP ME!"

Antonio chuckles and then blurts out, "Should I help her?"

Loukas glowers at him, and Antonio laughs. "I'm just joking. Yiayia, this is for calling me The F-Word last Christmas."

He puts up his middle finger and nods at me. "Galanos? You have this under control. My feet hurt."

Not exactly helpful, but not sabotage either, so I'll take it.

Antonio struts off, but his comment enrages me. No. I have nothing under my control. This was a simple assassination attempt and now every single one of my family members is here and my dog just let go of Yiayia's leg, which now spurts blood as she emits another shriek and then a dramatic groan.

"Fine," she says, "Leave me here to die."

Odin yaps a few times and then snarls. Loukas glances at Stavros and sighs, "We can't, can we."

"Um… yes, we can!?" the rest of us blurt out. Except Stavros.

"I mean… we can't kill her here," Stavros says, "We ought to kill her in Thessaloniki."

The room is quiet for a few more seconds until Fallon chimes in.

"Yes. She should at least die there," Fallon agrees.

Tisha shrugs. Latrice is the last to lower her weapon. After I nod at her and let her know it's okay.

Tisha blurts out, "So that's it? We're taking her back to Greece?"

"Take me to a hospital!" Yiayia shrieks at the top of her lungs. "PLEASE! A HOSPITAL!"

We don't take her to a hospital, but we get a doctor. Lou and Stavros scare Papa off. For good. I still haven't told my brothers about my brother. And I think I ought to confess Adam's existence soon. I also need to check on him. I pace urgently until the doctor arrives.

Latrice, Fallon, and Tisha help him attend to Yiayia, although they're all skittish around her. Yiayia tells the doctor that we violently abuse her, and she accuses Stavros of raping her and Tisha of sodomizing her.

Tisha tells the doctor that she has serious dementia, which shuts Yiayia up and successfully thwarts her plan to get us all shipped to an Athens prison. I pull Stavros and Loukas aside.

"I have a problem," I whisper to them.

"We solved your problem for you," Stavros grunts.

Loukas nods agreeably and explained, "We have her. All we have to do is kill her. Work up the courage to kill the most terrifying woman alive. She'll definitely haunt us."

Stavros snickers, "Trust me, she already haunts us."

The women aren't the only skittish ones.

"That's not my problem. My problem is... I have a brother."

"You have two brothers. And Papa probably has several more bastards."

"It's my mother's child. I... rescued him."

"Where is he?"

"My boat."

"You brought him to an assassination?" Loukas says. He's unable to help himself and thinks that because he's older, his criticism of me is automatically relevant. I give him an unimpressed look.

"I didn't plan a rescue. And you brought my dog to an assassination."

"Latrice has been training him to pick up Yiayia's scent," Loukas says, "She claims he was necessary."

"You let her come here," I snapped, "I should kill you for that alone."

"Let?!" Stavros snarls. "Do you think we control these women? They control us... Now don't let them hear us... Where is this child...?"

"Don't let us hear what?" Tisha says, popping out from behind Loukas with a terrifyingly curious expression on her face.

"Nothing, my angel," Lou says, turning around and kissing her, "Nothing to worry about at all."

"You're being sus."

"We're helping Galanos out of a tight spot," Stavros says.

He points at Latrice. And I know what he's saying. I have to tell her I adopted a five-year-old boy. And I do not know how she'll react...

FIFTY
LATRICE PAGONIS

The doctor gives Yiayia sleeping pills — a gift for us after she calls him a beta-male who can't keep his toupee on without super glue. The man asked her if she smoked, and that was her response. It only surprises me he didn't knock her out himself.

Greek doctors for our family learn discretion quickly or they suffer the consequences. Stavros drives the rest of the family down to the boat. Not my boat, but the one we're taking back to Greece.

I need to take Latrice to my boat now and meet up with Adam. She's eager to meet him and not angry at all. I step over blood on the floor from Odin's attack and open the fridge to find some of Yiayia's good snacks for Odin. Latrice looks worried.

"Why are you looking at me like that?"

"Aren't you mad at me for lying and telling everyone your secret so we could get ahead of your assassination attempt?"

"No. Hold the cheese."

She holds the cheese and rolls her eyes.

"Don't you get upset about anything?"

"Yes. Plenty of things. Latrice. We have a son."

"What? Galanos... we don't know if it's a boy or a girl yet and shut up, we haven't told your family yet..."

"I adopted a son. He's my biological half-brother, and I adopted him from my mother."

Latrice knows me so well that she asks the only question I want anyone to ask. "How was it seeing her?"

I sigh and lean against the fridge.

"I don't do feelings well," I answer. "That's all you want to know."

"Okay. So the half-brother? Is he safe?"

She's not angry either. All she cares about is that a hurt child is safe. I could have used her in my life when I was younger. I need her now to keep me human and safe.

"He's on my boat. We'll get him and then we'll head to the super-yacht. I just... I know it's a lot. You're pregnant but... he's innocent, and he deserves better."

"I think it's sweet you'd want to help. Seriously."

She kisses me and I feel all my worry fall away. Even so, I've failed her. Because Yiayia's still alive. If my siblings hadn't been there, I would have done it. I know I would have. But I don't want them to see how much of a monster she's made of me. Latrice... I'm not angry with her. I know why she did this... but I need to face this beast on my own.

"You cut your hair."

"Am I hideous now?"

"No. But you look strange... like Eminem."

"That's an insult. I'm going to kill myself."

"Don't say that!"

"Sorry."

She leans against me and kisses me again.

"We'd better get Adam," she whispers. "Come on. I want to meet this little Galanos."

And I have a plan.

Latrice, Odin and Adam instantly fall for each other. Latrice is excellent with him. They stand on the edge of the boat as I drive us to the super-yacht. Odin barks, and Latrice dazzles Adam with tales of Thessaloniki. They're hugging each other and planning a trip to the beach by the time Stavros and Loukas lift my boat to the yacht, and the four of us climb aboard.

Fallon and Tisha emerge from one of the back bedrooms, scowling.

"She's in bed, but she's running a fever," Fallon says, "It might be the bite."

"It's definitely the bite," Tisha mutters, "But she's tied up."

"We're tying up an old woman with a fever, how far have we fallen..." Stavros grumbles.

"To be fair," Loukas counters, "She deserves it."

We all nod and mutter that she does indeed deserve it. Latrice sighs and says, "I don't know how to say this, but it's exactly what Galanos would do... Screw, Yiayia! I'm pregnant, everyone!"

Tisha makes an inhuman squeal while Fallon gives a heart congratulations. We all hug her, and Odin barks with delight for a reason only a dog could understand. Adam hangs back a little, which I notice. I pull away from my family members and approach him, crouching.

"Hey. You okay?"

"Scared."

"You have nothing to fear."

"I want Latrice to play," he mutters.

Latrice hears her name and comes over. She grins and Adam smiles back. He wraps his arms around her. Latrice hangs out with Adam until he falls asleep. The rest of us take turns checking on Yiayia and making sure she stays medicated. I tire my family out every time it isn't my turn, talking relentlessly, making jokes and hoping... no, praying... that they all go to bed early.

I came to Lemnos to do something and I plan to do it. Fallon and Stavros fall asleep first. Stavros hasn't slept, and he has a dull sounding conversation with a fake plant. Tisha and Loukas make out until Antonio excuses himself to his room. Tisha drags Loukas upstairs.

Adam's already tucked into bed when Latrice approaches me and takes my hand. I know an excellent way to get her to fall asleep quickly, but she seems to have seen my scheme coming a mile away.

"I know what you're doing," she whispers.

"Do you?"

"You've been at it all day. You're transparent to me. I'm your wife."

"Go to bed, kitten. Let me do what I must."

"Alone?" she whispers. "Is that really what you want?"

I press her body against mine, loving her softness. Her lips press against mine and I want to sink into them and forget the terrible things that I must do to protect my family.

"I am not alone," I whisper. "I am devoted to you. To our family."

I press her stomach and Latrice gasps.

"Okay," Latrice says, "I understand. You need to do this alone. But after that, we're a proper family."

"You don't think Adam spoils it, then?"

"Children don't spoil our lives," she answers. "I've always wanted kids. I don't care how I get them. If he needs parents, we'll be his parents."

Her answer tugs at my heart. I have to do this for her now more than ever. I have to make sure that we live a safe and happy life. I owe it to my brothers. Yiayia nearly killed Tisha, she had Carlotta kidnapped, and she humiliated Fallon, intending to kill her, too. She won't stop until she punishes us for the crime of marrying women of a different race.

"Go to bed, kitten. Please," I murmur.

This is my burden. My job. I helped Yiayia so many times when I ought to have helped my brothers. Since Latrice, I've changed. I will give them this gift and plead for their forgiveness and hers.

"Tell me what you're going to do," she begs, "Let me know if I should help."

"Sleep. For me. For the family. Let me do the work I must do."

She takes Odin to our bedroom, and the ship is quiet. I visit my grandmother's room, shutting the door behind me and locking it. She's strapped to the bed and her eyes are closed, but she knows it's me.

"Galanos... you've come to free me," she whispers.

It's not like I expected her to change in her last minutes alive. Her breath is soft and I can't help but notice how weak she sounds. I don't feel like a monster, even if I know what I'm about to do. I spared a life already. Talia doesn't deserve her life, and I spared it, so I can't face judgment for this.

I tell my grandmother the last truth I want her to know about me. We have no scores to settle anymore.

I say to her, "I've married Latrice. We're having a child."

"Worthless..." she breathes.

"Yes," I tell her, "I may be worthless. But at least in five minutes, I'll be alive."

Her eyes snap open and she fights against the restraints gently, hoping that I won't notice. She turned me into a monster who couldn't help but notice.

"Don't," she commands.

"Yiayia, you are not in a position to command me. And believe me, I am very sorry for what I'm going to do. I promise you, it will be painless and dignified."

She scowls and hisses, "Too weak..."

I rip the pillow from beneath her head. She groans as her head rolls back and she laughs.

"Much too weak," she whispers.

"All you had to do was love us."

"I made this family strong," she whispers, "I tried."

I approach the bed, and she laughs. Louder this time. I don't bother telling her to stop laughing. I won't deny a dying woman her wish. She dies in exactly four minutes. I sit back against the door, my heart pounding.

I killed her. I really killed her. Her head turns to the side and her Aegean blue eyes bore into mine.

"Yiayia," I whisper, as if she can hear me. Maybe I'm testing to make sure she's dead. Sweat drips down my brow and I feel sick to my stomach. I don't think I enjoy killing. I don't. But this is the only way to keep them safe. To keep us all safe.

It's late and I'm alone when I wrap her in a blanket and throw her overboard with blocks from beneath the kitchen sink tied in her shroud. She's light, frail and incredibly dead. But there's no joy in burying bodies. Especially not hers. For all her cruelty, she was there for me. When no one else was.

I bite back tears as I throw her over the side of the boat. The fall would have snapped her neck if she wasn't dead. I watch until she sinks, and then I slink upstairs to bed where Latrice waits. I slide next to her and she gurgles in her sleep as her monster wraps his arms around her and murmurs, "I have killed for you, kitten. I hope this makes up for everything I've put you through."

I surprise myself by easily falling asleep with my arms around Latrice Pagonis. My wife. I will never fail to keep her safe again.

A VERY PAGONIS RETURN TO THESSALONIKI

Several Months Later...

The girls will be here soon. Three months after getting my negative STD test results, my daughters will be born. Yiayia's funeral was incredible. The land disputes started before we could bring the empty coffin into the church.

Papa tried to assault the priest for saying that his mother "was" beautiful instead of "is" beautiful. Fallon fainted from exhaustion toward the end of the day. Loukas cried so much, you'd think he didn't want Yiayia dead. Tisha, Carlotta and Antonio took care of the twins the entire time.

Latrice tried looking after Odin, but he stole the collection plate out of the hands of the altar boy and escaped for the street. Poor Latrice waddled after him and nearly fell over, which nearly made me lock her in the dungeon until the due date.

She fights more than you'd think, so I don't end up locking her away.

Now, I watch her sleep and my fingers walk across the large protruding stomach. *Twins.* It doesn't seem like it ought to be possible for all of us to produce twins, but that's the way it happens when you're a Pagonis. Yiayia always used to say we were fertile people and apparently, she was right.

Adam sleeps with Odin in his new bedroom a few doors down and I have my very pregnant wife all to myself. I touch her stomach and feel movement. They move so much more now. I touch the soft curve of Latrice's belly and she groans.

"Galanos… your daughters won't stop kicking me."

"They're Pagonis girls. They're meant to be active."

"Do you think you could tell them to rest for a second. I didn't sleep a wink."

"I know," I whisper, kissing her cheek, "I've been watching you."

"All night?"

"I'm not sleeping until they're born."

"Don't you think you're a little overexcited, Galanos? They're coming. And you haven't slept in three days."

"I haven't done cocaine, either. So I count that as a victory."

Latrice sits up, sleep in her eyes and her belly resting between her legs as she struggles to get her bearings.

"It's creepy that you watch me sleep," she grumbles.

"I thought you liked it."

"We watched *Twilight* together once and now you think I want a man who watches me sleep?"

"I don't know what you want? A kiss, maybe?"

"A kiss would be nice."

I kiss her cheek and she sighs, ruffling my unnaturally short hair, which I've kept dyed for the time being.

"I miss the blond, you know."

"I'll dye it again for you."

"No," Latrice sighs, "Don't bother. You're pretty hot either way."

"Finally…"

"What?"

"We're married and you've never admitted you think I'm hot."

She rolls her eyes, assuming I'm exaggerating.

"You have five million people on the internet telling you that you're hot every single day."

"Who cares about them? I want to know my wife appreciates my exercise routine and attention to detail. It takes a lot of work to look perfect."

Latrice sighs and makes a soft yelp before her gorgeous dark brown eyes snap open... *wide.*

"What's going on?"

"Galanos... I think it's... contractions. I think the girls are coming."

"But they were due yesterday."

"They didn't get born yesterday," Latrice says, pointing out the obvious with an angry beaver face.

I touch her belly and then look at her in terror.

"Are you sure?"

"ADAM!" Latrice calls, "ADAM! Can you snap Galanos out of his panic."

"I'm not panicking!"

"Why did you grab your gun?!"

Oh, yeah. I did. Instinctively, I reached over for it, but the last thing we need for Latrice to give birth to these babies is a gun. *Shit.*

Adam bursts into the room, dragging the prepared suitcase behind him.

"Gal! Put the gun down!" Adam says, "Take the bag."

The little boy speaks with all the authority of a Pagonis, even if we don't share a father. I think. I take the bag and Latrice demands her cellphone from the nightstand. Adam brings it to her and she calls Stavros and Loukas.

"He's panicking! Call in the reinforcements."

"I am NOT PANICKING!" I yell, firing three shots into the ceiling.

"GALANOS!" Latrice says, "YOUR DAUGHTERS DON'T NEED A STARTING GUN OWWWWWWW..."

"ADAM. WE NEED TO FIX HER. HOLY SHIT I'M PANICKING..."

Okay, I mess up a bit here. I start thinking about the ten thousand reasons I'm not ready to be a father and I blurt them all out until Latrice yells one last time, "Galanos! We rehearsed. The midwife's on the way and the hospital room is literally one floor down. Breathe!"

"I should be the one helping you!"

"Then help!"

We go back and forth like that for a while, but I eventually Get Latrice settled before the band of Pagonis family members and midwives come in. Fallon and Tisha go to be with Latrice, who doesn't want me anywhere near her. I pace anxiously with Odin. My brothers try to comfort me, but they're idiots and they do a horrible job.

Stavros solemnly says, "If you're lucky, they'll get Latrice's facial features. She doesn't have such a large head."

Loukas nods along and points out that at least my height makes up for my enormous head. *Brothers.* Cass and Helen wait at home for news and in case anything goes wrong. Carlotta's with Papa for the weekend in Italy on his new boat with seventeen of her newest "friends".

Blindness hasn't slowed down my niece's social calendar at all. The day moves in a blur until the midwife emerges with a brilliant smile on her face.

"Congratulations, Galanos. The baby girls are here. Latrice is holding them and she wants you to meet them."

My heart pounds and I am nearly too scared to enter the room. My daughters... my beautiful, perfect daughters. I have gone through hell to make sure they don't live in terror and fear the way we have. It burns how much I love them before even meeting them.

It *scares* me.

I push the door open and Latrice drips in sweat, with an excited smile on her face. Baby girls, one in each arm, look like tiny loaves of bread against her chest.

I can't help myself. I love them so much, I start crying. And it's like all the feelings that I'd ever suppressed come out. I steady my shaking as I hold my daughter. My first born in one arm and the midwife hands me the other.

"Girls..." I whisper, "They're our girls..."

"Layla and Athena Pagonis," Latrice says, "Just like we agreed. We did it, Galanos."

"You did all the work," I whisper, "Now it's my turn. To love them. To protect them. To keep them safe."

"You loved me," Latrice said, "You protected me. So I know you'll do the same for them and for our family."

"I love you," I whisper, to all of them, finally free to mean it.

THE END.

Turn the page to start a new dark & spicy bwwm romance series FREE.

ABOUT JAMILA JASPER

The hotter and darker the romance, the better.

That's the Jamila Jasper promise.

If you enjoy sizzling multicultural romance stories that dare to *go there* you'll enjoy any Jamila Jasper title you pick up.

Open-minded readers who appreciate **shamelessly sexy romance novels** featuring black women of all shapes and sizes paired with smokin' hot white men are welcome.

Sign up for her e-mail list here to receive one of these FREE hot stories, exclusive offers and an update of Jamila's publication schedule:
bit.ly/jamilajasperromance

Get text message updates on new books:
https://slkt.io/gxzM

EXTREMELY IMPORTANT LINKS

ALL BOOKS BY JAMILA JASPER
https://linktr.ee/JamilaJasper
SIGN UP FOR EMAIL UPDATES
Bit.ly/jamilajasperromance
SOCIAL MEDIA LINKS
https://www.jamilajasperromance.com/
GET MERCH
https://www.redbubble.com/people/jamilajasper/shop
GET FREEBIE (VIA TEXT)
https://slkt.io/qMk8
READ SERIAL (NEW CHAPTERS WEEKLY)
www.patreon.com/jamilajasper

JAMILA
JASPER

Diverse Romance For Black Women

MORE JAMILA JASPER ROMANCE

<u>Pick your poison...</u>

Delicious interracial romance novels for all tastes. Long novels, short stories, audiobooks and more.

Hit the link to experience my full catalog.

FULL CATALOG BY JAMILA JASPER:
https://linktr.ee/JamilaJasper

DARK MAFIA ROMANCE PREVIEW #1

Sample these chapters from my best-selling Amalfi Coast Brotherhood Italian mafia romance series while you wait for my upcoming romance series.

If you enjoy dark & twisted mafia romance stories, you can binge the entire completed series on your eReader.

Enjoy the free chapters.

Click here to sign up for text messages about my new release: bit.ly/textjamila

A BWWM DARK MAFIA ROMANCE

FORCED TO
Surragate

JAMILA JASPER

DESCRIPTION

The last thing Jodi remembered was a shot of tequila.
Next thing she knows,
Italian sociopath Van Doukas has her chained in his basement...
And he's claiming she agreed to become the mother of his child.

There's a detailed contract and everything... with her signature.
Jodi will do whatever it takes to get away from him...
But she doesn't count on the 6'7" Italian Stallion being skilled with
his tongue and excellent in bed.

SERIES TITLES

Forced To Surrogate
Forced To Marry
Forced To Submit

CONTENT AWARENESS

dark bwwm mafia romance

This is a mafia romance story with dark themes including potentially triggering content, frank discussions and language surrounding bedroom scenes and race. All characters in this story are 18+. Sensitive readers, be cautioned about some of the material in this dark but extremely hot romance novel. The character in this story is **forced by circumstance** into her situation.
Enjoy the steamy romance story...

ONE
PRODUCE A PURE ITALIAN HEIR

VAN DOUKAS

There aren't enough cigarettes in the world for meetings with my father. The boss. Tonight, I meet with him to discuss something 'very important'. He calls everything 'very important', but tonight, I know exactly what he wants from me.

He wants me to kill again, this time for my foolish sister, who can't seem to keep herself out of trouble. Everyone in the family heard about what happened to Ana by now. That idiot Jew was foolish enough to put his hands on her with witnesses and expect nothing to happen? That's not how the Doukas family works, which he'll soon learn.

You mess with the Doukas family, we retaliate. If the Jew had any wits about him, he would disappear from the Amalfi Coast and head for the mountains or Sicily, or somewhere we don't have ears. He could go to Albania like Matteo. Maybe then we wouldn't find him. But fuck, I don't want to carry out another hit. Why can't that lazy fuck Enzo do it? Or better yet, Eddie. I carried out my first hit when I was two years younger than him. We spoil the new generation and wonder why our family falls apart.

None of this would be my responsibility if Matteo would get over himself and come down off his fucking mountain.

I stop my motorcycle and approach my father's front door. The all white old European style mansion sits on an excessive and opulent lot on the coast, right above the cliffs with a long path to the beach, a 'fuck you' to the tax collectors and the government who want to stop us from doing business.

Most of my siblings still live here, but I prefer keeping myself far away from papa and his... associates.

I can hear the party from the entrance. Seriously? On a fucking Tuesday afternoon? I assumed he called this meeting because he was working for once. He's intertwined in a different business based on the noise filtering outside. Please, Lord, let me not walk in on my father having sex with a model... *again*.

I open the front door to our old family home without knocking and immediately regret it when a completely naked foreign woman runs giggling toward the door, too high and drunk to feel self-conscious, exposing her completely nude body to a stranger. At least I didn't find her twisted in bed with papa, although this isn't much better.

"Oh! Good afternoon, sir!" she teases me in crude Italian, spinning around to show off her assets. *Whore. Foreigner. Her tricks possess little interest to me.* My brothers Lorenzo and Matteo would sway more easily.

"Where's my father?"

She giggles and spins around again. Fucking hell, I wish the ground would swallow me up. My father's prostitutes do not interest me.

"Your papa?" she says, standing to face me with her legs slightly apart, daring me to ogle more of her body. I have no interest in whores and I want her to answer my fucking question.

Before I can answer, another one of my father's toys saunters into the foyer, naked. This one is young—she looks eighteen just about—far too young for my father. I grimace and keep my gaze firmly fixed away from the nude females. Just because the men in my family are bastards doesn't mean I have to follow suit.

If we don't conduct ourselves with respect, how can we expect the respect of the Amalfi Coast?

"Yes. My father. Sal," I grunt, failing to hide the irritation in my voice.

The woman ignores my irritated tone with her response.

"Oh, he's in the back with Boyka. I can take you there after we take you to bed upstairs."

How much is he paying these women? We're still struggling to get Jalousie off the ground and he spends all his money on Slavic hookers.

"Not interested. I have a meeting with him."

"Are you sure?"

I don't dignify them with a response. I walk past the girls, keeping my eyes away from their bodies. Where the hell is my father? I pass the long hallway with the family portraits and follow the loud music and the louder giggling from near the pool. The familiar sound of pool jets betrays papa's location.

He's in the fucking hot tub again, I know it. He spends all fucking day in the hot tub, dishing out orders and expecting work to happen without him lifting a fucking finger. It's a fucking miracle anything gets done around here.

My father chuckles loudly, and I brace myself before approaching him. He's the boss and you don't question the boss, even if he's your father and even if he cares more about partying and women than our family — than our future.

When I enter the back patio, the pungent smell of tobacco and marijuana surrounds me. Judging by the bottles of vodka on the ground, the piles of cigarette butts and the other piles of detritus, they've been at this fucking party since last night.

Fuck. I put the cigarette tucked behind my ear into my mouth and approach my father's outdoor speakers, unplugging them and stopping the little dance party happening around his hot tub. Three women, each wearing next to nothing with their tits out belly dance for him while he chuckles loudly, his fat stomach causing waves in the hot tub. When the music stops, they stop too and look up at me indignantly.

They don't have to ask who I am. The ones who don't know Van Doukas can tell that I'm related to Sal. I have my father's eyes, but thankfully, I don't have his overweight body or his bald head. The girls make booing sounds at me, but I brush them off.

"I'm here for our meeting," I say sternly to papa.

He chuckles and nods. "Yes. The meeting. I almost forgot."

Almost? He doesn't look like he's fucking prepared for a meeting.

Papa dismisses the girls, except for one — Boyka. She slides into the hot tub next to him, twirling his thick plumes of chest hair around her fingers and sliding his freshly cut cigar between his lips. Nauseating. Papa coughs after a puff and taps the cigar over the edge of the hot tub.

"You're early."

"I'm twenty minutes late."

"Oh?"

"Papa, you said it was important. Shouldn't we conduct this business alone?"

None of the girls are dumb enough to rat on Salvatore Doukas, but unlike my father, I don't see the sense in taking risks.

Boyka's hand moves down my father's chest and I don't want to imagine what sorry shriveled part of him she touches next. I just want my orders so I can get the fuck out of this bachelor pad.

"I'm getting old, Van," he says. "I'm getting old."

He didn't call me down here to bitch about his old age. I furiously puff on my cigarette, waiting for him to get to the fucking point. Papa grunts as Boyka touches something... sensitive. Cristo...

Watching my father grunt through a hand job might be the only thing worse than watching him stick it to a woman.

"Do you mind postponing your fucking hand job until later?"

Boyka's hand rises guiltily from the water and I choke down bile.

She really was touching the old fuck. I shouldn't swear at him or set him off. Papa might seem old, but he can have me killed. Any of my brothers would do it if he gave the command. Tread carefully, Van.

"Maybe I should leave," Boyka says, giving me a flirty glance as she plays with her tiny pink nipples.

"Yes," I snap. "Please get the fuck out of here."

Papa scowls. "Be respectful, Van. Boyka is a very dear—"

"I said please."

Papa smirks. "Boyka, return in thirty minutes. If we're not done..."

"We'll be done," I interrupt, glowering at my father. I don't have all afternoon for his games when I have the club to attend to.

Boyka reluctantly leaves.

"Are the women in this house allergic to fucking clothes?"

"None of them are allergic to fucking anything."

I'm not doing this with the old man today.

"Why did you call me here?"

I start another cigarette. I keep swearing I won't touch another, then I spend five minutes around papa and change my mind.

He leans back in the hot tub, displacing several pints of water over the edge.

"I'm tired, Van," he groans, leaning back and rubbing his forehead.

"From working?"

My father doesn't pick up on the sarcasm. He hardly leaves his fucking hot tub anymore, and he hasn't done anything even remotely resembling working at either of the nightclubs, restaurants, apartment complexes or construction sites around town.

If it wasn't for me and Enzo, he wouldn't have the fucking time to boink Boyka or whatever the fuck he does with all these young Slavic women.

I still have to tread carefully around him. He's still my father, my boss, and I must obey him.

"Yes," he says, coughing. "From working. I need someone to take my place and lead the family soon. I want to retire, Van. You and I both know I need a break."

He spends every fucking day on vacation while his sons and nephews run his businesses. Vacation? We're the ones who need a fucking vacation.

"Perhaps you should contact Matteo about that."

My older brother spent his entire life preparing to be the boss. It's not my fault he fucked off, leaving his worthless children with us, I might add. I'm already halfway through my fucking cigarette and he hasn't closed in on the point.

Papa scoffs. "Matteo hasn't left Albania in four years. He left his children, his business, his fucking money, and he's not coming back. Give up on him."

"You're the one who trained him for the role. Send Enzo after him. Better yet, send his fucking son."

I don't want to go into the mountains to bring my jackass older brother back and I don't want to have this conversation with my father.

"Why don't you go to Albania?"

"Every time I'm in the same room as Matteo, he tries to kill me," I remind papa. I love Matteo, but he isn't exactly easy to get along with.

I'm surprised a woman tolerated him long enough to allow him to give her Eddie.

"Fair. But I need a replacement, Van. I don't want to be the boss anymore. I can't take the stress much longer."

Stress? What stress? Does my father seriously think sitting in his fucking hot tub banging whores counts as a job?

"Have you considered the role?" He asks before I can spew something disrespectful in my father's direction.

"Why would I want to be the boss of this fucking family? It's filled with degenerates, fuck-ups, people who need more violence to be kept in line. I kill enough as it is. You don't want me to be the boss and nobody in this fucking family wants me as the boss."

"People respect you, Van."

"People fear me. There's a difference."

Papa nods. "Exactly. Personally, I think you would make a good boss."

"I disagree."

But I don't completely. Yes, the job would be horrific and I'd have even more blood on my hands than I do now by the end. I could bring honor back to our family, clean the streets of our scum, stop the Jews from fucking with our shit... but I can't. Not with Matteo gone. Even in the fucking Albanian countryside, he would find out what I did and Matteo would kill me.

"No," Papa replies calmly. "You don't. But I agree with your assessment that you're not quite ready."

"I never said that. I said I didn't want the job."

Nobody smart wants my father's job. He spent twenty years walking around with a target on his back before he built up enough trust, enough loyalty, enough captains in the streets of Italy to ensure his safety. I don't want to lose my freedom.

"You didn't have to say anything. I know my son."

"Hm."

Arguing with my father is entirely senseless.

"You need an heir, Van."

"What?"

"I will give you the leadership of this family without the ritual, without the sacrifice and without the financial investment required. All I want is an heir."

"Why don't I go up to fucking Albania, then? Because I can't produce a child out of thin air."

Papa chuckles. "Don't you have women? If you want a woman... I filled this house with them. I have very young ones too. Eighteen. Nineteen. They make good mothers."

"I am not interested in fucking teenagers."

"Then find a whore like that old Greek Pagonis fuck. I don't care how you get the heir. You can prove how serious you are by giving me a child. I'll be generous. I'll give you a year."

"I don't want this role," I snap. "So the likelihood I'll produce an heir is slim."

Papa laughs, which only infuriates me further. There's nothing funny about bringing a child into the world.

"You can't lie to me, Van. You were always the most ambitious child. Maybe it's because you were smack in the middle and we didn't pay any attention to you. Who fucking knows?"

My father spent little time raising any of us, except for Enzo, and look how that fucking turned out.

"Thank you for the psychoanalysis."

Every time I visit my father, my desire for alcohol increases exponentially, along with my cravings for nicotine. He brings the worst out of everyone, especially me.

"No problem," he says, again ignoring my sarcasm.

"What happens if I don't produce an heir? Eh? You still need someone to take your place."

"I make this offer to Lorenzo if you don't produce what I want."

"What?" I would have at least expected him to mention one of our cousins, one of the very obedient captains from the northern coast, or even fucking Eddie, Matteo's 18-year-old son, would be better than my irresponsible fuck of a brother. That old fuck really knows me well because he just said the only thing that could get me to reconsider his stupid fucking offer.

"You heard me."

"Lorenzo would ruin this family. For fun."

"I know. And it would become your responsibility to save it. You would have to act as the boss to save Lorenzo from himself. You might as well earn the position."

Fuck this old man...

"I don't want a family life, papa. I don't want the fucking wife or the fucking family. I want this life. It's what I'm good at. Business. Killing. More killing. That's who you taught me to be."

I'm not a man who can picture himself kicking around a football with my children or taking them to the beach. I'm not built for seducing women for more than a night and dealing with the danger of introducing them to my life or worse, hiding it the way papa did with our mother.

He can pretend it's not his fault what happened to her, but we all know the truth. No woman deserves our life. I can't afford to react. He loves when he can draw a reaction out of me.

Papa continues, as if my reaction is irrelevant. "Part of this life means having a family. I can't expect my other children to carry on my bloodline."

"Matteo has a son. You have a fucking bloodline. Why don't you make him the fucking boss?"

"Eddie? Eddie will not survive long the way he lives."

"That's a way to talk about your grandson, eh?"

"Have another cigarette, Van."

I'm already on my fucking third. But I'm not in a position to turn down his offer, considering the shit he wants me to deal with right now. An heir? I thought he wanted me to kill someone. Producing an heir in a year... It's just fucking impossible. I stick the cigarette in my mouth and light it.

"You can't let the family fall apart. We aren't the only people who would suffer. What would happen to our people, good Italian people, when the only people around they can get money from are the fucking Jews, who hate our guts?" He says.

I can't let his guilt trip work on me.

"I want an heir."

"Hm."

"Consider what you would sacrifice by turning down my offer, Van. It's not just about the family. It's power. You act like you're a fucking saint, but you are my son. You enjoy power. You're just too much of a stuck up cunt to let yourself enjoy it."

"Thanks papa."

"You're welcome. Now, onto the matter of the Jew."

Fuck. I hoped my father would only piss me off one way today, but if we're discussing the matter of the Jew, I won't leave here tonight without an assignment. Someone else could easily do this job, but he wants me to kill. Because I'm good at it.

"I suppose none of my other brothers have the free time to do this?"

"I don't care. I need you to do it. The cunt offended this family."

"Perhaps we waste too much time retaliating for every offense. Ana told you to drop it."

I'm taking a risk just questioning his order, but he's pissed me off so much that I stopped caring.

"Decision making isn't women's work. It's our work. The man signed his own death warrant. I want it done soon. Call me when you finish the job."

"Hm."

"If you don't like the way I run this family, Van, you know what to do. I want to retire. Make an old man happy."

Drugs and whores are the only things that make my father happy.

"An heir," I scoff. "You want me to have a fucking bastard child to continue your bloodline? A bastard won't have any loyalty to his family. Children have a mother and a father, a mother they spend all their time with. If I fuck some poor woman, you won't have an heir. You'll have a problem on your hands."

"Then get creative. If you need to get the baby and kill the mother, do what you must."

What's happening to this family? When did we lose our way and talking about murdering women for our own ends? Papa… This life changed him. It was slow, but it changed him completely. Too bad there's no getting out.

"Thank you for the advice."

"You're welcome. Now get Boyka back in here and get the fuck out. I need relief."

"Good evening, papa."

I drop my cigarette on the ground without bothering to step on it. Maybe my father's right — it's time for him to retire. But how the fuck will I get an heir? I need help.

There's one person I can call on for assistance in these matters. I don't like involving the Greeks in Italian business, but... they're our cousins. She answers after a few rings and it sounds like she's at a nightclub. She has an inordinate amount of time for parties...

"Ciao?"

I can barely hear her over the sound of the music.

"Miss Pagonis. It's Van."

She giggles. "Duh. What's happening? You finally have work for me?"

"How soon can you come back to Italy?"

Click here to learn more about where to buy the book:
https://www.jamilajasperromance.com/blog/forced-to-surrogate

MAFIA PLAYMATE
PREVIEW #2

https://bit.ly/bostonirishmafia1

BOSTON IRISH MAFIA ROMANCE SERIES

Mafia Playmate

Mafia Property

Mafia Surrogate

Mafia Possession

Mafia Stalker

Click here for the complete collection:

www.jamilajasperromance.com/catalog

CONTENT AWARENESS

Read this passage if you require content warnings for sensitive material. I do not give detailed content warnings that will spoil the plot, but be aware of this note.

This is a mafia romance story with dark themes including potentially triggering content of **all** varieties, violence, frank discussions and language surrounding bedroom scenes and race.
All characters in this story are 18+
Sensitive readers, be cautioned about some of the detailed romantic material in this dark but *extremely hot romance novel.*

DESCRIPTION

A large pink box arrives on Aiden's doorstep with a woman inside.
His mail-order bride arrives in her birthday suit and tied up in knots
with a pretty pink silk ribbon.

Aiden never requested a dark-skinned beauty...
His family would never approve of such an impure connection.

Who is this woman? What does she want?
A note in the box reveals the truth...
**The woman in the box - *Valentina* - is a gift from an anonymous
sender who wants something dark and twisted in return.**

CHAPTER
ONE
AIDEN

You have one job in the Murray family. You grow up, you get your marks, you listen to Pa, you marry a nice Irish girl, preferably a blond or a redhead with lighter features.
You do what Padraig Murray asks.
You pray everyday and you keep your rosary wrapped in your pocket. You stay loyal. You keep our bloodline strong.

Pa demands a meeting with me now that I'm back in the city. He claims it's important, but it can't be that important if he wants to meet me during the Red Sox game. It feels good to be home. There's something special about Boston, but maybe that's just it – paradise is wherever our family is.

After Pa, I'll go home and see Roscoe, my Rottweiler. Then get my shit together and call my younger brother Darragh to check in on his training and find out if Rian's around. Over the weekend, I'll head to Leominster to visit Callum and then Sunday after church, stop by to see Ma and Odhran. I brought a gift home with me for Tegan, Rian's daughter, and I can't wait to see my niece's face light up when I give it to her.

If there's one thing I don't miss about being home, it's a never ending list of shit to do.

I meet my father at our usual casual meeting spot, Mulligan's, a place where we aren't afraid to celebrate Irish pride. A place where you can catch the Red Sox game and no one can catch your conversation. *It's as much home as anywhere else.*

I spot my father hunched over the bar from the street, his face illuminated by a warm orange bulb as he watches the pre-game announcer talk. I prefer football to baseball, but Pa bets on all their games, so he likes to keep his eye on the Red Sox each season.

When Pa calls, you answer, and he's desperate to know about the affair with the Italians – what the fuck happened, have I found the renegade cousins who pissed off the Italians, and whether I've killed them yet. *I haven't.*

It's all bad news and my ass is on the line if I don't find a way to sort out all the shit that happened in Long Island. At least we're guaranteed peace with the vicious Italians. *Those greaseballs aren't any better than the blacks. 'Trust 'em as far as you can throw them', Pa told me. But for now, we have peace and that's what matters. At least to me.*

I enter Mulligan's and the conversations fall to a hush. *Aiden Murray's back.* I clear my throat and the conversations continue. But there are more phones pulled out than before and two guys sitting in the back leave. I don't hate the reputation I have. Most of the bar fights I earned this cutthroat reputation in were Darragh's fault, but that doesn't change what people say about me.

Darragh, my younger brother, can still throw his weight around in the ring, but he got his practice here, in this fucking place. Our last fight here was over a girl. Darragh kicked some Puerto Rican's ass and a few of our boys jumped him outside... I don't know what happened to the guy after.

My father slides a twenty-dollar bill across the bar to the

bartender, Finnegan O'Malley, a one-eared ex-hitman, who in turn fills up two glass pints of amber Sam Adams. Pa's already several drinks ahead of me. *Great. The news can't be that bad then.*

I pull out a bar stool next to my father, who barely acknowledges me, although he must've caught me entering the bar through the reflection on the glass behind the bartender. He shoves one of the pints across the bar towards me. He knows I prefer Guinness, but I don't mind starting with this. I can see my dad's reflection in the glass. He looks older than I remember. He's pushing 70, so I shouldn't be surprised by the large streaks of gray through his slick hair which was once blond, but changed color throughout his life, settling on a dark chocolate brown, like Rian's.

I glance at the television to check the score, but the game hasn't even started yet. I can smell the alcohol coming off of him already.

"You can have a Guinness after you drink this," he says. "I heard you did good work with the Italians."

He sounds raspy, but calm. My tension dissipates. This is just a normal, father-son meeting. Nothing to worry about.

"I didn't find Eoin or Robert. Haven't heard fuck since they all screwed with Vicari," I say as I take a sip of my beer.

"Maybe the Italians killed them," he says. "They're a violent, vicious group of people."

"Yeah."

Like we're ones to talk. Pa's done with his Sam Adams already and waits patiently for me to catch up, as if I could catch up to a man who's been drinking for an hour. At forty, it's not so easy for me to keep up with long nights of drinking. I don't know how he does it.

He waits for me to have a few more sips, his eyes glued to the television. Chris Sale throws the first pitch. It doesn't go so well. My father glances down at his glass and sighs. "It's going to be a long night."

"That bad this season?" I grunt, glancing up at the Detroit batter sliding into second.

I've been too busy to keep up with baseball. My father grunts. Yeah, it has been that bad.

"Any other news?" I ask him, finishing off the Sam Adams. Dad grunts and snaps his fingers for the bartender, Finnegan. The buff, tattooed bartender hustles over as dad orders two Guinnesses without opening his mouth. Bad news if he's drinking Guinness.

"Cops got Rian last week. They're charging him with manslaughter."

Manslaughter?

"What did he do?"

"What the fuck do you think he did?" Dad responds calmly. "He killed somebody, they caught him. That boy's not careful enough and I have to pay to get his ass out of trouble. Maybe some prison time would do him good."

"That's what you said the first three times," I grunt. Sale throws a good pitch and my father's face visibly brightens.

"If it weren't for Tegan, I'd let him spend a few extra years behind bars," Dad confesses. "Your mother won't let me do that to his daughter."

"What's going to happen to her?"

"I don't know," my father says. "No one has seen the kid in a week."

"What?" I growl, sipping at my beer and hoping this is my father's idea of a joke since he sounds dangerously unconcerned.

"What do you mean no one's seen her? Is she with her ma?"

My father shrugs.

Rian's notoriously bad taste in women landed him with a child he should have never brought into the world. She's a sweet girl, but doomed by a mobster father and a whore mother.

Her ma doesn't live in Boston anymore. She wants nothing to do with Rian.

"Where does he say she is?"

"Last time he saw her was the night he got arrested," Pa says before taking a sip of his beer.

"What about the cops? Did they give her to his lawyer or something?"

I don't have a single paternal instinct in my body, but my mind courses with worry over Tegan, despite my father's calmness.

"She'll turn up," he says, pouring more alcohol down his throat.

Fuck, Rian. My brother must be an even worse parent than our father. His daughter's missing and he's behind bars and there's no one else to look for her except...

"I can find out where she is. Once I get Roscoe and take care of–

"It would serve him right if something happened to her," my father says coldly. "Her mother isn't Irish. He keeps fucking up. I'm tired of cleaning up his messes. Now *drink*. This is not why I asked you here."

I bristle at his comment, but it's just Padraig Murray. This is who he's always been and my brother should have had the good sense to keep his dick in his pants. I made it to forty without fathering bastards all over Boston. Rian should have been more careful. I drink a few more sips, but I can't let this go. *Who else will worry about the fucking kid if not me?*

"How the hell did Rian let this happen? Can I talk to him?"

"Best that none of us talk to him. The cops listen to everything. I can get messages into the prison and messages out, but I don't want you talking to him."

"Fine," I grunt, finishing off my first round of Guinness and ordering us another. I try to pay, but my father stops me and then finally answers my other question.

"Your idiot brother trusted a woman," he says. "He wants a mother for that little girl so badly, that he's willing to do anything. He's willing to kill for a woman who doesn't deserve him."

"I didn't know he had a woman," I grumble.

"*Had* is correct," Pa says. "She's dead."

I wish I could tell you a chill ran through me, or I had some other human response to my father's announcement. I don't need a university degree to understand what he's implying. Rian had a woman, she got him locked up, so my father had her killed.

"Will that affect his case?"

"No," Pa says. "It was very clean."

"Who?"

"None of your business, Aiden. You worry about your shit, I'll worry about your brother."

I want to feel sorry for Rian, but he deserves it for crossing our father. This is what happens when he pisses off Padraig Murray. More problems for all of us.

"How much time is he facing?"

"Three years since he's been in jail before. I tried to get that stupid motherfucker to get his life together, but your brother just wants to be a fuck up."

"Who's the lawyer?"

"Someone from Nigel & Bancroft."

At least he isn't cheaping out like he did for Rian's first case. I don't want to push my father's buttons, and despite his outward calm, he must be furious at Rian for drawing more attention to us, but Rian has his uses.

"It's Rian," I remind him. "Crazy fucking Rian. We need him out soon. There are some jobs only Rian has the balls to handle."

Padraig snorts. "He takes after my father. Too proud and too violent for his own good."

We created the monster Rian Murray is. He's our responsibility.

"He needs another woman."

"He needs a woman who isn't a fucking spic," my father spits. "At least the child looks white."

"What about this previous woman? What'd she look like?"

"It doesn't matter," he grunts. "She's dead. Now drink. We have more important things to talk about than your idiot brother and his shitty taste in women."

I drink because Pa commands it. I do everything he commands

and have since I was a child. I have the burns and scars to remind me of what happens when you disobey my father. At first, I hated him for what he did to me, but to keep an organization like ours together, you need to inspire fear.

You have to be cruel to survive – that's just how the world works. I can't let Tegan go. The second I see Darragh, I'll ask about her and track her down.

I drink so I don't lose my temper. He doesn't give a fuck about Tegan. No one does. Maybe he's wrong and one of my sisters took her in. But who would do that? Evie's saddled with her drunkard husband and two unruly kids of her own – Katie and Patrick. Kiara's off at university and Maeve's sixteen, too young to have any involvement.

"I need to tell you something important," my father says somberly, as if there could be something more important than my missing niece right now. I'm burning with desire to leave, but if I get up without my father's dismissal, he'll hurt me. Or someone I care about. Not like there are many of those people yet. It's foolish to get close to people in this life.

"Then tell me."

If he notices my tightening tone, my father doesn't acknowledge it.

"There's a plot against my life. I don't know who. I don't know why but… there's someone out there trying to kill me," my father says, the faded tattoos on his knuckles even more wrinkled than I last remember. He's getting older, but aside from his physical appearance, he shows no signs of slowing down. If anything, he's desperate to prove himself more. If he wasn't ordering more killings than necessary, maybe Rian wouldn't be locked up.

I don't want to dismiss his concerns as paranoid, but he's the leader of our family. There's always a plot against his life. It comes with the territory. My father doesn't have to worry because he has us. *Family.*

"Fuck that," I grunt. "No one would be stupid enough to try to kill you. April 2013, four days after the bombing. An entire decade ago. That's the last time anyone tried."

I was thirty back then, old enough to be the one who ended that war before it started. Back then, we only killed when necessary. I got five tattoos that year, one for each kill. Each a painful release, each representing a necessary act to keep my family safe.

My father smirks and keeps drinking. He shrugs. "That's what I thought. But I'm serious. This time is different. This time the bastards might just get me. I'm getting old, Aiden. Most guys in our line of work don't make it this far."

"What happened?" I grunt, urging my increasingly drunken father to get to the point. His cheeks blaze tomato red with alcohol and his blue eyes swim with tears, again brought on by drinking rather than any emotion. He grunts and knocks his biggest gold ring against the bar's surface contemplatively.

If anyone tried to kill him, surely Darragh would have mentioned it. He's responsible for keeping our father alive.

"I feel it in my bones," Pa replies. "Someone wants to destroy our family."

"Yes," I grumble. "Our cousins. But they're gone and if they were anywhere near this city, we would have heard about it."

"I don't know. Something big is coming for us. I feel it."

"We can make decisions based on feelings now?"

"Cut the shit, kid. You know my instincts are good because you're like me. You can smell shit before it hits the toilet bowl."

"I'm home. If anyone tries to kill you, they'll have to get through me, Darragh, and Callum."

My father smirks. "My boys. I'm proud of all of you. Except Rian. He's a piece of shit."

Ah, Padraig. Honest as fuck, especially when he's drunk.

He might not be proud of Rian, but he still loves my brother enough to spring for decent lawyers and to make sure Tegan goes to the best day school in Boston. Once she's old enough, she'll go to Milton or Dana Hall, or another nice private school where she can meet someone to untarnish her sullied blood, that is as long as I can find her. If Rian's behind bars, she could be anywhere. Hopefully not with her mom's people.

She belongs with us, even if Rian made mistakes. She looks like us and that's good enough to cover up his shameful behavior. I don't know what Rian was thinking with that Puerto Rican chick. Tegan's mother was low class.

Let's hope my brother's behavior doesn't come back to haunt all of us. Let's hope his daughter is safe, sound asleep somewhere and protected.

"Thanks, Pa," I mutter, uncomfortable with even this much emotional closeness between us. I love my father, but trusting him too much is dangerous. Rian found out the hard way that it isn't worth it to defy our family beliefs, and it definitely isn't fucking worth it to screw around with the wrong women.

"And Aiden? I need you to hurry the fuck up and find a wife. I'm getting old and I want to retire, but I need a family man to lead this family. You're the oldest. Why the fuck can't you keep a woman? Do I have to send you back to Galway?"

He wants a real answer.

"Not interested in chasing after girls, dad. All they want to do is take your money and ask where the fuck you're going. I've had enough."

"That old dog won't take care of you when you get old."

"Neither will some Boston snob who could take my ass to the cleaners in a divorce."

He laughs, which is the best reaction I can hope for. He quickly moves along to talking about the game and his plans for the business, and then asks me questions about Long Island. They're a mess out there, but doing better under John Vicari's leadership. We're developing a few buildings together and are prepared to make a lot of money in the real estate game. John does cleaner business than his father. Too bad the old man died of a heart attack... that's the word anyway.

"I need you to find a nice girl," my father reminds me once he's almost blackout drunk. He can barely keep his head up. *Great.* I'm not dragging his ass outta here tonight. If he wants to get so wasted he can't sit up straight, I'll leave him for Finnegan.

"We have this conversation every time we talk."

"This time, I'm serious. I want to retire. I don't want you bringing home no spics either like the Duffy boys."

"Fuck's sake, Pa. You can't talk like that around here anymore."

"I can say whatever the fuck I want. I want Irish children. Irish fucking children and I need you to have a wife so I can retire."

"Retire any old fucking day you want," I growl. "It'll be good for you to stop worrying about who I fuck or marry or the fate of the fucking family."

"The fate of the family matters," he says, taking another sip of his newest glass of beer before rubbing condensation off the sides with his napkin.

"I'm too old to have kids," I growl. "I'm too old to get tied down. You and mom were lucky you even found each other."

That's bullshit and we both know it. They stay together because they're Catholic, because back in the eighties, my dad killed someone for her father and won my mother like a prize. He also put a baby in her quickly and then kept her pregnant. There's nothing romantic about their love story or marriage in the Murray family.

"If you can't find a girl, I'll find one."

"The last girl you found me was a crazy fucking redhead who wanted to bring Roscoe Jr. into the bedroom. No thanks."

My father shrugs. "She was white. Do you know how hard it is to find a white girl around here who hasn't been fucking ruined by some fucking Puerto Rican or black guy?"

"What do you want from me, Pa?"

I know what I want. I want an end to this conversation, and I want my father to give me a fucking break about women and dating. All the Irish and Catholic women in Boston know to stay away from us, and the ones who don't learn their lesson pretty fucking quickly.

"Find a nice white girl with big tits and blond hair and get her pregnant so I know you're fucking serious about family. That's what I want."

"Give me time."

He continues, getting to what I suspect was the original point he wanted to make before the liquor got to him. "And get your ass to the site in Back Bay tomorrow bright and early."

"Why?"

This is the first I'm hearing about something wrong at the Back Bay construction site. I know something's wrong because my father doesn't do anything bright and early unless there's a problem to solve.

"You'll find out tomorrow. You just got back. Go home. Pet the dog. Your mom's tired of walking that big fuck. He nearly knocked her over near Harvard Square."

"How is mom?"

"Pissed off."

"Why?"

"Eh. Upset about another woman. It's nothing."

It's nothing. Dad just got his second mistress pregnant and even if we all know about it, we're all supposed to pretend it's no big deal that our elderly father knocked up a Irish teenager who he supposedly hired to clean the construction company office.

I hate how he treats our mother. What's the point of having a family or a woman if you hurt her? There's no getting through to him, but I have to try for my mother's sake.

"You treat her better, pa. Seriously. She needs you."

He grunts. "Get your ass home kid and get a white girl pregnant."

"Thanks, dad."

"If you can't find one, I'll find a good Irish girl who needs a green card and bring her over to you!"

My father is the last person I want picking my romantic partners. I mutter something to him about cutting back on liquor, then I pat my father on the back and leave the bar. This is the closest we've felt in years, but there's still a wall between us and there always will be. I felt closer to him when I was younger, when it was easier for me to justify the life I led. I know I'm a screw up, I know I don't belong anywhere near a woman or a family or any of the fucking things my father wants from me.

He knows it's wrong to bring a kid into this life, but he did it anyway. He knows that we're villains, but he doesn't care. Fuck, I don't care either, I suppose. I'd just rather not ruin a perfectly good woman.

I drive out of the city listening to rock classics on the radio. Just as I turn down my street – I live at the end of a cul-de-sac – I notice the large box on my front step. There are only five large houses at the end of this cul-de-sac, all of us with wide open well-maintained lawns around traditional New England colonial houses.

The box on my front step is fucking enormous – and I don't remember ordering anything for delivery. My hand moves swiftly to the pistol under my seat. I feel no fear as I reach for the gun and slip a mag out of my pocket. I feel ready.

Leaving the city for any amount of time always carries a risk, especially since I didn't exactly leave the place with a house sitter. The last time my teen brother Odhran house-sat, he trashed the place and had a threesome in my bed. I hop out of my black GMC Sierra with the gun under my coat and approach the box slowly, glancing furtively over my shoulder for anyone who might have eyes on me.

The box has holes in it. It's large. Pink. Wrapped in a bow. I reach for the bottom of the box and try to lift it. *Fuck*. It's heavy. I drop the box and I swear I hear a sound coming from inside it. *Is that possible?* I try to peek through the holes but it's too fucking dark and something's telling me opening this box will be a shitshow. It has to weigh about a hundred pounds. Maybe more. I'm no weakling, but it still takes a measure of back strength to lift a box that fucking heavy.

I open my front door and greet Roscoe Jr., my rottweiler, as he bounds towards the door to greet me. His coat looks shiny, the nub of his docked tail wags back and forth. Pa's choice, not mine. He runs up to the box and sniffs at it a bit.

There's definitely something in there and it gets his attention because Roscoe utters a low bark.

"Roscoe, go lie down."

Once he heads off to his bed, I throw my doors open wider and eye the giant box to decide how to carry the fuckin' thing. I would call Rian if his stupid ass wasn't in jail. I could call Callum, but he's still hung up on some fucking girl and won't answer my calls because I won't sugarcoat my opinion of him. Then there's Darragh... He's probably twice as drunk as Padraig. Not a good option either.

I'll have to carry the box myself. I stretch a little and then grab the edges of the box and grunt as I carry it a few feet inside my doorway. I set the box down more gently. *Is there something alive in there?* If it were an animal, I suspect Roscoe would be barking from his spot in the house, but he's laying down as I commanded, gazing at me curiously and wagging his tail.

He's probably wondering why I'm not taking him for a walk since I'm back. *At least he didn't bite the sitter this time.* I close my front doors and then search for an opening on the giant pink box. Finding none, I start with the ribbon and peel it away. The box comes up to my waist. It's *enormous*.

If it didn't weigh a hundred fucking pounds, I would assume it's a novelty gift or something extra special from one of my brothers. Which of my piece of shit brothers would get me a welcome home gift? It's not like either of them are here with a six pack of Guinness right now...

I peel the top of the box open and there's another box inside it, also pink. I open the second box and stumble backwards as I expose the contents. I don't mean to act like a fucking idiot, but I nearly fall over, because this is the last thing I expected to find on my doorstep. I just got back to Boston... How long has that box been out there?

Holy fuck, why isn't she screaming?

I gain control of myself and approach the box again, heart pounding because my second assumption is that the human female in the box might be dead and that's the reason she hasn't made a sound. The sick thought twists my stomach into an unyielding knot.

I slowly approach the box again, ignoring my heavy breathing, focusing instead on taking in as much information as possible about the situation. I move the flaps of the box open and stare at the woman's face.. Suddenly, her eyes snap open before swiveling around and looking me directly in the eye..

Holy fuck, this woman is alive.

"What the fuck is this?" I grunt to myself. Not to myself. I'm not alone. I dry swallow and run my fingers through my hair. She's black. Someone tied up a black woman in a pink ribbon, wrapped her up like a gift and put her in a box on my doorstep. This has to be a sick joke.

I'm almost too scared to reach into the box and touch her, but I have to touch her to get her out of the fucking box. Whoever this woman is, she ran into the wrong fucking people and ended up in the wrong living room.

I have tattoos and vows of loyalty to prove how I feel about people like her. "Don't worry. I'll get you out of there."

I don't know why I'm bothering with comfort. I reach into the box and grab her at the base of her spine before hoisting her out of the box and gently setting her on the ground. My stomach lurches. This is some sick, twisted shit. Whoever did this to her stripped this woman naked, bared every inch of her dark skin, the color of Arabica coffee, and wrapped her in a pink ribbon, contorting her limbs and running the ribbon over her bare breasts, between her thighs and in loops around her body so she's wrapped up like a chocolate present.

My body has an unconscious, primal reaction. I could unwrap her like the present she's been wrapped up to be, but I need answers quickly.

She has a gag in her mouth, a round white ball that keeps her lips spread open and hooks at the back. Her eyes roam around the room in terror as I reach into my pocket for my knife. I've killed people with this knife and now I'm using it to save someone.

Her skin prickles with goosebumps as I touch her. I apologize, but I need to brace myself against her to get her free. I press the serrated edge to the ribbon and make the first cut.

I cut her legs free. She groans as her legs fall in a curled heap. She cries out and tries to jerk them again, but however long she's been in that position was far too long for her to have full control of her legs and hips.

"Don't move," I remind her. I touch her skin again and my stomach lurches. Fuck, her skin is so dark. I look pale as fuck touching her and even putting my hands on her drives guilt through me. She's black. She's the wrong kind of person. I run my tongue piercing over my lower lip as I focus on all the parts of the ribbon I have to cut free.

When I have her limbs mostly free, she rolls onto her side, groaning in pain as her arms and legs curl in an awkward and splayed mess next to her. Even her wrists bend at an unnatural angle. I know she's alive, but the woman still looks dead.

I swallow slowly. What the absolute fuck is this?

"I'll take the gag out, but you can't spit or bite or do anything of that nature. Do you understand?"

She stares at me, but she can't say anything. I approach her mouth slowly and reach around her to find the clasp of her ball gag. I unhook it and take it out of her mouth. She groans again and winces in visible pain as she attempts to close her jaw. She slowly moves her hand to her face and rubs her cheek, groaning.

I crouch next to her, staring at her in awe, knowing that I shouldn't but am completely incapable of taking my eyes off the naked woman in front of me. If her nudity makes her uncomfortable, that hasn't sunk in yet. My cock stiffens inappropriately in my pants and I clasp my hands in front of my dick, refusing to take my eyes off her.

Her breasts are small, but they protrude forward in tiny, dark orbs with nipples that are even darker than her extremely dark skin. Holy fuck, I didn't know nipples came that dark. My eyes widen inappropriately and I pray she doesn't notice my leering. Who sent this woman to me and what exactly did they send her for?

Christ, Aiden. Get a grip. You're staring at her crotch now and it's obvious.

She's waxed completely and my gaze snaps to the bare, dark brown lips. I wonder what this strange woman conceals between those lower lips and what color her flesh is between those thin, toned legs. I clear my throat.

"Who are you?"

"Read the card with the gift," she manages to say, with a raspy voice and an accent I can't place.

"I asked you a question."

"Read the card with the gift," she repeats.

I raise an eyebrow and walk towards the box. There's a large card at the bottom, about 8 x 10 inches, printed on thick paper. I pull it out of the box and read the note, muttering it out loud to myself. *What the fuck is this?*

Dear Mr. Murray,

We hope you enjoy your object. Your task is simple. Use the object wisely. Have unprotected sex with the object and film a 4K quality video.

Compress the video file and send it to the email address below.

The object may be initially unwilling but both of you will face strong motivation to comply. The object understands that documentation of her existence belongs to us and if she fails to comply enthusiastically, we will destroy her identity.

If we do not receive the video within one week of today's date, you will both lose what's most important to you.

Tegan Murray counts on you to succeed. We have possession of the girl and you would be wise to listen to our orders if you or your family want to see her safe.

Do not call Padraig Murray. Do not call anyone else, or you will both suffer.

It takes less than a second to fire a bullet.

You must comply. When you're finished with said object, it is yours to keep.

Sincerely,

Your Benefactors

OA

"What is this sick shit?" I growl, throwing the card back into the box, causing the woman still kneeling on the ground to flinch. My heart thuds.

These people have Tegan and this woman might know where she is and who they are. I won't be a part of this sick fucking game.

Click here to order Mafia Playmate:
https://bit.ly/bostonirishmafia1

PATREON

13 SEASONS OF SERIAL CHAPTERS

NEW preview chapters published WEEKLY on my Patreon.

Read all 6 seasons of *Unfuckable* (Ben & Libby's story)...

UNFUCKABLE

For a small monthly fee, you get exclusive access to over 375 chapters of my first completed bwwm dark and spicy serial romance, as well as the spin-off serial...

DESPICABLE

The second serial, despicable has 300 chapters available for all Patreon subscribers to access instantly and... we officially have a **third completed spin-off bwwm romance series.**

And yes you get access to all of this at the $5/month tier with more benefits at more pricey tiers.

The third serial is about Clover + Thomas. Thomas has a shocking connection to a character in the second serial and Clover is an all-new African American female lead.

POWERLESS

This series has three *very long* "seasons" of chapters, the length of five full-length novels all-together.

You will probably have over three months of binge-reading before catching up to current content, making this one of the most 'bang for your buck' author Patreon subscriptions out there.

Don't take my word for it.
Check the post history:
www.patreon.com/jamilajasper

PATREON HAS MORE THAN THE ONGOING SERIAL...

⚡ INSTANT ACCESS ⚡

- NEW merchandise tiers with **t-shirts, totes, mugs,** stickers and MORE!
- **FREE paperback** with all new tiers
- **FREE short story audiobooks** and audiobook samples when they're ready

- #FirstDraftLeaks of Prologues and first chapters **weeks** before I hit publish
- Behind the scenes notes
- Polls and story contribution
- Comments & LIVELY community discussion with likeminded interracial romance readers.

LEARN MORE ABOUT SUPPORTING A DIVERSE ROMANCE AUTHOR

www.patreon.com/jamilajasper

THANK YOU KINDLY

Thank you to all my readers, new and old for your support with this new year.

I look forward to making 2023 an INCREDIBLE year for inter-racial romance novels. I want to thank you all for joining along on the journey.

www.patreon.com/jamilajasper

Thank you to my most supportive readers — my Patreon subscribers!:

Queen Ke

Jamie C

KimW

Warrior_pprincess

SavageSam

Roslyn H.

Katrina

LMSYT

Lainey R.

Naomi

GrumpyMillenial

Jay

Asia A.
Angela D.
Danyelle C.
WakeupMakeup Slay
Jocelyn F.
Nikki O.
Cdublu
Carla
Jonathan
Kelly
Jessica
Jasmine
DARSHELL
Dawn
Tiabuena3
Leigh
Yvonne
Ashlee
Crystal
Marshybabyyy
Shout
Quaniquequia
TK
Kayla
Shronda C.
Ma-Eyongerie
Kayla
Chantell
Kheiara
ophelia
Vickie
Cass
Kamil
Kaela

Love

Miryam

Charlene

Summer

Lola

Eryn

DD Davis

Symone

Deborah

Beatrice

Valescha

Khadija

makhalaab

Kaya

Glitter Garden

SavageSam

sybil arroyo

Ncsportsfan79

Jessica G.

Danielle

Yola

Joslin

Alexciz

Stacia

Ayanna

Asia

Hailey

Kaya

Nikki

Naomi O.

Jessica J

Chakiya

Noelle

kourtnee

Martha
Nikki Valentina
xjkpop
Valeria
BlkBae
SweetS
Msteeq
Rhonda
Darrah
Killa
Shavon
Misty
India
Kassandra
Imani
Nala
Chantell
Benvinda
Roger
Lexi B
Zapphire
Vbrooks
Tasha G
Kiera
Valencia
Stacy
YANITZA
Texansgurl76
Emma
Tinette
Jenny
Mariah
Nale
Tanisha

Trenita

Shelle

dulcemaria413

Shanice

Letarsha

Tania

Neeka

Julia

Linda

Lisa

Jiannie

Jillian

Tameka

Asia

Scarlette

Olwyn

R W

Fayefaefee

Brianna

Tiffany

Katie

Diamond

Kera

Tia

Love Reading

Dominique

Sheria

Jennifer

Georgette

Monique

Wendolyn

King Turtle22

Jessica

Nic M.

JustChill

DJC

Atira

TheeLastHokage

Yvonne

Chrissy

Janelle

Rian

LaRonda

LaRonda

Deanna

dlawson382

Jasmine

Haley

Belinda

Sercee

Yvonne

Jadelock

Farah

Tamiya

Quin

J.Payton

Geek Girl

Ashley

Rubi

Pilar

Sandra

Jurnee

Anni

Shannet

Joneesa

GlitzyHydra

Amanda

Barbara

Brianna

Jamica

Lyons

MARY ANN

Marketia

SarahD

LoverofHawaiiHearts

ceblue

Yolanda

MonaGirl Lewis

Dianna

Mary

amna

Nysha

fayola

Ty

Abria

Shyra

Andi-Mariee

Jamila

Naee's World

KEISHA

Jennett

Fredericka

Candece

Chante

Pholuv

Lydia A

Sabrina

JM

Jackie

Mo

Natrilly83

Ashaunte

Tolu

Margaret

Wendolyn

Lori

Dionne

ZLB

Kristina

Nicol

ELBERT

A. Harris

Jesi

Brenda

Desiree

Angela

Frances

LaShan

Only1ToniD

Debbie T.

Tiffanie

April L

shawnte

Kay

Lisema

Yvonne F

Natasha

Colleen

Julia

Amy

Jacklyn

Shyan R

Kiana B

Pearl

Javonda

Sheron

Maxine
Dash
Alicia
margaret
Love2Read
Juliette
Monica
Sandhya
MaryC
Trinity
Brittany
June
Ashleigh
Nene
Nene
Deborah
Nikki M
Dee
TyKira
Kimmey
Laytoya
Shel W
Arlene
Judith
Mary
Shanida
Rachel
Damzel
Ahnjala
Kenya
momo
BJ
Akeshia
Melissa

Tiffany

sherbear

Nini J

Curtresa

REGGIE A.

Ashley

Mia

Tink138110

Phia

Sharon

Charlotte

Assiatu C

Regina

Romanda

Catherine

Gaynor

BF

Perpetua

Tasha G

Henri Ann

sara

skkent

Rosalyn

Danielle

Deborah J

Kirsten

ANA

Taylor R.

Charlene

Louanna

Michelle

Tamika

Lauren

RoHyde

Natasha
Shekynah
Cassie
AnnaBooms
Keitheena
Nick R
Gennifer M
Rayna
Anton
Jaleda
Kimvodkna
JaTonn
Jazmine
Anoushka
Raynischa
`Audrey
Valeria
Courtney
Donna
Patrisha
Jenetha
LaKisha J.
Ayana
Taylor
Christy
Monica
FreyaJo
GRACE
Kisha
Christine
Alexandra
Amber
Natasha
Stephanie

LaKisha
kristylove7
Cynthea
DENICE
Latoya
monifacd .
Doneishia
Mariah
Gerry
Yolanda T
Yolanda P
Susan D
Phyllis H
Alisa K
Daveena K
Desiree S
Kimberly B
Robin B
Gary S
Stephanie MG
Georgette A
Kathy
Marty
JanetDaniels
Megan
Shelle
Delores
Janet
Lydia
Phyllis
Freda
Charlott R

Join the Patreon Community.

www.ingramcontent.com/pod-product-compliance
Lightning Source LLC
Chambersburg PA
CBHW021140160726
47994CB00001B/23